The Shoeshine Killer

Marianne Wheelaghan

To Stuart
with best wishes
and nice to see
you again!

Marianne x

Published 2015 by Pilrig Press, Edinburgh, Scotland

A CIP catalogue record for this book is available on request from
the British Library.

ISBN 978-0-9927234-3-9

www.pilrigpress.co.uk

Printed in Great Britain by Imprint Digital

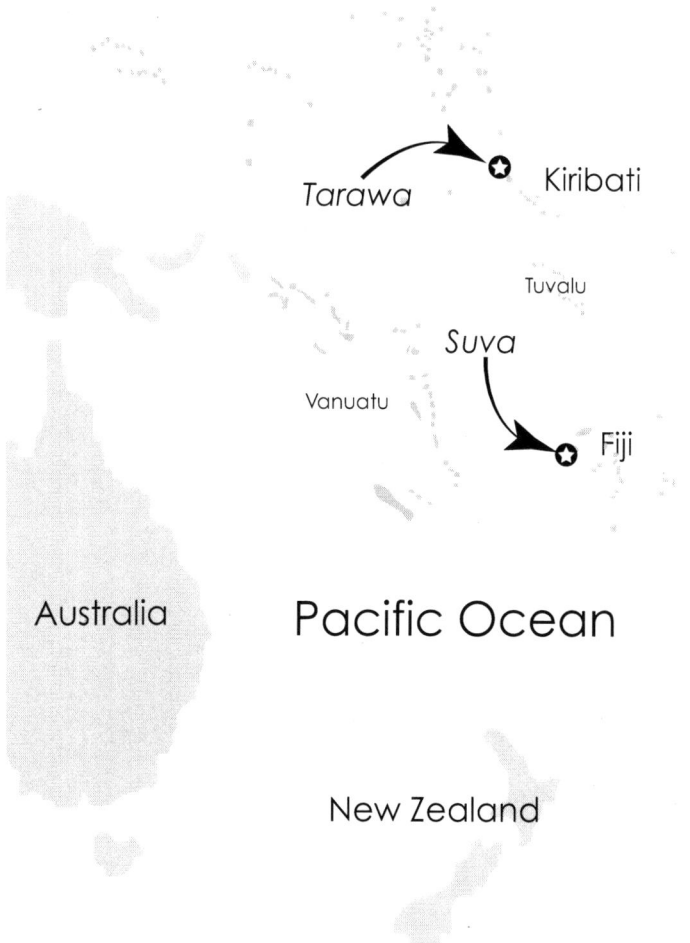

Tarawa

Kiribati

Tuvalu

Suva

Vanuatu

Fiji

Australia

Pacific Ocean

New Zealand

About the author

Before becoming a writer, Edinburgh-born Marianne Wheelaghan was a croupier, a marketing manager, a chambermaid, a cashier, a Brussels sprouts picker, but mostly she was a teacher. Marianne taught English and Drama in Germany, Spain, the Republic of Kiribati and Papua New Guinea. She also wrote plays. Marianne now lives back in Edinburgh with her family.

When she is not writing, she is running the online creative writing school www.writingclasses.co.uk.

About the book

DS Louisa Townsend has moved from Edinburgh to work for the Kiribati Police Service on Tarawa, a remote coral atoll in the middle of the Pacific. Locally she is known as the Scottish Lady Detective.

Louisa is in Fiji for a money laundering conference. From the moment she arrives in the country things go wrong, including some weird perv breaking into her room while she sleeps and mucking about with her underwear. But that pales into insignificance when she stumbles upon the murdered body of a new friend. Louisa wants to help find the truth and the killer. But DI Vika, the officer in charge of the investigation, tells Louisa to keep out of it.

Louisa isn't happy. Not one little bit. The slime-ball snooper is still breaking into her room, and although Louisa doesn't know how or why, she's sure there's a connection between the break-ins and the murder. Determined to get to the truth, and with the help of Fijian colleague Constable Makereta, Louisa embarks on a journey which takes her into Fiji's underworld and fighting for her life.

The Shoeshine Killer is the second book in the Scottish Lady Detective mystery series featuring Detective Louisa Townsend.

1

The twin propellor aeroplane, full with sixteen passengers, landed on the Suva airport runway with a loud clatter. The bald passenger in front of Louisa yelped. Louisa rolled her eyes. A wonky landing was nothing compared to being six hours late, which she now was. An officer from the Fijian Police Service was supposed to pick her up. Would he still be waiting? Probably not. No, revise that, definitely not.

The delays had started even before she'd left Tarawa, her home for the past two years. She and her fellow passengers had boarded the big Boeing 737 on time only to wait on the tarmac for two hot and uncomfortable hours. No explanation given. As if that wasn't bad enough, a fuel stop en route had lasted three hours instead of thirty minutes. Again, no explanation given. Louisa had finally landed in Nadi just in time to catch the last domestic flight of the day to Suva. Twelve hours to fly two thousand kilometres was a long time even by Pacific standards.

The small plane taxied to a halt. Louisa peered out the tiny passenger window. Sheets of bluebottle black raindrops battered the ground outside. She shivered. No one told her Fiji would be wet. Tarawa was hot and dry. She was missing it already. A small illuminated sign above Louisa's head told her she could undo her seat belt. At last.

The dimly lit airport was tiny, more of a large shed than the terminal for Fiji's capital city. The luggage from the plane, half a dozen lumpy holdalls and cases, had been dumped, dripping wet, in a lonely hall that appeared to double up as an arrival and departure lounge. Louisa's case wasn't with them. This was not good.

An irritable man at the lost luggage desk confirmed her worst fear: Louisa's case had accidentally been left in Nadi. The soonest she could get it was the next day. Her heart thump-thumped. Fast. Faster. All she had with her was what she was wearing. Having no clean clothes to change into when she woke up was nothing short of a disaster. The voices could start. Louisa took a long, slow breath. In. Out. And again. She needed to trick her body into thinking she was calm. In. Out. She would deal with the clothes problem later.

Outside, protected from the rain by the sloping terminal roof, Louisa looked around for her lift. As she'd anticipated, there was no police car waiting for her. Or any other car, for that matter. Not even a taxi. Or a bus. Not that Louisa did buses, but she could in an emergency, and this was rapidly turning into one. How was she going to get to her hotel?

'Wait!' yelled a tall Caucasian man, coming from the terminal. He pulled an upright wheely suitcase and waved his mobile phone in the air.

Louisa tensed her body, ready for danger. 'What's wrong?' He was the balding man who had sat in front of her on the plane. His fingernails were painted black.

'There has been a coup!' he shouted. 'My mother has told me on the phone.'

'The army have taken over?' Police Commissioner

Nakibae, her boss back on Tarawa, had said nothing about political unrest in Fiji.

'Yes.' He nodded his head feverishly. 'It was on the news back home. Mama says the army have all the guns and everyone must do as they say.' He put his phone in his shirt pocket. 'That is why there is no one here. They are all scared.'

'Is your mother sure?' He looked forty something despite his Pillsbury Doughboy cheeks and garish board shorts and shirt.

'My mama does not phone me up to tell me lies,' said the man, pouting furiously.

'All the same, I think I'll ask someone inside.'

'You are not listening!' His voice was shrill. 'There is no one. They pushed me out and have run away out their back doors.'

'Let's keep calm, shall we?' Louisa gave the double door into the terminal a shove. It stayed closed. Bugger. They were locked out.

'I am worried.' His lips trembled. 'I have never been in a country where there has been a coup.'

'I'm sure there is no cause for alarm.' Had the army really taken over? Was that the reason for the flight delays? 'We need to find someone to ask what's–'

A loud CLUNK followed by a HISS stopped Louisa in her tracks.

'Agh! I can't see!' The man grabbed Louisa's arm.

'Stop panicking!' Louisa shook him off and peered around. The terminal behind was in darkness. 'They've switched the lights off. Probably a timer. Our eyes will get used to the dark in a minute or so.'

'We are sitting swans for an attacker!' wailed the tall

man, sounding close to tears.

'No one is going to attack us. And it's ducks,' said Louisa. 'Sitting ducks.' She listened. Apart from the man's whimpering and the splitter-splattering of the rain as it hit the sloped roof above their heads, there was silence. Were they really the only ones there?

'I do not care what it is,' sniffed the man, nibbling on his thumb nail, 'I do not like it.'

'How far are we from Suva city?' The emergency situation was rapidly turning disastrous.

'No idea.' He looked glum.

Louisa scanned the area. A sliver of a crescent moon meant she could just about see. They appeared to be surrounded by fields. 'We're in the countryside somewhere. I'm going to start walking.' She wasn't fond of the dark but hanging around the deserted airport was pointless.

'Walk?' The man sounded confused. 'To where?'

'A village or a house to ask for help.' She stepped from out of the shelter of the roof. The rain had all but stopped.

'No. No.' The man shook his head adamantly. 'I think we should stay.'

'You stay then.' Above her head palm fronds rustled in the warm, damp breeze, sending random rain drops scattering onto her head. She shivered.

'But we have to remain together.'

'No, we don't.' She started walking and suddenly felt like Dorothy setting off on the Yellow Brick Road, but not as chirpy. Definitely not as chirpy.

'Stop!' wailed the man.

Louisa ignored him. Then she felt a pang of guilt. But it didn't last. She was a police officer on Tarawa. It was her job to protect and serve the people there. People in Fiji were not her concern, especially not some random cowardly tourist with bad taste in nail varnish.

'But I don't want to be alone!' he wailed. 'Wait!'

2

His name was Edwin. He was from the Netherlands. An only son, he lived with his mother in Utrecht. Like Louisa, this was his first time to Fiji. As they walked he constantly looked around, like a sparrow watching out for a cat. 'Mama said the soldiers are everywhere.'

'We don't know for sure there's even been a coup,' said Louisa.

'My mother would not call me from the other side of the world to tell me a fiction!'

'I meant the news report on the radio could have been wrong,' said Louisa, silently wishing Edwin had stayed at the airport and not followed her. His incessant talking was doing her head in. They'd been walking for half an hour and he'd not stopped. But worse than that, they'd not seen a single person or building. And in the dark the coconut palms and grassy fields all looked the same. For all she knew they could have been walking in circles. Orienteering had never been her thing.

'What if they shoot us?' said Edwin, rattling his suitcase behind him.

Louisa threw her hands in the air in despair. 'Why would they?'

'They could believe we are dissidents.'

'If we meet any soldiers, we'll explain we've just arrived.'

Louisa had heard everything now. Edwin a dissident? Not even with his black varnished nails.

'But what if they don't believe us?' Edwin paused to catch his breath.

'I'm a police officer with the Kiribati Police Service. Fiji and Kiribati are neighbours. They'll believe me.'

Edwin steadied his upright suitcase and sat on it. 'My mama said the police and the army are not friends, not any more. You being a police officer will not help us.'

'Let's be positive, shall we?' said Louisa, marching ahead. 'At least the rain has stopped.'

'You are going too quickly!' Edwin scrabbled to his feet, grabbed his case and hurried after her. 'Wait!'

She ignored him. He was clearly unfit and Louisa didn't like unfit people. Then she felt guilty again. She was being mean. It wasn't his fault it was dark and late, or that they were lost or that she'd been made to come to Fiji on the whim of her boss. She stopped walking and waited for Edwin to catch her up. She envied him his luggage. How had his arrived and not hers? She shivered. Remembering she had no clean clothes to change into made her feel anxious. There were worse things, but not for Louisa. She had to focus on something else, not let the thought of the germs multiplying all over her body take a hold.

'What do you do in Utrecht?' she said when Edwin was next to her.

'I am a car driving inspector. People think it is a boring job. It is not. It is a very important job but it can also be a dangerous job.'

'Oh?' She doubted that very much. The previous year she'd headed a murder investigation and had nearly got killed in the process. She could tell him a thing or two about danger. 'In what way dangerous?'

'I failed one young man. The day after the test I was sitting in my car. His father he came to me. He knocked on my window and asked to talk to me. I thought he wanted to go over his son's performance. I wound the window down and he punched his fist into my face.'

'Ouch!' Louisa was genuinely surprised. 'I hope you reported him to the police.'

Edwin gasped. 'Look!' he pointed ahead. In the scant moonlight a group of five burly men in black sweat pants and hoodies headed towards them.

'Shit!' said Louisa. The men were huge. If they wanted to cause trouble, they could.

'Let's go back?' whispered Edwin, tugging on her arm. 'Please, they have not seen us yet. Let us go back.'

'Back where?' she hissed, shaking him off without taking her eyes off the supersized men.

'The airport,' whispered Edwin, his voice full of desperation. 'Anywhere but here. They have not yet seen us.'

'Oy!' The shout came from the biggest man in the group. 'Where do you think you're going?'

3

A four by four Toyota Land Cruiser Prado pulled up behind Louisa and Edwin. A gaunt Caucasian, middle-aged man leaned out of the passenger window. 'Do you need a lift?'

'Let me do the talking,' whispered Louisa.

'We are lost and those men are shouting at us!' blurted

Edwin, ignoring Louisa's furious look and hurrying towards the car.

'Jump in. This isn't a safe area to be wandering about,' said the man. 'I'm Rick, this is Stewy.' Rick nodded to the driver.

'How's it going?' said Stewy. He was slightly built with long brown hair, tied back in a pony tail and a postage stamp of a purple beard on the tip of his chin.

'I'm Louisa,' said Louisa, climbing into the back of the air conditioned Prado after Edwin. It smelled of new carpets and beeswax. Squeaky clean. 'There were no taxis, so we started walking.'

'My name is Edwin. I wanted to stay at the airport but Louisa insisted we leave,' said Edwin pulling a face.

Louisa laughed silently. Both a coward and a liar. 'Is it true the army are in charge?'

'You bet,' said Stewy, pulling away. 'Commodore Bainimarama seized power earlier today.'

'My mama phoned me about it,' said Edwin. 'Some people didn't believe me.'

Louisa ignored him. 'Has anyone been hurt?'

'No casualties so far,' said Rick.

'The prime minister is under house arrest,' said Stewy. 'Some people would say he's a casualty.'

Rick shook his head wearily and looked out of his window.

'My mama said there is a lockdown in Suva centre,' said Edwin, 'that no one is allowed on the streets.'

'It's not so much a lockdown as a curfew,' said Stewy. 'It runs from eight at night to eight in the morning. It applies only to the city centre. Is that where you were headed?'

'The Holiday Inn,' said Louisa, watching with relief as

they sped past the burly men on the road. They could have been friendly, but she was glad she'd not had to find out.

'I am booked to stay there also,' said Edwin.

'Not tonight you're not,' said Stewy, 'it's in the centre.'

Louisa groaned. 'Are there any hotels outside the centre?'

Stewy shook his head.

'But what will we do?' said Edwin, his voice full of anxiety.

Stewy glanced sideways at Rick. 'They could crash at ours?'

Rick nodded his head and turned to face Louisa and Edwin in the back of the car. 'We live outside Suva centre in a suburb called Tamavua. You're welcome to be our guests until tomorrow.'

'Yes, please!' said Edwin, beaming.

'That's very kind, ' said Louisa. Yes, the men were strangers but they didn't look like people traffickers. And if she was really lucky, their house would be as clean as their car.

'What you doing in Suva, then?' said Stewy, concentrating on the road ahead. 'Business or pleasure?'

'I am a tourist,' said Edwin. 'I'm here for pleasure.'

'And I'm here on business,' said Louisa. 'Definitely not pleasure.' Stewy sounded Australian.

'Oh? You're not an item?' said Stewy.

Edwin hooted with laughter. 'No. No. No! Officer Louisa and I have only just met.'

'The police?' said Rick.

'Detective Sergeant Louisa Townsend to be precise. Presently working for the Kiribati Police Service. In Fiji for a conference on money laundering in the Pacific.'

Rick nodded knowingly. 'At the Holiday Inn.'

'That's the one.'

'You're Irish, right?' said Stewy, glancing at Louisa in the rear-view mirror.

Now Louisa laughed. 'Close. I'm Scottish, from Edinburgh. I've been living on Tarawa for the last two years.'

'A bit of a change from Scotland?'

'My mum is from the island. My dad is Scottish. He went to work there, they fell in love and had me and then my brother. We left when I was eight to go to Edinburgh. I returned two years ago to work for the police service.' Louisa did not usually talk about herself. She decided the relief at not wandering aimlessly any more was making her lightheaded. 'And you two?'

'I'm from New Zealand,' said Rick. 'I used to be a teacher. Been here a while. Set up my own business. We've had a few hiccups recently, but nothing we can't handle, isn't that right?' The last comment was addressed to Stewy.

'I'm sure these lovely folk don't want to hear about our tiresome problems,' said Stewy, dryly before suddenly laughing. 'Now me, I'm from God's Own Country, Australia. Came here to visit ten years ago, fell in love and stayed.'

'And what about the coup?' said Louisa.

'I wouldn't worry about it too much,' said Rick. 'This is the fourth coup I've witnessed in the last twenty years. I've survived them all, as has Fiji.'

'But is it safe?' said Edwin.

'Safe as any country with a military dictator in charge,' said Stewy, winking at Edwin via the rear view mirror.

'Not that safe, then,' said Louisa. Was Stewy flirting

with Edwin?

'Commodore Bainimarama has promised to hold elections as soon as possible. He's only doing what he thinks is necessary,' said Rick.

'Isn't that what Hitler said?' said Stewy. He glanced at Louisa and Edwin via the rear view mirror. 'Laisenia Qarase, our prime minister, was effectively placed under house arrest earlier today. He's asked Australia to send in the troops, and I'm with him.'

Rick slammed his fist on the dashboard. 'Australian and Fijian troops firing on each other will not help! No one has been hurt, we want it to stay that way!'

Stewy clamped his mouth shut and drove on in silence. Edwin cleared his throat as if to speak then seemed to think better of it and looked down at his hands folded on his lap. Louisa sighed. It was going to be a long drive.

4

They'd been in the car for forty minutes. Louisa stared out her window. She couldn't see a thing and had no idea where they were but at least they were away from the men with the hoodies. She shivered. Who knew what would have happened if Rick and Stewy hadn't stopped and picked them up? Sure, Rick was a little moody, and she had no time for moody people as a rule, but it was a small price to pay to be safe. The car flew over a bump. Edwin squealed. Louisa was flung upwards and stopped from making contact with the roof by her seat belt. The car jerked over a second bump and Louisa was catapulted out of her seat a second time. She grabbed the door handle to steady herself. Bloody hell. Where was the hurry?

'If you don't slow down, we're going to have an accident,' said Rick. It was his first words since his earlier outburst.

'Keep your hair on,' said Stewy, grinning. He looked at Louisa and Edwin in the rear view mirror. 'Sorry about that. The roads in Fiji are lousy.'

'You do not need to apologise,' said Edwin, beaming. 'I trust myself in your safe hands.'

'Awe, thanks, mate,' said Stewy, smiling at Edwin. 'You say the nicest things.'

Edwin giggled at him. 'You are very silly!'

Stewy winked again and Edwin blushed.

Louisa couldn't believe it. Edwin and Stewy were actually flirting with Rick sitting there. Was Rick aware of what was happening? Louisa glanced at him. He glared ahead. Oh, he knew alright. Louisa groaned silently. She hope there wasn't going be another outburst. She hated that sort of emotional stuff. The trip was turning out to be one big disaster. Why hadn't she told her boss, Nakibae, to stuff his conference?

When Nakibae had phoned her, just two days earlier, he'd talked about Louisa going to the conference in Suva in his place as an exciting opportunity. He'd got last minute funding to participate in an international crime forum in China and, as everyone knew, the expenses for travelling to China were ten times that for Fiji. It was a no brainer for him. But she'd had other plans for this week. Namely, catching up with her boyfriend, Mataio, who'd been away visiting his sick mum. A hop and a skip by local plane, but Mataio may as well have been in Timbuktu. There were no phones on Mataio's mum's island of Beru, not even satellite phones. As a consequence Louisa had not been able tell Mataio she wouldn't be there when he got back. Ironically, his flight landed a couple of hours after hers took off.

If she knew Mataio, and she did, he'd be wondering why Louisa hadn't picked him up at the airport as agreed. And been surprised not to find her at home. But he would have seen her letter by now, in the middle of the dining table. In it she explained why she was in Suva and gave him the Holiday Inn phone number. She imagined he'd have already dialled it and would be worrying why she wasn't there, especially under the circumstances – if news about the coup was on the radio in Holland it would be on the radio in Kiribati.

'Not long now,' said Rick.

'Thanks,' said Louisa.

Louisa had assumed Rick and Stewy were a couple but maybe she'd got that wrong. Rick was a middle-aged, clean shaven man with an Imperial Leather soap smell about him. His grey hair was crew cut short. He wore a white, pressed, short sleeved shirt and beige chinos. And, unless she was mistaken his nails were manicured. For some reason she imagined he did press ups in the morning. Stewy was younger and with his pony tail and tiny purple beard, way more funky than his friend. She noted he wore a chunky gold chain around his neck. Smart but casual in a black T shirt and jeans. Although he was slight, he also looked like he worked out. A jogger probably. The men seemed opposites. But they said opposites attracted, didn't they? Look at her and Mataio. Or, were the men simply friends, not gay at all? She glanced at Edwin now dozing next to her. She was in no doubt about his sexual orientation.

'Here we are,' said Rick as Stewy pulled the car to a

halt in front of a high and wide solid gate. An illuminated sign on the wall next to the gate said The Garlands Bed and Breakfast. 'The guest house is a new venture for us.' Rick flicked a small remote control towards the gate. 'I'd appreciate you letting us know what you think.'

'Of course,' said Louisa watching the giant gate rumble sideways to reveal a super steep drive. With a name like that, she imagined pink knickknacks everywhere.

'Yep, welcome to our very own home, sweet home,' said Stewy, dryly as he drove the big car up the hill towards a floodlit colonial style house. He wasn't smiling now.

5

Louisa fell asleep as soon as her head touched the starched white pillow. Eight hours later she awoke refreshed and rested. She loved The Garlands. It was all creams and polished wood and sparkling cleanliness. If she ever came back to Fiji she would happily pay good money to stay there. Rick and Stewy were clearly as obsessed about cleanliness as she was. Not that she thought of herself as obsessive, more fastidious.

On Tarawa Louisa had a very specific cleaning regime and made Reteta stick to it. Reteta was her cousin and her cleaner. Louisa hadn't wanted a cleaner but Reteta had been very persuasive. Eventually, Louisa had agreed to let Reteta clean for her a couple of days a week, which was when Reteta set up camp in Louisa's back garden, bringing her husband, mother-in-law, three children, Daisy the boy dog and a pig with her. Reteta became the sister Louisa never wanted.

On the plus side, Reteta kept the house spotless and never questioned Louisa's cleaning rules; maybe she thought all foreigners were this fastidious? Mataio never mentioned her cleaning thing either, not even on the bad days when Louisa reverted to the rule of four and washed her hands four times after touching something. As long as everyone stuck to the regime, the voices stayed away.

Louisa snuggled under the starched sheets and looked around the sumptuous guest bedroom. Would Mataio like to live in a house like Rick's? She couldn't say. There was a lot about Mataio she still didn't know. But only anecdotal stuff. About the important things, though, she was in no doubt: they were nuts about each other. Not long now and they'd be on their big trip to Scotland. Mataio was due to arrive in Fiji on Monday. They'd leave for Scotland on Tuesday. Flying from Fiji instead of Tarawa wasn't a big change to their schedule, although expensive. She hated for her plans to be mucked up, though. Uncertainty made her anxious. And until she talked to Mataio, she would worry he'd not found her message.

Time to get dressed. Louisa had put it off as long as possible. The thought of wearing her stinking clothes from the day before made her feel sick. She hoped her suitcase would turn up sooner than later. She stood up. At least she'd been able to shower and had her travel straighteners and ruby red lipstick with her. As long as she had her lippy on and her unruly chestnut kinks were under control, she could face just about anything.

She glanced at herself in the mirror on the wall opposite and groaned. Her hair, inherited from her dad's side of the family, was even worse than usual. A cross between a hedgehog and a haystack. She was not unattractive even if she said so herself, but she looked her age of thirty-five. Older, even. No grey hairs but plenty of those tiny wrinkles around the eyes. Where had they come from? Her mum always said she'd be stunning if she wasn't so angry looking. Thanks, Mum! Luckily, Mataio didn't give a shit about appearances. It was what she liked about him. That and his body. She smiled at the thought of being with him. Three weeks was a long time to go without sex.

Louisa turned to get her bra and pants. She'd hand washed them the night before and left them to dry on the towel rail at the bottom of the bed. She gasped. No! The white straps of her bra lay across her white pants. No! No! No! Drying items did not touch! Not ever! Not negotiable! It was one of her things. She would have never left her underwear like that. Someone had been in her room. But she'd locked the door. The key was on the bedside cabinet where she'd left it. She pulled the door handle. It resisted. Still locked. How had the intruder got in? Did they have a key? Had she been robbed?

Louisa grabbed her handbag and tipped it upside down over the bed. Everything tumbled out. Purse. Passport. Tickets. Pen. Paracetamol (two packets). Notebook. Warrant card for Kiribati Police Service. Warrant card for Lothian and Borders Police (which she should have handed in before leaving but had not). Empty wet wipes packet. Empty paper tissue packet. Mini toilet bag: lipstick, mascara, brown eye liner, soap in soap box, mini hair straighteners, hairbrush, mini hairspray, Clinique perfume, toothbrush, small tube of toothpaste, dental floss, mini packet of cotton buds, ear plugs, manicure set, eye mask. One folded sarong.

Louisa sat on the bed next to her stuff. Everything was there. Why would someone break into her room, move her underwear and take nothing? And, more's to the point, how did they do it? The night before Rick had gone to great lengths to explain how burglar proof The Garlands was. The security wire in front of the windows was solid, impenetrable. Then there was the three metre high gate and huge wall surrounding the property, plus the state of the art burglar alarm, imported from Sweden. The intruder must have been in the house already and had a key. It had to be Rick or Stewy, or both of them. Had Edwin been involved? But why? Did they have some weird fetish for women's clothes? Ugh! A quick examination of her bra and pants revealed no semen. What a relief. Still the thought of any of the three men touching her delicate bra and pants and then her having to wear them made her skin crawl. Bastards!

6

Louisa waited at the kitchen table in Rick's pristine kitchen. No one else appeared to be up. She wanted to talk to the men as soon as possible. She'd assumed either Rick or Stewy had been her intruder, but if Rick's security system had been compromised, all the rooms could have been broken into and she'd been jumping to conclusions. A phone rang somewhere in the house then stopped. A minute later a bleary-eyed Rick appeared at the kitchen door, wearing white cotton boxer shorts and nothing else. His body was all angles and corners.

'There's a call for you. From Scotland,' he said.

Louisa was stunned. 'No one in Scotland knows I'm here.'

'The woman said she phoned your house on Tarawa and someone called Reteta gave her our number,' said Rick.

'Ah!' Louisa had forgotten. Rick had let her call Tarawa the night before. She'd wanted to let Mataio know she was safe. Mataio hadn't been in so Louisa had left Rick's number with Reteta, just in case. She wished they had a mobile network on Tarawa. 'Is it my mother?' said Louisa, slowly getting to her feet. In the two years Louisa had been overseas her mother had never phoned. Not once. It was always Louisa who called her. This was not good.

'It is an older woman,' said Rick, gently. 'I didn't catch her name. Look, Stewy took Edwin for a jog but I imagine they'll be back any minute, Edwin doesn't look like a jogger to me. Take the call in my room. It's more private.'

Louisa followed Rick into his bedroom. She had to prepare herself for the worst. Shit! The phone sat on a bedside cabinet next to the king size bed. The receiver lay facing upwards on the cream quilt. Like her room, Rick's room was all whites and natural polished woods and spotless.

'Take the chair there,' said Rick, nodding to a oak dining chair next to the polished bedside cabinet.

Louisa sat. She leaned over and picked up the receiver. Her fingers trembled.

'Hello?' she said, cautiously, while watching Rick slip out of the room.

'Louisa, hen?' said a voice, bursting with life.

Whoever it was sounded too cheerful to be her mum. 'Yes?'

'It's me, Jean.'

'Jean?' Louisa had a vague memory of a small, skinny woman sitting with her mum on the sofa, Laurel and Hardy like. Then she remembered: Jean was a shopping channel buddy. 'What is it?'

'It's your mother. She's had a wee fall. Nothing serious. It was climbing out of that bath of hers. I told her to get one of those wet rooms. She was in the hospital–'

'Hospital?' said Louisa, her voice breaking.

'Don't you worry, there's no bones broken, just a bit of bruising and a knock to her confidence. She'll be as right as rain in a few days.'

'Are you sure?' said Louisa relieved.

'Oh aye. The thing is, hen, she's all worried about you coming home next week, what with you bringing your fiancé with you.'

'She doesn't need to worry about us.' Louisa laughed silently. Trust Mum to refer to Mataio as her fiancé. 'We'll look after ourselves.'

'Aye, but she needs a wee bit of help about the house, just until she's properly back on her feet.'

'I can help!' Louisa relaxed in the chair. A fall. Nothing serious. 'She must focus on getting better.' They'd never hear the end of it when they got there but that would be fine. As a healthy, if overweight, seventy-five year old, her mum was demanding enough. With an injury she'd be insufferable. Louisa would manage a week, though.

'That's what she told the carers.'

'The carers?' Louisa sat up.

'The hospital arranged carers to cook her meals, do a bit cleaning and her toilet. But with you coming she cancelled them.'

'Her toilet?' Louisa stifled a gasp.

'Just a bit of topping and tailing for a few weeks. No fuss.'

Louisa couldn't bring herself to ask what "topping and tailing" was. 'But you just said that it was nothing too serious.'

'Aye, it's not serious. But you don't recover from a nasty fall like that overnight, not at your mother's age. So, will you help, hen?'

'Of course, I will.' What else could she say? It was her mother. She'd prepared a packed holiday for Mataio, intending to show him the splendour of the Highlands and Islands of Scotland in all their wintery wonderfulness, now there would have to be changes. 'I'll give her a ring.'

'Don't bother. She can't get to the phone, hen.' Jean chuckled. 'I'll keep an eye on her till you get here. She called you the calvary, hen. Imagine that! Ta ta!'

The phone went dead.

Rick was at the end of the bed. He was still in his boxers. He had a glass of brandy in his hand. Worry lines creased his forehead. 'I'm so sorry, Louisa. Is it very bad news?'

'Yes. I mean, no. My mother's had a fall. She was in hospital. But she's out now.'

'The poor love,' he said sympathetically. 'Falls can be tricky things.'

'I'm flying home Tuesday. I'll be able to give her a hand around the house until she gets better.'

'That's good.' He sat on the bed opposite her. 'She'll appreciate you being there.'

'Yes,' said Louisa slowly. With sinking certainty it was dawning on her what she'd committed herself to.

'Who's helping her till you arrive?'

'A neighbour.'

'You have no other family?'

'A brother.' Louisa laughed. 'The blue-eyed boy lives in the south of England and visits her less than I do while living at the other side of the world.'

'He's the favourite, is he?' said Rick, nodding knowingly.

'The prodigal son.' She sighed. 'And I'm the daughter she never wanted.'

He nodded knowingly. 'My mother never accepted the fact I was gay. She was Latvian. Very old world. She did all her own baking and cooking until she died four years ago last June. There's not a day that passes that I don't miss her.'

'Oh, I'm so sorry for your loss,' said Louisa, awkwardly.

'You wait and see,' said Rick, gently patting her shoulder. 'You'll have a wonderful Christmas with your mother.'

She tried not to flinch. It wasn't his fault she had a thing about strangers touching her. 'I'm sure I will,' she lied, taking the glass from him and downing the brandy in a oner.

7

Rick drove in silence while Louisa stared out of the passenger window of the Prado. Slate coloured raindrops rattled red flowering hibiscus bushes and groaning banana palms. Here and there flurries of sodden people huddled under black umbrellas. Were they waiting for a bus? Going to work? Rick had insisted on taking her to the Holiday Inn and she'd accepted. Why wouldn't she? It was chucking it down and his car was both super clean and comfortable.

Besides she'd not got the first idea how to get there.

Of course, she shouldn't have downed the brandy in a oner. She was a lightweight drinker at the best of times. The rush of alcohol on an empty stomach, coupled with the awful thought of "topping and tailing" her mum, had given her a fit of the giggles. Rick had pretended not to notice while going into super cook mode and rustling her up a hearty breakfast of poached eggs, mushrooms, grilled bacon and toast. To her delight and surprise, Rick was good company and full of funny stories about his weird and wonderful mother. Louisa was enjoying herself until it became clear that Stewy and Edwin had returned from their jog and left again without telling Rick. In an instant Rick's mood had gone from fun, kind and solicitous to silent and sinister.

Thump! The Prado bumped in and out of a pot hole. Rick shook his head crossly and carried on driving. Louisa frowned. She had no time for moody people. Her dad had had moods. They'd got worse when they'd moved to Edinburgh. One day she'd be daddy's favourite girl, the next a stupid, filthy bitch – not the kindest of endearments for a nine-year-old to hear. Her mum had called him a drunk often enough for her to know alcohol was to blame. At least, Louisa told herself, it was the drink that made him behave the way he did. It was easier to believe that than consider he might have really meant the things he said.

Back in Edinburgh, when she was much younger, she'd used to sit on the outside step and wait for her dad to come from work. Long strides, head up, was good, that meant he'd had a drink. Short fast steps, head down, was bad. That meant he was sober. Sober equalled nasty. Not that he ever hit them. He didn't need to. His words did more damage than physical punches every could.

A row of drenched magnolia trees bursting with white blossoms seemed to wave at her. If a chattering monkey had suddenly swung out from one of the branches she'd not have been surprised even though she knew it was impossible. The car wound downwards, the rain stopped, a rainbow appeared across the sky and the tropical vegetation at the roadside was replaced by chunky walls and solid gates.

Mood or no mood, though, someone had come into Louisa's room and snooped about and she wanted to know why. As a police officer she'd signed an oath to always have the courage to hold herself and others accountable for their actions. She intended to do just that. She liked Rick, especially after he'd been so thoughtful about the phone call and her mum, but his abrupt mood swings suggested another, possibly darker, side to him. As the owner of the guest house he was the obvious intruder. Besides Stewy and Edwin weren't around to ask. She would have to choose her words carefully. Wait for the right moment. Timing was everything when it came to questioning, especially when someone was in a mood.

They passed a snake of shopping trolleys parked outside a glass fronted supermarket; a petrol station with a packed forecourt; half a dozen soldiers in combat fatigue, and a massive faux Greek building, topped with a golden statue of a man blowing a trumpet on the top of it – a large sign said it was the Mormon temple. The road widened to two lanes on either side and the traffic doubled. Ancient yellow taxis with Japanese lettering along the sides appeared as if from nowhere and nipped between the other vehicles. Battered buses, like prehistoric dinosaurs, roared after the taxis. Beep! Beep! Traffic lights flashed Walk! Don't Walk!

Louisa tried not to be overwhelmed. Her home of the last two years was a sleepy hamlet compared to Suva.

Rick jerked sharp right. Louisa gripped the car door to steady herself. They headed down towards a sweeping basin of blue, surrounded by cloud smothered mountains.

'Suva Bay,' said Rick. 'We're coming to the city centre.'

'Ah!' she said, relieved that he was speaking at last.

'I always think of Rio De Janeiro when I see this view. There's no giant Jesus or Sugarloaf mountain, obviously, and Suva Bay is much smaller than Guanabara Bay, but nevertheless there is something spectacular about the view.'

'It's very pretty,' said Louisa, although comparing Suva to Rio seemed a stretch. They flew through a set of traffic lights. To the left, stalls displaying sarongs and saris tumbled on top of each other in a dishevelled, makeshift market. To the right, rows of buses throbbed in an open air bus station full of muddy puddles. Ahead, in the window of a department store, a plastic green Christmas tree sat on top of a large chest freezer next to a poster advertising a Clarins moisturiser promising Youthful Vitality. Louisa shivered. She didn't want to think of Christmas. A week with her mum was bad enough, never mind two or three. Mum had never forgiven Louisa for going back to Tarawa. She'd accused Louisa of being selfish and abandoning her in her old age. The fall would be all the ammunition she'd need to emotionally blackmail Louisa into feeling an even worse daughter than she already did. As for "topping and tailing" her? No. No. No. Louisa wasn't going to go there.

The traffic became more erratic. Rick guided the Prado between lorries and buses as he pushed forward. He nodded to a mass of colourful stalls stacked high with mangos and pineapples and green plant stuff Louisa didn't recognise. 'That's our local market. Worth a visit.'

'Cheers,' she said. And, suddenly, there was Edwin. He stood by the entrance to the market. His left foot rested on a small wooden box. A skinny youth, wearing a dark baseball cap, a bright orange singlet and baggy shorts squatted by the box and polished Edwin's shoes. Sweat dripped down the lad's skinny tanned shoulders. A homemade sign propped next to the box said, "Killer Shoeshines here!" The black painted lettering was wobbly. It looked as if it had been written by a child or an older person with an unsteady hand.

And then Louisa saw Stewy. He came from the direction of the market. He carried a leather satchel slung over his shoulder and cradled two pineapples in his arms. When the shoeshine lad saw him he stood up and grinned. Louisa couldn't bet on it, but it looked as if they knew each other.

8

'That's Edwin,' said Louisa. 'And Stewy.'

'Where?' demanded Rick, quickly looking around.

Louisa nodded towards where the men stood. 'At the entrance to the market. There.'

Rick screeched the car to a halt. Louisa jerked forward. A cacophony of horns tooted behind them. 'Wait here!' said Rick, jumping out of the vehicle.

'You can't stop in the middle of the road!' Louisa yelled after him. Rick ignored her. Shit! Louisa hoped Rick wasn't going to do anything stupid. She undid her seatbelt, jumped out of the car and ran after him, ignoring the manic beeping behind her.

'Give it back,' demanded Rick.

'What?' said Stewy, offering one of the pineapples to Edwin.

Rick slapped both pineapples out of Stewy's hands. The fruit went flying. Edwin gasped. The shoeshine lad looked at his feet.

'What the fuck are you playing at, mate?' said Stewy, dropping his satchel on the ground and picking up the pieces of fruit.

'I know you took it,' said Rick. 'And I want it back.'

'Rick,' said Louisa, 'you're causing a traffic jam. People are getting angry.'

'And you're behaving like a dick,' said Stewy, furiously.

'You must move your car!' said Louisa, watching some of the drivers stuck behind the Prado get out of their vehicles and head towards them. 'Now!'

'After I've dropped Louisa off at the Holiday Inn, I'm going directly back to the house. I expect to see you there,' said Rick before marching back to the car.

Stewy gave Edwin one of the pineapples he'd just picked up and shook his head wearily. Louisa hurried after Rick.

'What's going on?' said Louisa, getting into the Prado and slipping on her seat belt.

'Nothing,' said Rick, pulling away and ignoring the furious car owners hurling abuse at him.

Louisa looked out her window. The timing was bad. Very bad. But she wanted to know who had snuck into her room in the night and why. Rick had just demonstrated he had a temper and was unpredictable. Who knows what he got up to when no one was looking? And if she didn't ask him soon, she would be at the Holiday Inn and it would be too late. She cleared her throat.

'Someone broke into my room last night.'

'Pardon?' said Rick, braking suddenly as a boy pushing a wheelbarrow top-heavy with root vegetables dashed across the path of the Prado.

'Nothing was stolen,' said Louisa, clutching the passenger door handle to steady herself as Rick pulled away again. 'But even though the room was locked, someone entered and picked up my underwear.'

'They did what?' said Rick, his cobalt blue eyes throwing her a sideways glance before focussing back on the road.

'They moved my underwear.'

Rick suddenly began to chuckle. 'This is a joke, yes?'

'No, it's not!' said Louisa calmly. How dare he laugh at her!

Rick frowned. 'You actually believe someone was in your room?'

'I know someone was.'

'I see.' His face stayed serious. 'Sorry, but if you locked your door that's impossible.'

Louisa shook her head. 'I always hand wash my underwear and leave it to dry in the same way. It's one of my things. When I woke up this morning, the items were not as I had left them.'

'And one of my things,' said Rick, seriously, 'is to make sure my guests are safe. Burglary is a serious problem in Suva. It is impossible for anyone to have got into the house and your room without triggering the alarm.'

'Then it had to be someone who was already in the house.'

Rick shook his head. 'There are only two keys to your

room. You had one and I have the other. I did not go into your room.'

'What about Stewy? Could he not have taken your key?'

'Stewy?' Rick laughed again. 'Why on earth would Stewy want to touch your clothes?'

'You tell me,' said Louisa, adamantly.

'Are you serious?' said Rick.

'Very.'

Rick shook his head. 'Stewy may be a stubborn, single-minded pain in the backside, but he has no reason to sneak into guests' rooms in the middle of the night and he has no interest whatsoever in women's underwear.' Rick glanced at Louisa, looked back at the road and sighed. 'You were very tired last night, weren't you? Is it not possible you're remembering wrongly?'

Louisa shook her head. 'No.'

'Then we'll have to agree to disagree.'

'No. Someone came into my room and if it wasn't Stewy it had to be you.'

Rick frowned. 'Are you calling me a liar?'

'Are you calling me one?'

Rick's face hardened. 'If you feel that strongly I suggest you contact the local police.'

'I don't think I need to do that,' said Louisa, sinking into the back of her chair. 'I just want to know what happened.'

Rick stared ahead and said nothing. Louisa looked out her window. It couldn't have gone more badly. But no matter how much Rick believed it was impossible to get into her locked room, he was wrong. When it came to her clothes, especially her underwear, she didn't make mistakes.

'I forgot to tell you,' said Rick abruptly. 'I called the

airport earlier. They said your suitcase has turned up. It's already been delivered to the Holiday Inn.'

'That's brilliant news! Thank you.' She'd have kissed him had she not just accused him of being a liar. As soon as she got her case she'd chuck the dirty, filthy clothes she was wearing into the bin, especially her underwear. The items would never feel clean enough for her to wear again. And fuck the intruder, whoever he was. She wouldn't be in the country for much longer.

Louisa heard oom-pah music. She looked out of her window. It came from a park in the middle of the centre. Three jolly looking musicians sat in a round bandstand, playing an accordion, a trombone and a clarinet. In front of the bandstand giant speakers amplified the music and two rows of grinning blue uniformed policemen and women kicked their legs and jiggled white gloved hands in time to the music. They appeared to be line dancing. If Louisa didn't know any better she'd have thought they were laughing at her.

9

The receptionist at the Holiday Inn was called Jyoti. She was tall and slender with almond eyes, silky long black hair and a beaming smile. She looked as if she'd just walked off a Bollywood film set. There was no message from Mataio or any record of him having called the hotel. It was the second thing Louisa asked Jyoti, after enquiring about her luggage. Louisa was surprised Mataio hadn't phoned. He must have read her letter by now, or at least got her message from

Reteta. Just as soon as Jyoti came back with her case, Louisa would call Mataio from reception.

Fifteen minutes later, and counting, Jyoti was still not back with Louisa's suitcase. Louisa wished she would hurry. More and more smartly dressed delegates for the No More Money Laundering in the Pacific Conference 2006 (NMMLP06) were gathering in reception and Louisa felt conspicuously scruffy – and she hated being scruffy.

'Are you the Scottish detective lady?' said an imperious voice.

'I'm a detective and from Scotland, yes?' said Louisa, looking up at a tall, rectangular woman with big hair, clear, coffee coloured skin and ice cool eyes with just a hint of make up.

'Commissioner Nakibae told me something unexpected has come up, that you will be representing Kiribati in his place.' Her mouth smiled while her eyes gave Louisa's casual T-shirt and chinos an icy glare.

'Yes. I'm delighted to have been given that privilege,' said Louisa, not really sure what the tall woman meant by represent. The woman's name tag, which was pinned to the lapel of a purple frilly blouse buttoned up to her neck, said she was DI Vika, Central Division, Fiji. The purple blouse matched her purple maxi skirt.

'I assume you will be freshening up before the conference?' said DI Vika, smiling coldly.

Louisa blushed despite herself. 'Air Pacific lost my luggage.' She didn't want to apologise for her appearance but felt she had to. 'But it has turned up and was delivered here earlier. The receptionist is getting it for me now. As soon I have my suitcase I'll be getting changed.'

'Good,' said DI Vika, seriously.

'Excuse me?' Jyoti was back.

Louisa sighed with relief. 'At last!'

'I am so very sorry.' Jyoti's head wobbled from side to side. 'There's been some confusion. The airport people did bring your suitcase here but our register had not been updated with your name – we still had Mr Nakibae down as staying.' She cleared her throat. 'The luggage was taken away again.'

'You what?' said Louisa, not wanting to believe her.

'I called the airport and they confirmed that after leaving here they took the suitcase to a guest house in Tamavua called The Garlands. That is where they left it.'

'Bloody, fucking hell!' said Louisa before she could stop herself. Swearing wasn't on in the Pacific. She could see DI Vika flinch. But she was mad, so fucking mad! 'I've just come from Tamavua!'

'So sorry,' said Jyoti blushing. 'So very, very sorry. Of course we will arrange for someone to pick it up for you.'

'How long will that take?' said Louisa, trying not to shout.

'We can have it here by this evening.'

'So I have to wear these stinking dirty clothes till then?' snapped Louisa, aware she sounded like a prima donna but unable to control her frustration. 'No way!'

'No,' said DI Vika, po-faced. 'I am sure Commissioner Nakibae would not want you to attend the conference dressed as you are. I will have someone take you to Tamavua. You will get your luggage and still have plenty time to return and smarten yourself up before the opening conference speech at eleven.'

Detective Constable Makereta was on orders from DI Vika

to take Louisa to Tamavua to get her luggage and come straight back. Louisa could have walked faster than DC Makereta drove. Sure, they were in the middle of another torrential downpour and caution was advisable, but at this rate they'd miss the whole of the conference, never mind the welcome address. Not that Louisa gave a shit about the conference. She just wanted to get out of what she was wearing. Where her clothes touched her, she felt contaminated. Polluted. Unclean. It took all her self control not to tear the filthy items from her body. It made no difference knowing that it was all in her mind. Or that the voices could start up at any minute. She was beyond that now.

'Do you enjoy being on Tarawa?' said Makereta, 'Pardon?' said Louisa, looking at the smiling woman as if for the first time. Thick, long brown hair, parted in the middle framed wide brown eyes in a round tanned face. She was about Louisa's age and height. She wore a purple nylon bolero over a smart black dress with a thin gold belt around her plump middle. No make up. Flat shoes. Attractive in a mumsy sort of way.

'What's it like being a police officer on Tarawa?' she said. 'DI Vika said you worked there.'

'It's fine,' said Louisa curtly.

'And which church do you belong to?'

'I don't,' said Louisa. She so did not want to make small chat with some random constable who couldn't drive faster than five miles an hour.

'But everyone goes to church,' said Makereta, still smiling.

'No, not everyone. Sorry.' If Makereta thought Louisa had been rude, she hid it well.

'But if you don't belong to a church, what will happen to your soul?'

Here we go, thought, Louisa. The amount of people on Tarawa who were concerned for her soul was surprising. And now here in Fiji too. 'My soul will have to look after itself.'

Makereta looked puzzled. 'You don't care about your soul?'

'No,' said Louisa.

'I can't imagine what it'd be like not to care about my soul.'

'Look,' snapped Louisa, 'can you put your bloody foot down!' So what if she pulled rank on her. Being a constable was all about doing what you were told.

'You don't need to shout,' said Makereta, no longer smiling.

10

The bottom gate to The Garlands was open and Rick's car was parked at the top of the steep driveway. Louisa heaved a sigh of relief. She'd worried there'd be no one home. 'You can park next to the Prado at the top there,' said Louisa. 'I'll not be long.'

Makereta drove the Rav4 slowly up the steep hill. She'd not said a word since Louisa had told her to go faster. Now they were at The Garlands Louisa felt seriously guilty about her outburst. It wasn't Makereta's fault that Louisa was a loony! Because that's what she was, stressing about imaginary germs in her clothes. Louisa sighed. Her New

Year's resolution would be to be more gracious and not lose her head as much. On the way back to the hotel, she'd be nice. Ask Makereta about her life. If she was married. What it was like being a woman police officer on Fiji. It couldn't be easy. Not if Louisa's experience on Tarawa was anything to go by.

'Any other orders?' said Makereta flatly, pulling up behind the Prado.

Was she being sarcastic? 'No. Thanks,' said Louisa, looking out at the torrential rain. 'I'll not be long.' Makereta gave her a blank stare. Louisa jumped out the car and dashed to the shelter of the front porch.

No one answered when Louisa knocked. She gave the screen door a pull. It was locked even though the front door behind it was wide open. Louisa called Rick's name. No answer. Had he been amused when the airport people had dropped her off her suitcase? She hoped Stewy wasn't around, or Edwin. She didn't want to witness another argument. She shouted for Rick again. More silence. She peered through the mosquito screen door into the house. The long hall was empty. Where the hell was he?

'No one home?' shouted Makereta from the car.

'Someone has to be in,' yelled Louisa above the noise of the rain. 'The front door's open and Rick's car is here. I'll look round the back.'

'You'll have to hurry. We're running out of time if we want to get back for the opening speeches! Wait a second. I'll come with you!'

Louisa wondered if Constable Makereta thought her physical presence would somehow hurry things up? That was rich given the speed she drove at.

'Here,' said Makereta, opening a giant yellow umbrella

and inviting Louisa to get under it. 'Might help keep you dry.'

'Thanks,' said Louisa, feeling slightly sheepish. The woman seemed like a nice person. Louisa was going to have to learn to be less judgemental.

Together the women walked round to the back of the house. A wall of tall avocado trees kept a rolling green lawn hidden from prying neighbours. There was a clap of thunder followed by a flash of lightning.

'Shit!' said Louisa, almost jumping out of her skin. 'Is this weather normal?'

'At this time of year,' said Makereta, looking down at her wet feet. 'Darn it, my shoes are wet through. I didn't expect to wear them outside.'

'Sorry,' said Louisa, wiping a necklace of sweat beads from her upper lip and forehead with a clean tissue. 'Can we please find your case and get back?'

Louisa knocked on the French door at the back. Nothing. She tried the handle. It wasn't locked. She went in, conscious she was dripping water all over Rick's pristine tiled kitchen floor.

'Goodness!' said Makereta, coming in behind her and lowering the umbrella. 'This is nice.' She checked her watch. 'Your suitcase?'

'It has to be here somewhere,' said Louisa, hurrying into the hall. She saw the crimson sliver. It seeped from under Rick's bedroom door, and stretched across the immaculate polished wood floor. For a second Louisa thought it was paint. A decorating accident. Rick had said they'd had a makeover. But then she smelled the familiar metallic smell of fresh blood and her guts twisted into a knot. This wasn't good. She whispered to Makereta who had followed her.

'Something's wrong.'

'What do you mean, wrong?' she whispered. 'And why are we whispering?'

'Look!' hissed Louisa, pointing to the floor. 'I think that's blood.'

Makereta's face became serious. She slipped her long dark hair behind her ears and looked all around.

'This is the police!' shouted Louisa. 'If there is anyone in the house, show yourself now!'

The women waited. Holding their breaths. Listening for a voice above the clatter of the rain battering down on the corrugated iron roof. Louisa shouted again. 'Police! Is there anyone in the house?'

Still nothing.

Louisa pointed to the door.

Makereta gave Rick's bedroom door a gentle push and it slowly swung open. The blood was everywhere. The walls. The bed. The floor, where Rick's motionless body lay. His white shirt was drenched in blood. It appeared to seep from multiple stab wounds to his torso. His face was untouched. Lifeless blue eyes stared upwards at the ceiling fan.

'I'm going to be sick,' said Makereta.

'No you're not. You're going to phone Vika,' said Louisa firmly. She remembered what it was like to see her first body. The ugliness of violence up close. The cold certainty that a life had been brutally extinguished. It was nothing like in the films.

11

Louisa stepped out of the hotel shower, slipped into her new indoor flip flops, wrapped a cream bath towel around her wet body and went into the bedroom. She placed a second bath towel on the hotel bed and sat down on it. The Holiday Inn room was like every other hotel room she'd been in, a tarted up concrete box with twin double beds in the middle of it. It was clean, though, and there was endless boiling water and four bath towels. Louisa could never have too much hot water or too many towels.

She only had a vague recollection of buying the bundles of stuff neatly arranged on the bed opposite. She was usually a meticulous shopper and picky. Not today. She'd been like a starving kid left alone in a sweet shop, or a dog allowed to roll in something smelly at the beach. She'd grabbed anything and everything, without even trying the clothes on first. She'd bought shoes, dresses, skirts, tops, bags, make-up, underwear, toiletries, deodorant, tissues, Chanel No 5 perfume, wax for her legs and bikini line – body hairs were another non-negotiable – and a brown leather case with matching overnight bag.

It wasn't the cost of everything that annoyed her, she could afford the stuff – she'd had nothing to spend her money on for the last two years. No. It was the amount she'd bought. Why three pairs of the same patent shoes, each a different colour, when she didn't even like a patent finish? She sighed. At least she now had clean clothes to change into. And finally, after an extremely long hot shower, her skin no longer felt on fire and the voices had gone away.

The voices had started at The Garlands shortly after Vika had accused Louisa of being involved in Rick's death.

Louisa had been furious. How could she have had anything to do with his murder? It was ludicrous. Vika had then made Louisa wait in the kitchen for four hours. Louisa had watched helpless as Vika's colleagues had trampled through the house, not a latex glove or pool shoe in sight, making rookie mistake after rookie mistake. It would have been laughable, had it not been so tragic. Rick deserved better. It was only while she was confined in the kitchen that Louisa realised her suitcase wasn't anywhere in the house.

The voices had started softly at first, like a Chinese whisper, before crescendoing into a full blown scream, 'You're disgusting! Unclean! Filthy! Take off your dirty clothes, you filthy bitch before you contaminate all of Suva! Whore! You are a danger to yourself and everyone you know!' She'd tried her best to ignore them but once they got going there was no stopping them. By the time Vika allowed Louisa to leave Rick's, Louisa knew the only way to stop the voices was to get out of what she was wearing. She'd hailed the first taxi she saw. And, despite it being a Shangri-la of matted cream fur, silk rugs and dangling three-headed Hindu gods with Bhangra music blaring from all sides, she'd jumped in and ordered the driver to take her straight to the shopping mall.

Suva Mall made the Saint James Mall back in Edinburgh look cheap and shabby. Luckily, they took credit cards – it was cash only on Tarawa, or cheque. It had been that long since she'd used her credit card, she didn't know if it would work. It had.

There were three floors of shops, reached by twin escalators. Each level was jammed with shoppers and decorated with dangling shiny red and green Christmas baubles and fake white and pink Christmas trees. Piped music played cheerful festive songs.

The top floor was almost all fast food stalls, Chinese mainly, not that Louisa would ever risk eating something from a fast food anything. The main store was called Prouds and was on the middle level. It reminded Louisa of John Lewis back home. Back on Tarawa you could only get cheap Chinese nylon imports or second hand clothes. Louisa didn't do cheap anything and especially not anything second hand.

She looked over the shopping on the hotel bed for a second time and picked up a pair of white silk low rise boxers. The material was deliciously soft. Delicate. Quite sexy. Not bad. What she'd really wanted though was a thong or even a string, something a bit more risqué, but not smutty. Mataio would be with her soon. Something positive to look forward to after a truly shitty day. Her first night with him after almost three weeks apart should be special. She placed the knickers back in the pink tissue. At least they weren't big pants.

She lay back on the bed and closed her eyes. All her instincts had told her not to come to Fiji. Why, oh why, hadn't she told Nakibae to stuff his conference? In Rick's kitchen Vika had asked her stupid question after stupid question. No, of course she'd not killed Rick. No, she didn't know who had. On and on it went. Vika had only let Louisa go when confirmation came from the hotel that Rick had been seen alive and well after dropping Louisa off earlier that morning. Had Vika actually thought Louisa had killed Rick? Really?

Louisa sighed. Maybe Vika had been right to treat her with suspicion. But when it became clear Louisa had nothing to do with the crime, why continue to treat her like a suspect? And why dismiss everything she said? When Louisa had told Vika about the intruder, Vika had said it was of no consequence. But Louisa knew from her own experience that when it came to murder, no incident could be dismissed, no matter how insignificant or, apparently, unconnected. Louisa was a trained detective, and a good one. She could be of help. But if Vika didn't want her assistance, that was fine by her. She'd be gone in a couple of days anyway. Louisa stood up. It was time to get dressed. She looked over at her shopping and groaned. How was she going to fit everything into the new suitcase?

12

The rain had finally stopped and there was a delicious warm evening breeze. Dining tables and chairs replaced loungers and deck chairs around the flood-lit pool area at the back of the hotel. Twinkling fairy lights connected a border of coconut palms and created a festive atmosphere. Two trellis tables just inside the entrance to reception groaned with standard BBQ fare: overcooked hamburgers, chips, chicken nuggets, chicken wings, coleslaw, green salad, rice, lettuce, slices of tomatoes, cucumbers and a sprinkle of coriander. Louisa grimaced. She didn't much like buffets, you never knew how long the food had been sitting on the table for or who had touched what. The place was mobbed with delegates. If she wasn't quick, she'd not get anything.

The men were mostly in Fijian Bula shirts, or Hawaiian shirts, and casual slacks or fawn coloured wrap-overs, like sarongs or lava-lavas as Louisa knew them from Tarawa.

Sandals replaced shiny shoes. Smart but casual. The women, the half dozen of them, had ditched their business blues and blacks and wore shimmering green and lilac evening dresses with glittery sling backs. Louisa was glad she'd bought the mauve swirl maxi dress she now wore. It was glam but not too ostentatious and in a weird way she fitted in, which was just as well. She hated standing out.

Louisa waited for a gap in the queue and helped herself to some chips and a burger and a dollop of ketchup. She couldn't decide on the chicken nuggets. A loud guffaw distracted her. It came from a chunky man at a table at the back of the pool. He was thick set and sat next to Vika and a small, skinny Indo-Fijian woman. Two more burly cowshed native Fijians joined them. Louisa recognised the men from the crime scene earlier but not the woman. Louisa was surprised to see Vika and her team here. Had they found Rick's killer already? It was possible. Stewy had to be in the frame. Especially after the row she'd witnessed. She'd told Maker and Vika all about it. Could Edwin be involved? Maybe. Not that Louisa could imagine either Stewy or Edwin carrying out such a brutal attack. But who knows? The mind of a killer was a twisted and complex thing. Vika glanced in Louisa's direction then turned away. If she'd seen Louisa, she'd not let on. Bitch.

Louisa decided against the chicken nuggets and scoured the area for a free seat at one of the tables. She hoped she wasn't going to have to eat in her bedroom. Eating in the same place that you slept was another non-negotiable. Someone called her name. It was Makereta. Her black dress seemed to have glitter in it, or was Louisa imagining that?

'Here!' said Makereta, patting an empty dining chair next to her.

'Thanks,' said Louisa, squeezing in beside her. 'Where did you get to earlier?'

'What?' said Makereta. The chatter from the delegates made it difficult to be heard.

'I said,' said Louisa, trying not to shout too loudly, 'What happened to you earlier?'

Makereta nodded towards where Vika sat at the back of the pool. 'I was dismissed. Apparently, there is no worse crime than not doing things by the book.'

'We did do things by the book!'

Makereta shook her head. 'According to Vika I had no authority to search the house and then when I did, I should never have let you come with me. You are officially a civilian – not forgetting a potential suspect. She said we contaminated the crime scene.'

'Bullshit! The killer could have still been around,' hissed Louisa. 'We needed to check to see if he, or she, was still on the premises. It would have been dangerous for you to have done so alone. And just so you know, I am not a suspect.'

Makereta shrugged. 'All I know is that Vika is the boss and I am most certainly in her bad books.'

'If I got you into trouble, I'm sorry.'

'It's not your fault.' Makereta hiccuped and a wave of cinnamon brown hair fell over her face. She swept it behind her ears. 'I wasn't in her good books before, if you see what I mean?'

Louisa frowned. Was Makereta drunk?

'Someone from my church knew Rick. She said he was a kind man.' She paused. 'They,' she nodded towards Vika's table, 'think his partner, Stewart Norris, is the killer. What do you think, you knew both of them?'

Louisa shrugged. 'I only met them both for the first

time yesterday. Rick was a bit moody and had a temper but I liked him and I liked Stewy. They seemed like nice people and they helped me out in an emergency.'

'Stewy is supposed to have a purple beard.' She scrunched her face. 'That's a bit odd, isn't it?'

Louisa laughed. Was she serious? 'It might make him a little eccentric but not a murderer. Has Vika questioned Stewy? What did he say?'

She shook her head. 'They can't find him.'

More guffaws came from Vika's table, the group were louder than everyone else. 'They don't seem to be taking the case very seriously.' Louisa scowled in Vika's direction.

'It's the curfew. We're all locked in now. You want a drink?' said Makereta, topping up her glass with red wine from one of the half dozen open bottles on the table.

Louisa shook her head. 'I don't drink.'

'Neither do I,' said Makereta seriously. 'Uh ho. Don't look now but here comes trouble.'

'Who?' said Louisa, glancing around furtively.

'It's DC Lavneet,' whispered Makereta. 'She's part of the murder team and Vika's snoop.'

'Hello.' It was the Indo-Fijian woman who'd been sitting at Vika's table. She nodded to Louisa, leaned into Makereta and whispered something in her ear. Makereta blushed and got up.

'Excuse me. I have to go.'

13

Louisa watched Makereta and DC Lavneet disappear into

the reception area. She wondered if Makereta was going to be okay. She'd not looked happy to go with Lavneet. Louisa glanced back at Vika's table. The group appeared to be sharing jokes instead of investigating a murder. But why shouldn't they? Jokes helped with tension and there was always tension around a murder. Who did it? Why? When? Was it premeditated? A crime of passion? Was the victim killed at the scene? Will they catch the killer before he or she strikes again? And Makereta was back.

'That was quick.' Louisa was surprised. 'I thought you were gone for the night. Everything okay?'

'Yes, thanks. All okay.' Makereta leaned over, took another one of the open wine bottles and topped up a random glass. 'You sure you don't want some? It's on the house. Comes with the conference.'

Louisa shook her head. 'So, who's Lavneet? And why is she part of Vika's murder squad when you're not?'

'Ah,' said Makereta, leaning towards Louisa and tapping the side of her nose. 'It's because she's special.' She nodded, lifted her glass and drained it.

'Special. How?' said Louisa. Was Makereta pissed?

'I work very hard. But any big case that comes I'm passed by. Vika doesn't like me. I don't know why not. But she likes Lavneet. Lavneet and Vika are BOMAS. You know what that means?' She didn't wait for an answer. 'Best of Mates Always. A foreigner told me that expression.' She hiccuped. 'You want to know another thing?'

'What?' said Louisa, sticking a fork into her last chip.

'Lavneet has just asked me to spy on you.'

A shiver ran up and down Louisa's bare arms. 'Spy on me? Why?'

'Oops!' Makereta laughed. 'I wasn't supposed to tell you

that. But I'm not a snitch.' She shook her head. 'Never have been. Never will be.'

'But what does she want to find out?'

Makereta's face crumpled. She stumbled to her feet. 'I don't feel well.' She fell forward and bumped into a man with big hair.

'Hey!' he said crossly.

Louisa quickly took Makereta's arm and guided her to the lifts. 'Maybe it's best if you have a lie down in your room, eh?'

'Good idea,' said Makereta, nodding. 'By the way, where is my room?'

Louisa sighed. 'Do you know your room number?' Bodily contact with strangers and drunks was something she usually avoided, but she couldn't just leave her, not in that state.

'It's thirty-six,' muttered Makereta, 'or is that my age?'

'We can ask at reception?'

'No, don't do that, they'll think I'm drunk.' Makereta's smooth forehead crinkled into a frown then she smiled. 'Yes. It is. Thirty-six. I remember thinking, oh, I'm thirty-six too.'

'And you have the key with you?'

Makereta opened her handbag and rummaged inside before waving a rectangular piece of plastic in the air. 'My key!'

'And you know where you're going?' said Louisa.

Makereta pulled herself up straight. 'I am not drunk!'

'I never said you were.'

'It's what you're thinking.' Makereta shook her head from side to side, causing her long thick hair to tumble back and forth over her shoulders in waves.

'I'm not thinking anything,' said Louisa.

'I don't feel well. That's all.'

'Here are the lifts. You want floor three.'

'I know!' said Makereta, before falling forwards, banging her head against the corridor wall and slumping towards the floor.

Louisa grabbed Makereta under her arms, heaved her back into an upright position and held her there. Her first night in Fiji someone snoops in her room while she lies asleep naked in bed. Her first day, her host gets murdered and she gets stuck looking after a lightweight drunk. What next? The lift doors opened. Louisa prised the plastic key out of Makereta's hand, manoeuvred her inside, pressed the button for floor three and watched the doors close in front of them.

Makereta's room was identical to Louisa's except Makereta's was a mess. Louisa almost gasped when she saw it. Clothes. Shoes. Toiletries everywhere. As if a bomb had gone off. How could anyone tolerate such chaos? She helped Makereta onto her bed and got a can of cola from the small hotel fridge. She placed the can on the bedside table. 'I think you should drink this.'

Makereta groaned where she lay, without opening her eyes.

'And here.' Louisa took out one of her packets of Paracetamols from her handbag and put them next to the can. 'Take two now and two again as soon as you wake up.'

Makereta opened her eyes. She peered at Louisa. 'Vika doesn't like you.'

'The feeling's mutual,' said Louisa.

Makereta's voice was hoarse. 'You don't understand, she

really doesn't like you. That's why she asked Lavneet to ask me to spy on you. Vika can make life difficult for you if she wants.'

Louisa laughed. 'I don't live here, how can she make life difficult for me?'

Makereta made a face and started to retch. 'I'm going to be sick.'

'Wait!' Louisa ran back into the hallway. She saw a maid's cupboard by the lift. She'd noticed a bucket and mop inside. Louisa grabbed the bucket and hurried back to Makereta's room. She smelled the sickly sweet, rancid vomit, before she saw it.

14

Breakfast was being served by the pool. All traces of the buffet from the night before had been removed. Louisa had enjoyed her fried egg and bacon and sautéd mushrooms, washed down with a piping hot black coffee, and was looking forward to having her warm croissant with blackcurrant jam. In half an hour she'd be talking to Mataio. She'd called the house on Tarawa on the way to breakfast. Reteta had answered. Mataio was having a shower. Louisa told Reteta to tell Mataio she'd call again in an hour. She could hardly wait.

Louisa sat facing the glistening Suva Bay. Noddy terns flew in and out of the coconut palms that edged the pool. Louisa preferred the terns to the fruit bats she'd glimpsed the night before. The temperature was deliciously mild, with only a hint of the sweltering humidity to come. The sky was a fresh blue and there were no insects biting, not yet. A mild honeysuckle smell mixed with the whiff of grilled smoked back bacon wafted around the pool. It felt good to be alive. She didn't see Makereta approach.

'I am so sorry about yesterday evening,' said Makereta, her face bright red.

Louisa shrugged. 'How do you feel?'

'Much better. Yes. Much better. I don't know how I got so drunk.'

'You drank too much.'

Makereta's round cheeks burned crimson. 'Obviously, but I didn't think I had. Thank you for cleaning up the sickness.'

'These things happen,' said Louisa.

'But not to me,' said Makereta, looking around. 'Wait a minute. I'll find a chair and join you.'

Louisa groaned. She hoped Makereta didn't think they were BOMAS. When Louisa had returned to the room with the bucket Makereta was on the floor covered in her own vomit. Louisa had dragged Makereta to the shower, washed her, found her a clean nighty, put Makereta in it and then put her to bed. Finally, she'd mopped up the few splatters of sick that had made it to the floor with a hand towel, opened the window to get rid of the sickly smell, dropped the towel in the bucket and left both items in the cupboard on the way back to her own room. It had then taken her almost an hour under the shower to get rid of the noxious smell and feel clean again. She didn't want to think about it again. Ever.

Makereta was back with a white plastic chair. She placed it next to Louisa's and sat down. 'I don't normally drink alcohol.'

'Next time try and drink water with the wine, eh?' said Louisa, rutching her chair a couple of inches away from her. Makereta had clearly never heard of giving someone personal space.

'There'll be no next time!' said Makereta shocked. 'Luckily, after I was sick, I felt much better.'

'I know, you wanted to go back down to the dining room.'

'Did I?' she blushed again. 'Well, I'm glad you made me stay. I slept like a baby. I never even heard Lavneet come in.'

'You share with Lavneet?' Louisa was surprised. No wonder there was so much stuff in the room. 'I got the impression that you and Lavneet didn't get on.

'We don't. If she'd seen me like that, she'd have told Vika for sure.'

'Lavneet really is a snitch?'

Makereta nodded. 'Oh yes, everyone knows Lavneet is Vika's snoop.'

'Why share a room with her then?'

'We're the only female officers in the central division, we have to share. It's too expensive to have our own rooms. Besides, if a woman has a room to herself everyone thinks she'll take a man back to it.'

Louisa laughed. 'I see. Because I have a room to myself everyone assumes I'm shagging men in it, yes?'

Makereta looked serious. 'You're not from the Pacific, we all know foreigners do things differently. It's how it is.'

'So, that's a yes?'

'That's not what I said,' said Makereta helping herself to one of the two croissants on the plate in front of Louisa.

'Help yourself, why don't you?'

'I have, thanks,' said Makereta, smiling.

Louisa sighed. They didn't do sarcasm in the Pacific just like they didn't do single women living alone. Had her cousin Reteta and her family lock, stock and barrel, and dog and pig, not moved themselves into her garden and squatted there from almost as soon as Louisa arrived on Tarawa, Louisa would have been considered a loose woman. In other words, fair game for any single man to pester, annoy, hassle, prey upon. Of course, now Mataio had literally moved in with her, it was different. She wasn't single any more, but Reteta was still camped in her garden. In the Pacific there was safety in numbers.

'What about Vika?' said Louisa, grabbing the last croissant on the plate before Makereta wolfed it down too. 'You just said she has her own hotel room.'

'She's the boss. She can do what she likes.' Her face fell. 'You know, I'd have liked to have been part of the murder investigation. How can I be promoted if I'm never given an opportunity to show what I can do? I don't know why she dislikes me so much.'

'I'm sure that's not true.'

'It is. And she really hates you, at least that's what Lavneet says.'

'Did Lavneet really ask you to keep an eye on me?'

Makereta leaned into Louisa. She whispered, 'Lavneet said that Vika thought you held the same rank as Commissioner Nakibae. That's why she told me to give you a lift to Tamavua yesterday. When she found out you were only a sergeant she was livid.'

'That's hardly my fault.'

Makereta grinned. 'She had arranged for you to have a car, you know a fancy one with the Kiribati flags on it. She says you made a fool of her.'

'She shouldn't have jumped to conclusions.'

'Well, just so you know, she wants information on you. Then, later, maybe in five months, or five years, or ten, your paths will cross and Vika will use what she knows against you and get her revenge.'

Louisa laughed. 'I'll hardly be here for another five days, never mind five years. So tell her what you want!'

'I am not a snitch!' said Makereta, her cheeks flushing with fury.

'I didn't mean to suggest that you were. All I'm saying is I don't care. I have nothing to hide.'

'Vika says everyone has something to hide.'

'Can we change the subject?' Talking about Vika was doing her head in. Louisa said, 'I assume you're attending the conference? Do you know what today's theme is?'

'How the Cook Islands deal with drug trafficking.'

'Positively fascinating!' said Louisa, sarcastically.

15

While Louisa waited for the hotel receptionist to connect her to the house on Tarawa, she saw Vika and Lavneet come out the lift, their heads bent in conversation. They hurried towards the pool area and presumably breakfast. Louisa felt a pang of envy. She remembered what it was to be on a big case. And she could understand Makereta's frustration at being excluded from Vika's team. Rick's murder was a big case. You could make a name for yourself being part of the team that found a killer. But what a horrible killing. Had they left the hotel ten minutes earlier yesterday morning, or if Makereta had driven that bit faster, maybe they would have arrived at The Garlands in time to catch the killer? It was even possible they could have prevented Rick's death.

Had Vika asked her, which she had not, Louisa would have said the killing appeared to be an opportunistic, passionate crime. Unplanned and frenzied. Yet, whoever had killed Rick had taken a cool, calm shower afterwards. The bloody towel in the en-suite bathroom was one of the first things they'd spotted. It required nerves of steel to take a shower in the house of someone you'd just killed. At last, the ringing tone for the phone on Tarawa. Louisa waited. No answer.

Mataio was probably out the back by the fire. It would take him a few minutes to get to the house. He never did anything in a hurry. Louisa let the phone ring on. She had a quiet chuckle to herself. What would he say when she told him she was a witness in a murder investigation? Talk about no luck chuck! Certainly, Stewy was the obvious suspect. Over eighty percent of murders were committed by close friends or relatives. And there was no denying Stewy and Rick had had some kind of major falling out. And then there had been the flirting between Stewy and Edwin in the car the evening before that. Not that "flirting" made them killers, but it did suggest Stewy and Rick weren't getting on.

Still no answer from Tarawa. Louisa waited some more. If Stewy had killed Rick, he would have had to have left the shoeshine spot almost immediately after Rick had confronted him. But neither Stewy or Edwin had looked in a hurry or as if they were about to commit a frenzied attack on Rick. Mind you, Rick had demanded Stewy meet him at the house. There was a good chance that Stewy had done so. Had Edwin gone with him? She shivered. If she were honest, though, she still couldn't see either Stewy or Edwin killing Rick. They didn't seem nasty enough, especially not Edwin. At the airport he'd been frightened of his own shadow. A killer? No. He was too much of a coward. Of the two, Stewy was the one most capable of killing. It didn't mean he did it, though.

The phone line went dead. Louisa asked the receptionist, an older Fijian man, to try the Tarawa number again. She waited to be connected. Again. The line clicked and she heard the familiar burr of the ringing tone. Not long now. In the light of Rick's killing, someone pawing her bra and pants paled into insignificance. The phone continued to ring and Louisa continued to wait for Mataio to pick it up.

She'd met Mataio not long after she'd arrived on Tarawa. He was one of the best things that had happened to her on Tarawa. Of course, being in charge of the investigator's training programme on Tarawa had also been good. Very good. But if she were honest, it had become boring. Training constables to be better detectives wasn't nearly as exciting as being a detective. Previous to coming to Tarawa, finding the bad bastards and getting them banged up had been her job twenty-four seven. And she'd worked hard to get there too. Gone to university. Studied when everyone else had partied. Passed her detective exams with the highest grades of her intake. Not that her mum was impressed. Being a detective was a man's job, and she'd made it clear she thought Louisa was wasting her time. But as far back as she could remember, being a cop was what Louisa had wanted to do.

When she'd joined the murder team it had been a dream come true. Not that she'd been much of a team player. That was her problem. Always had been. Unlike her brother, Mr Popular. When they were wee, he was always the first to be asked to join in on the games, she was always last, if at all. Billy no mates. That was her. Didn't matter what she said, it always came out bossy, opinionated, pushy. It made people think she was arrogant. A snob even.

Still no answer on Tarawa. Louisa put the phone down. What the hell was going on? Where was Mataio? She asked the receptionist to phone the number for a third time. He did. She waited. And waited. And waited. After fifteen rings she slammed the phone down. What was the bloody bastard playing at? Why the hell didn't he answer the phone? She would not try a fourth time. No way! She nodded to the receptionist that she was leaving and headed for the lifts. The lift doors opened. Two tall men exited.

'Their pool is bigger than the hotel pool here,' said the first man, nodding knowingly.

'Where do you suppose they got the money for that?' said the second man.

The first shrugged. 'You know it was the lover. He stabbed him with a knife.'

'There's no pool,' said Louisa, walking into the lift and pressing the button to her floor.

'There is a pool,' said the first man, scowling at her. 'A very big pool!'

'I was in his house,' said Louisa, as the lift door closed, 'and there's no fucking pool!'

16

Someone had been in her room. Louisa only did straight lines and her new leather case stood squint against the wall. Her lipstick was on its side, not upright as she had left it. She darted back into the hall. It was empty. She went back into the room. Checked through her clothes. Everything was there. Or was it a burglary? She'd used the room safe. A rookie mistake! Hotel safes were notoriously easy to break into, like their rooms. She checked the safe. Travel money, credit cards, airline tickets were all there.

Louisa sat on her bed. While she'd been downstairs having breakfast with Makereta, someone had come into her hotel room, raked through her stuff and left without taking anything. Louisa didn't like it. No, not one little bit. It was more or less a repeat of what had happened at Rick's. Who was doing this and why? Could it be Edwin? He had been at Rick's and he was supposed to be staying at the hotel. Either that or a total stranger was stalking her. But given she'd only just arrived in the country, that seemed unlikely.

But why would Edwin do such a thing? Was he working with Stewy? Louisa groaned. But, crazy as it seemed, and much as she was loath to do so, she would have to tell Vika about the intruder. No matter how slight, this was a connection to yesterday's killing, it couldn't be ignored. But first she had to clean the room and shower. The thought of someone rummaging through all her things, made her feel violated, dirty, disgusting.

Under the hot spray of the hotel shower Louisa slowly began to feel normal again. But thinking so much about Rick's death and the mysterious intruder-cum-pervert made her realise how much she missed detective work. It was nearly two years since she'd been involved in proper police work, a triple murder on Tarawa. She'd been lucky to survive that. Her last case in Scotland had been a big one too. One of the biggest cases Lothian and Borders Police violent crime team had ever had. Drugs. Murder. Rape. Prostitution. GBH. ABH. Smuggling. You name it, that case had it and it had involved a right bunch of bad bastards.

Every member of the murder team had worked hard. For twelve weeks they'd each of them had an average of four hours sleep a night. Then, bingo! She'd hit the bull's eye. All on her own she'd tracked down a witness. Reliable. Honest. Upright. Her evidence was irrefutable. It was the key. With it everything else fell into place like a line of dominoes. The prosecutor fiscal was in no doubt. The bad guys would go down. There had been pats on the back all round and she'd got the biggest ones. It had been the best day of her life. And then, as quickly as it had been the best day, it had became the worst day.

In front of the whole team, and out of the blue, her boss had lost it with her. Bawled her out. Called her arrogant and disobedient. Said that her insistence, against his direct orders, on working alone had led to confusion and misunderstandings. Louisa was totally taken aback. She'd not even realised she'd been working alone. He said they'd succeeded this time, but that had been down to luck. He'd warned her, if she didn't start cooperating with her colleagues, she'd find herself back on the beat or worse still, out of a job. There was no place in Lothian and Borders Police for mavericks like her.

17

'They're saying Stewy is the killer,' said Makereta, pointing to a bundle of newspapers on the reception counter.

'Stewy really did it?' Louisa picked up one of the papers. Makereta smelled of lemon and jasmine. 'Really?' She wasn't surprised but she felt somehow disappointed. She read out the lurid headline, '"Gay lover slaughters older boyfriend in jealous frenzy." Has Stewy been arrested then?'

Makereta shook her head. 'They still can't find him. He's not even been questioned.'

'These stories are lies then.' So, the press in Fiji were like the press everywhere, saying anything for a headline.

Makereta shrugged. 'Apparently a well known drug dealer has admitted to selling Rick and Stewy drugs and said that they were habitual users.'

Louisa glanced at a shoulder shot of Commodore Frank Bainimarama and a headline urging Fijians to stay calm. She frowned. 'I saw no evidence of any kind of drugs in the house, not even cigarettes.'

'A white powder was removed,' said Makereta.

'Cocaine?' She supposed they could have taken drugs. Why not? Half of the consenting adults in Edinburgh did.

'Lavneet said they also found porn video tapes of young boys.'

'Paedophilia?' Louisa was genuinely shocked. 'I can't believe that.'

'I quote,' said Makereta, '"New Zealander Rick Davies and Australian Stewart Norris used to invite young homeless boys back to their house on the pretext of giving them food and shelter. Once the boys were there the men plied the boys with drugs and drink and took advantage of them. This is what happens when gay people have too many rights. It's time to stamp out this vile curse, which is bringing shame to our beloved Christian country." Unquote.'

Louisa was stunned. 'Where are they getting their information from?'

'And there's more: "An anonymous witness exclusively told The Fiji Times that Rick Davies had a violent temper and was jealous of his younger partner, Stewart Norris, who was known to be a flirt. It is the opinion of our witness that it was only a matter of time before someone got killed."'

'That's hearsay and gossip. Is there any actual concrete evidence that proves any of these accusations? And how do the papers know about the cocaine and porn videos anyway, that's police business?'

'Someone from the police will have leaked it. It happens all the time.'

'The papers don't mention Edwin?' said Louisa. 'Why not?'

'According to Lavneet, he arrived at the hotel shortly after we left. Given Rick was murdered only minutes before we discovered his body, Edwin could not have killed him.'

Louisa inched closer to Makereta and whispered, 'Listen, while we were having breakfast earlier someone broke into my room. But just like at Rick's, the intruder left without taking anything.'

'Oh my goodness!' said Makereta, her brown eyes widening. 'That is very strange. But why go into your room and take nothing?'

Louisa shrugged. 'I don't know but I've only just arrived in the country so any interest in me and my things has to be connected to my stay at Rick's and therefore his murder.'

'Who could it be?'

Louisa shrugged. 'Whoever it is, I have to tell Vika about the incident.'

'Oh?' said Makereta, taking the newspaper from her and putting it back on the reception counter. 'Do you think that's wise?'

'It's too bizarre to be ignored,' said Louisa. 'Vika needs to check it out. Besides, I don't like the idea of someone snooping about my things. Who knows what they'll do next. Don't you agree?'

Makereta smiled then slipped her long thick hair behind her ears with one smooth movement of her hands. 'It is odd, I'll give you that, but DI Vika doesn't appreciate anyone telling her what to do, especially not a foreigner.'

18

Vika was with Lavneet at the pool still having breakfast. 'The first conference talk of the day starts in five minutes,' said Vika, glancing at her watch as Louisa approached. 'Shouldn't you be making your way there?'

'Someone broke into my room while I was down here having breakfast earlier.'

'Oh?' said Vika, picking up her coffee cup and taking a sip.

'It's the same M.O. as at Rick's. The intruder rummaged around then left without taking anything.'

'A matter for hotel security, surely?' said Lavneet.

Louisa shook her head. 'Possibly, but it is a coincidence,

don't you think, being broken into in the same way both here and at Ricks?' She addressed the last remark to Vika.

'The chambermaid could have moved your things while tidying up.' Lavneet again.

'I've already checked at reception, the maids have only just arrived. Everyone was late because of the curfew. I think there may be a connection with Rick's death.'

'Are you aware The Garlands guest house was in the news recently?' said Vika, putting her coffee cup down with a clatter.

'I saw this morning's papers. They accuse Stewy of the killing, which seems not only premature,' said Louisa, 'but prejudicial to any trial.'

Vika continued as if she'd not heard Louisa. 'Rick and Stewy advertised their guest house in Australia as a place to stay for gay holiday makers.'

'And?' said Louisa, wondering where Vika was going with this.

'Homosexuality is not only against the law in Fiji it is a sin in the eyes of our Lord God. If you went to church, you would know that.'

Louisa groaned silently. Another holy roller. Great! And how did Vika know she didn't go to church? 'But isn't discrimination also against the law in Fiji too? I'm sure Chief Commissioner Nakibae told me that.'

'Homosexuality is tolerated,' said Vika curtly. 'But that does not mean we want to encourage that sort of person to come to Fiji.'

'What has Rick being gay got to do with his murder?' Vika was not the first homophobic police officer Louisa had met and no doubt wouldn't be the last.

'It suggests the men were and are depraved and capable

of anything. When we find Stewart I am in no doubt he will confess to the crime.'

'He's still missing, though, and looking at my break-ins more closely may help you find him,' said Louisa.

Vika smiled then rested her rigid upright back slightly backwards into the chair, as if making herself more comfortable. 'You know what I believe?'

'What?' Was Vika finally going to include her in the investigation?

'It is clear to me that you have misremembered where and how you left your belongings.'

Louisa laughed. 'I didn't misremember!' Was there even such a word? 'Perhaps, I could have made a mistake once. But not twice. I am very particular.'

'Yes. I know. You have issues, don't you?'

Louisa stopped breathing. 'Pardon?'

'You have issues with imagining germs where there are none. And you believe these imaginary germs can kill people who are on the other side of the world if you don't scrub them away. If you can imagine such ridiculous nonsense I think it is very possible you can imagine your things had been moved.'

'You can stop right there!' said Louisa, her voice trembling. 'I have imagined nothing. Someone broke into my room twice. Once at Rick's and here again at the hotel. It may or may not have anything to do with Rick's killing, that is not for me to say. But, given the circumstances I thought it my duty to report what had happened. So why don't you do your duty and investigate it!'

19

Louisa should have listened to Makereta. Vika was a first class bitch! How did the sanctimonious cow know about her medical history? Louisa had told no one on Tarawa about it, never mind on Fiji! The only person who may have seen her medical record was Nakibae but that was unlikely as she was contracted by the European Union not the Kiribati Police Service. Nakibae wouldn't get that information. Then the penny dropped. The EU office for the Pacific region was in Suva. No doubt Vika had a friend, or a cousin, or uncle, or aunt, or whoever, who worked there and told her what she wanted to know. Clearly, as in Kiribati, nothing was private in Fiji. So what if she was fastidious about being clean and tidy? Lothian and Borders Police had had no issue with her medical history, so why did Vika?

Louisa stopped walking. Where hell was she? She'd left the hotel in such a rage she'd paid no attention to where she was going. Above her head bunches of bats dangled upside down from the branches of tall palm trees. They looked like giant shiny black fruits waiting to be plucked. Louisa shivered. Across the road a family of five picnicked in a large scrubby park area. To her other side, behind a metre high stone sea wall, the heaving purple Pacific thrashed into the roots of tangled mangroves. Something. Bobbing. In the musky water between the trees. Bulging. Bloated. Purple. She looked more closely. It was a dead pig. Legs facing skywards. Like a four-legged buoy. Ugh! Walking aimlessly was helping no one. Louisa turned and went back the way she came.

Regardless of what Vika thought, Louisa knew someone

had snooped in her room on two occasions. If Vika wasn't interested in finding out who the culprit was, then Louisa would check it out herself. She wasn't going to let some creep rummage through her things whenever he – she was sure the snooper was a he – felt like it. Besides, if there was a link between the break-ins and Rick's murder, she could be in danger. What else did she have to do? Go to the conference and listen to a handful of academics and bigwigs talk about themselves. She didn't think so.

She needed a plan. Didn't matter if she didn't stick to it, any plan was always better than no plan. The most obvious way forward was to talk to Edwin and Stewy. They had both been in The Garlands at the time of the first break-in. Louisa wasn't convinced Stewy was a killer, although jealousy could turn the kindest of people into crazed killers, but as Stewy was on the run, that left Edwin. She shivered again. The idea of Rick luring young boys to his house was the stuff of fiction, surely?

Edwin didn't answer his door. Louisa sighed. Stopped in her enquiries before she'd even started. How pathetic was that? She glanced around. The hotel corridor was deserted. The delegates were presumably at the conference. The other guests sightseeing or sunbathing or whatever it was tourists did in Fiji. Edwin was probably with them. She placed her ear against the room door. Silence. If she could only have a peek in his room. Just for a minute. What if he kept a diary? It was amazing how many people did.

The chambermaid was on the floor below, which was Louisa's floor. The last three doors in the corridor were open. The girl's trolley was outside the third last door. Louisa popped into the room. The girl was in the middle of stripping the beds. She looked about twenty. Sweet faced. All the better. Louisa asked if she'd mind opening her door as she'd left her key inside? The girl said Louisa needed to ask at reception. Louisa put on her best smile and said she'd been to reception but there was no one there. If she asked ever so nicely, would the girl mind helping her just this once? Louisa would even let her see her passport in the room to prove she was not a thief. The girl gave in.

The girl unlocked Louisa's door with her master key card, which she took from a pocket in the front of her nylon overall and Louisa got her passport and showed her it. The girl asked if she really was from Scotland. When Louisa nodded the girl asked Louisa what snow was like. Louisa told her: cold and wet. Louisa hated snow, especially when it stung her cheeks. Louisa then asked the girl where she was from. She was from Nadi. And had three children, which shocked Louisa. She looked too young. Louisa asked if she had a photo of them. She had. In her bag, which she kept hidden in her linen trolley. Together they went back to the trolley. The girl left the master key on top of the trolley, removed her handbag, hidden behind a stack of crisp white sheets, took out a photo of three smiley children, all under ten, and proudly showed it to Louisa. Louisa made a kind comment and thanked the girl. Then, while the chambermaid leaned over and hid her bag back behind the sheets, Louisa swapped the master key sitting on the trolley with her own room key.

If Louisa was lucky, the cleaner wouldn't be aware she had the wrong key: she'd only three rooms left to clean and as the doors were already open, in theory, she wouldn't need to use the key again for a while. And if, when the key was next used it wouldn't open the doors, it would be thought of as a technical glitch and the card would simply be recoded.

Back on Edwin's floor Louisa knocked on Edwin's door once, twice, three times. Nothing. She looked up and down the corridor. No one. She swiped the keycard over the electronic lock and she was in.

20

Louisa leaned against the back of the door and held her breath and waited. It was so quiet she could hear her blood rushing through her veins. What the hell was she doing here? If she got caught, she could get done for breaking and entering. That would be her career in the police over. Finished. Forever. But a minute was all she needed to look around. She grabbed the Do Not Disturb sign on the inside door handle, opened the door again and quickly posted it outside. If the chambermaid did come to do the room that would sort her.

She leaned against the back of the door a second time. She slowly exhaled and inhaled. The pungent, sweet smell of overripe fruit made her wince. A yellow pineapple sat on the bedside table, next to the phone. Was that one of the two that Rick had slapped out of Stewy's hands? Probably. She wouldn't have eaten it either, not after it had been on the ground.

The hotel room was similar to her own, but a different shape and much bigger. Whereas her room had twin double beds in it, this room had one giant bed. The wastepaper bin was empty. It looked like the chambermaid had been and gone.

Edwin's suitcase sat on a luggage rack opposite the bed. It gaped open. Louisa clocked a couple of shabby T-shirts, a black thong – she grimaced at that – and two stray socks, not matching. The wardrobe was empty. As was the ensuite bathroom. No toothbrush. No hairbrush. Nothing. Edwin may have checked in but he wasn't staying here. So where was he? Hiding out with Stewy?

Louisa flopped down on the armchair by the window. Why check into a hotel and not stay there? And where did that leave her theory of Edwin as the snoop? It wasn't a good start. She scanned the room. Had she missed something? Anything? Suddenly she had a deja vu. She'd been in a room like this before. It was on that fateful day in Edinburgh when her boss had bollocked her out for being a maverick.

That day had almost been as bad as the day she'd come home from school to find her dad had left them. Her life would have been so different if she'd not let her police colleagues drag her to the Three Sisters in the Cowgate to celebrate. Telling off or not, she'd won them the case. They'd insisted on buying her a drink. They'd told her not to take the boss's dressing down to heart. They'd all been where she was standing. The stress of the case had got to him. She was not to worry.

Ironically, for the first time it felt as if she belonged. But when the others left the Three Sisters to go to another pub, she'd quietly stayed behind, silently seething. Too angry to go home and face her mother. Then the boss had appeared, pissed as a fart, looking for the others, and had the cheek to ask her where everyone was. She'd told him. He'd gone to leave then changed his mind. Said he was sorry he'd been so harsh. That it had been for her own good. That she could be a good officer, a very good officer, especially for a woman, but she had to follow the rules. She'd laughed, especially for a woman, eh?

He'd thought her laughing meant she'd accepted his apology. That she had understood where he was coming from. He'd plonked himself down. Almost sat on top of her. She'd pushed him away. He'd resisted. If she'd had a brick, she'd have smashed it in his face. She'd got the evidence that got the bad guys, and he'd been too weak to admit his own mistakes, blamed her instead. Too mean to give credit where credit was due. Angry because she, a woman, had been right, and he, the boss, hadn't had a clue. How the hell had he got the job? He'd sat there, leaning his drunken dead weight into her body, muttering about responsibility and pressure. He'd even offered to buy her a drink. She was about to tell him to take a flying fuck. But then she had the idea. The one she shouldn't have had. The one that changed everything.

21

The centre of Suva was heaving. Louisa had left Edwin's room with the sweet scent of the overripe pineapple lingering in her nostrils. It was her only clue and a long shot, a very long shot. But the shoeshine lad from the day before had seemed to know Stewy. In fact, she'd bet money on he did. In what context? That was another matter. For now she didn't want to think about the accusations in the newspapers, she just wanted to talk to the lad and ask him if he knew where either of the men could be.

Louisa pushed through the noisy crowds. She saw the box first, it nestled between two market stalls. It was impossible to miss the scrappy sign with the words 'Killer Shoeshines here!' scrawled across it. The lad squatted next to the box. He wore the same baseball cap and sunshine orange vest. He polished the shoes of a tall, fat Fijian man in a dark blue suit. A suit, in this weather? Louisa stood next to a jumble of people queuing at a stall selling mangos and avocados, waiting for the lad to finish. Someone pushed into her. She stumbled, fell into the fruit stall. For a second she thought the fruit would tumble on top of her. How had her glittering career come to chasing a phantom snooper, whose worst crime was to have touched her bra?

But she knew why. She should have reined herself in that fateful day in Edinburgh. If she had, she wouldn't have had to leave her job. But when her boss had sat down next to her in the Three Sisters and offered to buy her that drink, she'd acted without thinking. All it took was a little bit of flattery and a little bit of looking into his eyes in that certain way. An occasional grin and accidentally brushing his hand. More drinks helped. How could he have believed she would want to sleep with him after the way he'd humiliated her? But he had. She'd help him stagger to the Holiday Inn Express in the Cowgate. Booked a room with his card. Sex didn't happen, he couldn't even get his clothes off, never mind get it up, not with the amount of alcohol he'd consumed. But he didn't know that. She'd helped him undress. Took a couple of compromising snaps with her mobile, just in case he tried to deny he'd been with her, and left him there comatose.

The next day she'd lied blatantly and reported him

for abusing his position and her. It was wrong of her on every level. Wrong! Wrong! Wrong! What had possessed her? It was her word against his word. They took her word. Turned out there had been complaints made against him before but that still didn't justify her behaviour. When had she become a liar and a snitch? It was a moment of badness. He'd had to take early retirement. His wife left him. The others blackballed her, you didn't snitch on your own. It was the only rule. Work became unbearable. And the worse thing was, they were right, she'd have blackballed herself if she could have.

'You want me to clean your shoes, missus?' The young man grinned, his front teeth were black stumps. The big man had gone.

'No thanks, but I would like to ask you a question, if that's okay?' He looked about sixteen. Maybe older. Scrawny. Bare feet. Poor.

'You want to know where Albert Parade is? I can give you directions, you give me money?' He held up his grubby hand.

She smiled. 'No, I don't need directions. It's to do with someone who had their shoes shined yesterday? You were here yesterday, yes?'

'I'm always here,' said the youth. 'You're a tourist? Do you need a Fiji driving licence? I can get you one for tomorrow?'

Louisa laughed despite herself. 'No, I don't need a driving licence.'

'You want hashish? I'll get you a very good price.'

'Nothing like that.' What would he offer next? 'Yesterday morning, around half past eight you polished a foreigner man's shoes. The man was white and very tall.'

The boy looked blank. 'I polish the shoes of many foreign men.'

'He was with another man, also a foreigner. But this foreigner lives here in Suva even though he is an Australian. His name is Stewy. He has a small purple beard on the tip of his chin.' She pointed to her chin as if to emphasise the point. 'He's difficult to forget. Another older man came to talk to him. I was with them. You remember us?'

The boy looked vague. Shook his head. 'No. I don't remember the men, or you.'

Louisa laughed. 'You were right here.' Louisa, pointed to the ground. 'The older man knocked two pineapples out of the man called Stewy's hands.'

The boy's face turned ugly. 'I told you, I don't know you or your friends. Now go away.'

'You've heard about the foreigner who was murdered? It was in all the papers today. Well, it was that older man who was killed. The police want to talk the man with the purple beard about the death. Are you sure you have no idea where he, or his tall friend, might be?'

'You stop asking questions!' The lad swept his shoe cleaning paraphernalia into a blue plastic carrier bag, grabbed his box, and headed across the road. 'Go away!'

'Wait!' shouted Louisa. Why did he lie? She was good with faces. He was the same boy she saw with Stewy and Edwin. She went to run after him but he'd vanished. Bugger! She'd stuffed up. She should have been more tactful. Less pushy. He was scared. That much was clear. But why? Louisa rounded the corner. She saw a second shoeshine boy, further down the road. He looked even more ragged than the one she'd just talked to, like something out of a Dickens novel. He squatted by a small box, on top of which he was arranging a handful of brushes in a neat row. If Louisa didn't know any better, she'd have said he was doing a stock take.

22

'Hello,' said Louisa, wiping sweat from her neck with a tissue.

The young boy looked up. He smiled. He had all his teeth. 'You want a shoeshine?'

She shook her head. 'Can I ask you a few questions?'

The boy grinned and stood up. 'I am very good at answering questions.'

'Thanks. I was talking to another shoeshine lad. He sat back there,' she pointed to where she had just come from, 'but he had to leave quickly and I didn't get a chance to ask him his name.'

'That's Wame's spot,' said the boy.

'Wame?'

The boy nodded, still smiling.

'Is he always there?' Louisa reckoned this lad was thirteen, if that.

'Yes. It is a good spot but this one is better. You really, really don't want me to shine your shoes?'

She shook her head. 'Was Wame there yesterday morning, around about 8.30?'

'For sure. He is always there.'

'Yesterday morning Wame cleaned the shoes for a friend of mine, called Edwin, a tall, bald foreigner from the Netherlands. He was with another man, an Australian, who has a tiny purple beard. He's called Stewy. I wanted to talk to Wame about the men.'

The boy frowned. 'I don't remember seeing them. But it was busy yesterday. I don't see everything when I am busy.'

'What are you doing?' It was the Fijian man in the suit Louisa had seen earlier. His round face dripped sweat.

Louisa stood up slowly. 'That has nothing to do with you.'

'Your questions are stopping my boys getting customers. If you don't want your shoes polished, you clear off!'

'I'll leave when I want to,' said Louisa.

'You go!' he said. 'And you?' He thumped his big hand into the boy's head. The boy cried out and dropped to his knees.

'Stop that!' said Louisa

The man ignored her. 'What have you been saying?' He lifted his hand to hit the boy again.

'No you don't!' said Louisa, grabbing the man's arm and twisting it behind his back. The man roared in pain. She pressed his bent arm deeper into his sweaty back. 'Hit him again and I'll take you to the nearest police station and have you for assaulting a minor, but not before I've broken your arm. Got that?'

'Let me go,' hissed the man, his eyes bulged with fury.

'It didn't hurt!' cried the boy, on his feet. 'Please, let him go!'

'Now, as it happens I do want my shoes cleaned,' said Louisa, catching her breath.

'You are a dead person!' growled the man.

She squeezed his arm tighter.

'Stop!' he hissed.

'I repeat, if you hit the boy again, I will report you for

assault. That's not a warning that's a promise. Do you hear?'

'My arm!'

'Stay still and I'll let you go.' She remained tense. Ready. For an attack. Just in case. When she felt his massive body relax, very slowly she loosened her grip on the arm. Inch by inch, until the arm was free. She moved away.

'Bitch!' He cradled his arm to his chest, his eyes watered. 'I'll get you for this!'

'Now,' she said to the boy, taking her purse from her bag. The arm would hurt. She'd really twisted it. Being smaller than him was to her advantage. It'd take him a while to get over the shock and to use it again. She had time. She looked at the young boy. 'How much?'

'A dollar,' whispered the boy. She could hardly hear him.

'Good.' Louisa gave him a dollar.

The boy's hand trembled so much he almost dropped it. 'Put your foot on the box,' he said quietly.

Louisa placed her foot on the crate.

Head down, the boy picked up his buffer and started working on her sandal.

'I am going to fucking kill you, bitch,' said the fat man staring at her, his arm gripped to his chest, his eyes glowing with hatred.

'Where I come from hitting defenceless little boys is as bad as being a lassie basher.' She would not panic. His right arm would be hurting. It would be her bad luck if he was left handed. She had time. She wasn't going to let him scare her. The bastard. She took long deep breaths. But she was scared. Bloody hell! What had possessed her to twist his arm like that? She had no authority here. He could do her for assault! She'd gambled he'd not want the police involved. But what if she'd been wrong? Worse still, what if he'd seen the armlock coming and known how to get out of it? Her breaths tumbled out of her nose and mouth. Short. Erratic. No air. She would not panic. She made herself breath. Slowly. She would not lose control. Not now. Out. In. Out. In. The man began to wriggle his bent arm. Christ! She had to leave. Now.

'Other foot, please,' whispered the boy, without looking up.

Louisa smiled and swapped her right foot for her left foot.

'I will make you disappear,' said the man under his breath, sounding less and less angry and more and more confident.

Louisa smiled back at him. 'Yet, here I am.' What was she doing? She was so scared she could have screamed. The answer was simple, she had a death wish. Yes, that was it. Otherwise, why, oh why, ask the boy to clean her shoes? Subconsciously, she was wanting to be killed. The boy coughed. Her sandals were done.

'Worth every cent,' she said. He laid his small brush on the box and refused to look up. 'Thank you.'

'When I find you I am going to kill you!' growled the fat man.

Louisa wanted to give him the finger but instead she walked away. Every one of her senses on red alert. Ready for anything. Just in case. What a bastard. The poor boy was even more scared of him than she was.

23

Louisa waited to cross the road. The traffic was mad. Cars, lorries, buses and taxis of all sizes hooted and tooted and stopped and started. The fumes from the vehicles mingled with the earthy market smells created a noxious mix. She didn't want to look back but she had to know if the man was following her. She looked. The man and the boy were gone. She sighed with relief. Suddenly. A sinking feeling. What if she'd made things worse for the boy? She hoped not. What had possessed her to twist the man's arm back like that? She was losing the plot. The big man clearly had power over the shoeshine boys. Did he run some kind of protection racket? Imagine having to pay protection money for a shoeshine spot? She'd heard everything now. Maybe the boss man took a percentage of their earnings? Or maybe he employed them?

There was a lull in the traffic. Louisa nipped across the road. She'd met the boss man's kind before. Bullies, who picked on defenceless people who couldn't fight back. All talk. All show. No action when challenged. A coward. He didn't scare her. She shivered. Who was she kidding? She had provoked him big time. No getting away from it. He'd probably break her legs if he got the chance. So, why take the chance? But she'd have to come back. The boy called Wame had lied to her and she wanted to know why. A tall, gangly, balding white man walked into a car park a block down. Was it Edwin? If she was quick, she could catch him.

Louisa looked up and down the packed car park. Monstrous four-by-fours sat squashed next to cars half their size. Some vehicles looked blocked in. Others seemed to be parked slap bang in the middle of the access road. Pedestrians, pushing full shopping trolleys, ambled between the cars. The man who had looked like Edwin had vanished at the entrance to the car park.

There a security guard sat in a metal box, which looked like a giant upright sardine tin. Louisa smiled at him. 'Excuse me.' It was a long shot but why not? 'I'm looking for a friend of mine. A foreign man, bald, tall and thin. He came in here a minute ago. Did you by any chance see what direction he went in?'

The guard shrugged. 'Most people who come in by foot are going there.' He leaned out of his box and jabbed a fat thumb towards a giant shack at the back of the car park. 'The Aussie Second Hand Clothing Shop.'

Young women, older men and couples with children sifted through rails of denim jeans, full length dresses, jackets and jumpers. Two tall floor fans just inside the glass door entrance wafted musty, warm air over the heads of the people. The smell turned Louisa's stomach. After her dad had upped and abandoned them, overnight her mum had started buying their clothes from charity shops. Once, when she was with her mum looking for a school uniform, she must have been in her early teens, an old man came into the shop. He told the old ladies behind the counter that his elderly mother of eighty-eight had passed away. It had been very sudden. He'd wanted to give them all her things. He'd brought bag after bag into the shop: books, ornaments, pots, pans, plates, cups, jewellery, shoes, reading glasses, towels, clothes and more clothes. With the last bag he broke down into tears. A grown man crying? She'd felt embarrassed. Since then, she associated second hand shops with her dad leaving them, old people and death.

She looked up and down for Edwin. He wasn't there. Had he even come in the shop? It had been a long shot. Just in case he was skulking in the shadows, she went up and down each of the sweltering aisles once again. What a waste of time! She was hungry and tired and desperately wanted a shower. Time to go back to the hotel. Outside, the bright sunshine dazzled her. She licked her lips. She also really needed a drink. She had to be careful, though. What if the big boss of the shoeshine lads was looking for her? Thump! Something against her head. Pain. Darkness.

24

It was unpleasantly hot. Louisa's throat felt thick and sticky and her head throbbed badly. Was she going to be sick? A smell. In the air. Of rancid cooking oil. Whoosh! This morning's breakfast surged up into her throat. She gulped the acidic bile back down. Ouch. The back of her head. She touched it. A lump. Some bastard had bashed her. She opened her eyes. A tall woman. Next to her. Big hair. Someone else, a younger girl, with big eyes and a sweet face holding a plastic cup to Louisa's lips.

'Are you okay?' said the woman.

'What happened?'

The woman nodded towards the girl. 'She found you outside.'

'You were on the ground. I came back inside and got help.'

'Did you see who hit me?' said Louisa.

The girl looked blank. 'There were many people in the

car park.'

'You rest. I have called the police,' said the woman.

'I am the police,' said Louisa, trying to sit up then thinking better of it. 'I mean, I am the police in Kiribati.'

The woman either didn't hear or didn't care. 'When they come they will help you.'

Louisa didn't know why she'd told the woman she was with the Kiribati Police Service. It didn't matter. 'Thank you.'

The woman shrugged and wandered away. The girl handed Louisa her water, smiled briefly and followed the woman.

Louisa gently leaned back in her chair. It was hard white plastic. Like a picnic chair. Where the hell was she? She couldn't remember anything. She looked around. Red square Formica tables. Scuffed lino, cracked, crumbling, disintegrated. Cigarette stubs. Grime. A skinny, scabby dog, tits hanging so low they almost touched the ground. White washed brick wall dripping dirty grease marks. A rancid cooking smell. A counter. Three heat lights warming chicken wings and chips, chunks of taro. She was in a greasy spoon. Louisa retched. It didn't get much more unhygienic than a greasy spoon café. The last thing she wanted was for the voices to start up again. Not here. Not now. She tried to get to her feet for a second time. The movement made her want to throw up again. She sat back down. Closed her eyes and then opened them again.

The café was packed. People chatted. Lounged. Munched their food in the stifling heat in the stuffy room. A steamed up picture window looked onto the car park beyond. Another surge of nausea forced Louisa to put her head between her knees. Who had hit her? Think! Think!

Think! Yes! She remembered! She'd been following the man who looked like Edwin into the second hand shop-cum-barn. He'd disappeared. She'd come out of the shop. Looked around. Vaguely recalled a café sign. That's when it must have happened. Of all places to be attacked, outside a greasy spoon, and a dirty one at that. But the voices were silent. Nothing. Not a peep. They were like that. Totally unpredictable.

The voices had started the day after she'd become a teenager. It was a Saturday. She'd turned thirteen on the Friday. She'd been to the corner shop to buy some rolls. When she'd dropped the bread rolls on the kitchen table as usual, she'd noticed some dirty marks above the cooker. From out of nowhere she thought the marks harboured thousands of germs, and if she didn't clean them, her mother would die a painful death. It was such a stupid thought she'd laughed out loud. But it wouldn't go away. Even after she'd given in and wiped the wall down, a voice in her head kept telling her the wall was still dirty, contaminated. She washed and scrubbed the wall for a further hour before the voice went away. From that day she'd been obsessed about keeping the house germ free.

As soon as someone or something touched a work surface Louisa had to clean it, again and again and again. It drove her mum nuts, and cost a fortune in cleaning products. They argued about her incessant cleaning but Louisa never told her mum why she was doing it. She'd tried to stop. Until then she'd always hated housework. But if she ignored the voice telling her to clean, it got louder and louder. If she still did nothing, another would join in, and another, accusing her of also being dirty and saying her mother would die because of her. She knew the voices were her own thoughts. She'd worked that out. But it didn't make it any easier to deal with them. Then one day her mother said she'd had enough of her crazy behaviour and marched her to the doctor's.

25

Makereta's brown eyes were wide with concern. 'The owner of the cafe got your name from your conference badge.' Makereta nodded to the delegate's badge on the lapel of Louisa's blouse, which Louisa had forgotten she'd had on. 'She called the hotel, said you were mugged. I came straight away. What happened?'

She pointed to the back of her head. 'Someone hit me and it hurts.'

'Nothing was taken from your bag?'

Louisa shook her head.

Makereta made a puzzled face. 'Did you see anyone acting suspiciously before it happened? A drunk? Someone on drugs? It is very rare for foreigners to be attacked, but it can happen.'

'One minute I was standing looking across the car park and the next I was out cold.' Louisa looked around at the busy café. 'Are there no witnesses at all?'

'No. It was probably very quick. One blow. Bang. You fall down. He, or she, makes an attempt to rob you but is disturbed and so he or she disappears. Over in a second.'

'Maybe? But what if it has something to do with the break-ins. Or even the killings?'

'Like what?' said Makereta, looking doubtful.

'I don't know,' said Louisa, suddenly feeling exhausted.

'If you were knocked out, you'll have to go to the hospital to get checked over.'

'I'm fine. I just need a minute to catch my breath.'

'I don't know about that.' Makereta pulled up one of the white plastic chairs and sat next to Louisa. 'What were you doing here, anyway?'

'I felt like some fresh air so I came to the market,' she lied. 'Before I was attacked I saw someone who looked very much like Edwin. I was following him.'

Makereta looked visibly shocked. 'You can't go about following people, you've no authority here. If Vika finds out she will be very angry.'

'I won't tell her, if you won't.'

'I won't say anything but the man you were following may do so.'

It was then Louisa remembered the shoeshine boss. She groaned silently. Could he have attacked her? Very probably. She was ashamed of twisting his arm. It had been impulsive, foolish and dangerous. If Makereta thought following someone was a crime, she'd have a field day if she knew Louisa had assaulted a member of the public, no matter how justified. Louisa decided not to tell Makereta she'd talked to the shoeshine boys or their boss.

'Do you feel well enough to walk?' Makereta stood up.

'I think so,' said Louisa, gingerly getting to her feet. And probably best not to tell Makereta she'd broken into Edwin's room either.

'Good,' said Makereta, leading her out the café, 'because I'm going to take you to the hospital.'

'There's no need. I'm fine, really.' This much Louisa did know, the lad called Wame had lied. And there had to be a reason for that.

'No, you're not,' said Makereta. 'There's blood dripping down the side of your neck.'

26

Someone somewhere was singing. Soft melodic notes. Louisa didn't recognise the tune or the words, which were in a language she didn't understand. Was she imagining the singing or was it real? Was she finally going mad? Really mad? She pushed open her eyes, the lids felt heavy. For some reason she could only go in slow motion, as if her body was on melt down. As the room came into focus, Louisa became aware of a gentle throbbing at the back of her head. More of a dull ache than all out banging. She was in her hotel room. She was sure of it. But there was stuff everywhere. Dresses. Sandals. Shoes. Toiletries. And none of it hers. She tried to sit up. The throbbing in her head got worse. Makereta appeared from the en-suite bathroom with a towel, turban-style, wrapped around her hair, wearing a hotel towelling dressing gown. She stopped singing when she saw Louisa.

'How do you feel?'

'What are you doing in my room?' said Louisa, sounding more aggressive than she'd intended.

Makereta frowned at Louisa. 'You don't remember?'

'Remember what?

'Someone hit you. Yesterday. You were bleeding.'

Louisa groaned, that's what the big lumpy thing was at the back of her head. She touched it with her finger tips.

Ouch.

'You needed stitches.'

Yes. She did remember. Makereta had taken Louisa to the hospital for a check up. They'd waited hours in the decrepit, germ ridden, rambling Edwardian building before a nurse finally appeared, superglued her together and slapped a dressing over the wound. She'd said Louisa had been concussed and had to stay overnight. Louisa had refused. Staying in the same building as hundreds of sick people was never happening. The nurse got a doctor. The doctor would not discharge her.

'Has the pain gone?' said Makereta sitting at the end of Louisa's bed, her big eyes full of concern.

'I have a terrible headache.' She wished Makereta would get off her bed.

'I'm not surprised. You can take these now.' Makereta pointed to some tablets on the bedside table next to a bottle of water. 'Two, every four hours. They'll help.'

'But why are you here?' said Louisa again, taking two of the pain killers from the packet.

'You were concussed. I offered to keep an eye on you,' said Makereta getting up and pouring Louisa a glass of water.

Louisa groaned. It came back to her. Makereta had assured the doctor on duty that she knew about the tell-tale signs of concussion – slurred words, loss of balance, confusion, persistent headaches. She'd agreed to stay with Louisa overnight to "keep an eye" on her. They'd got back to the hotel just before the curfew. Louisa had only realised Makereta really intended to stay the full twenty-four hours when she dropped her suitcase off in her room.

'Think you can eat something?' said Makereta.

Louisa shook her head. 'Look, I'm fine now, you don't have to stay any longer.'

Makereta frowned. 'It's not been twenty-four hours.'

'If anything was going to happen, it would have happened by now. You've already been very helpful.'

'Only six more hours,' said Makereta cheerfully, turning to survey the clothes scattered across the floor. 'Besides, I'm happy to help you, especially, after the way you helped me.'

Louisa screamed silently. She wouldn't last one hour! The sight of Makereta's clothes scattered across the room was giving her a panic attack. As for the germs Makereta was depositing everywhere by not taking off her shoes – ninety percent of the dust and dirt that came into a room came from people's shoes.

'I'm thinking of wearing this,' said Makereta, holding up a black dress against her dressing gown.

'It looks good,' said Louisa. She had to get Makereta to leave.

'It's my cousin's. I borrowed it for the conference. I'm not sure if it's me.'

'Try it,' said Louisa. Not that it would be easy to get rid of Makereta. Louisa had thought she was a pushover but she'd got that wrong. Makereta had insisted on staying the night and nothing Louisa had said or done had persuaded otherwise.

'I will put it on.' She smiled and took the dress into the bathroom. 'Back in a moment.'

Louisa touched the dressing on the back of her head for a second time and winced for a second time. It still hurt. The attack could have been random, she acknowledged that. But, equally, the attack could have been as a direct result of her questioning the shoeshine lads about Stewy and Edwin. If that was true, the big boss wanted to scare her off. Or maybe he simply wanted to batter her for what she had done.

'What do you think?' said Makereta, standing in front of Louisa's bed, hand on hip.

'You suit it,' said Louisa genuinely. How had she got changed that quickly? Louisa would have taken at least twenty minutes to consider how it looked from every angle before showing anyone else. 'Very nice. Now, I really think it really is safe for you to leave me.'

Makereta laughed. 'It's only a few more hours and I like being with you. You're much more fun than Lavneet. Lavneet doesn't like chatting. '

'Chatting?' Louisa pushed herself higher up in the bed. She didn't like chatting either.

'Mataio sounds so handsome and kind.'

'I told you about Mataio?' She never ever talked about her private life. To anyone. Ever. Absolutely not negotiable. Even telling Rick she didn't get on with her mum had been a moment of weakness, which she'd put down to shock. That hit to the head must have done more damage than she thought.

There was a knock on the door. It was Lavneet. DI Vika wanted to see Louisa in the incident room. Immediately.

27

The incident room was like all the other small hotel meeting rooms Louisa had ever been to: stuffy, despite air conditioning, floor-to-ceiling white net curtains covering double glazed picture windows, bland magnolia walls, blue needle-cord carpet, an oval conference table and a white board on the wall. Louisa gave a start. Her name was in the middle of the board in big, red capitals and circled in black: LOUISA TOWNSEND. Two lines of purple linked her name to two circles on the left, one on top of each other. RICK DAVIES was in the top circle and STEWART NORRIS in the bottom one. To the left of these circles was the biggest question mark Louisa had ever seen. What was her name doing up there? Unless, Vika believed that Louisa's break-ins were linked to Rick's death, after all?

The door flew open. Vika swept in, followed by Lavneet and Makereta. Makereta threw Louisa a sympathetic look. Louisa's heart sank. If Makereta was feeling sorry for her it couldn't be good.

'We have found your suitcase,' said Lavneet.

'What?' said Louisa. This was the last thing she'd expected.

'We need you to identify it,' said Vika.

'Okay.' They were in the middle of a serious murder investigation, yet here was DI Vika wasting time tracking down her missing suitcase. Was this for real?

'Go!' Vika snapped her fingers at Lavneet, who darted out the door. 'While we wait, please tell me about the attack in the marketplace yesterday?'

Louisa shot a glance at Makereta, who looked away, then said, 'There's not much to tell. Someone hit me.'

Vika frowned. 'You have no idea who or why?'

'None.' There was no way she was going to tell Vika about the incident with the shoeshine boss or that she might have seen Edwin. Not while her name was on that white board. Vika had used her position to find out about Louisa's medical history and then used that knowledge to discredit Louisa. She distrusted her completely. 'So, where did you find my suitcase?'

Vika ignored the question. 'Why were you at the market yesterday and not at the conference?'

Louisa shrugged. 'I wanted some fresh air and went for a walk. Before I knew it I was lost,' she lied. 'Was the suitcase at the airport?'

'It was left at the guest house,' said Makereta.

'Constable!' said Vika, throwing Makereta a vicious look. Makereta looked away.

'Where in the house?' Louisa was puzzled. 'We searched everywhere.'

'It wasn't inside–' said Makereta.

'Constable Makereta!' snarled Vika, 'Keep your mouth shut!'

Makereta blushed.

'You found it outside? In the garden?' said Louisa. What the hell was going on?

The door flew open for a second time. It was Lavneet. 'They're bringing the case now.' She was panting, as if she'd been running.

'Be ready to identify it,' said Vika, waiting next to Lavneet and Makereta by the door.

'Sure,' said Louisa. This was crazy stuff. Why all the fuss about her suitcase? Louisa looked at her name on the white board. She would like to know why it was there but she wasn't ever going to ask Vika. Footsteps. In the corridor. At least two people.

'To be honest,' said Louisa, 'I've replaced all the items in the case now. The contents can be given to charity. All except a present I got for my mother. I might keep that, if it's still there?'

'I can confirm the item was not in your case when we found it,' said Vika.

'Yes, it is no longer in the case,' said Lavneet.

They were a double act now? 'You don't know what the present is, so how do you know it's not there? Unless the case is empty. Ah, is that it? Everything's been stolen?'

Lavneet shook her head. 'The case was not empty.'

'I don't understand,' said Louisa, feeling frustrated. 'Either my things were in the case or not?'

Vika held up her hand. 'Late last night we found the body of Stewart Norris. He was in a suitcase that we very much believe belongs to you.'

'What?' Louisa didn't know what shocked here more, that Stewy was dead or his body was found in her suitcase.

28

Two burly Fijian police officers carried what looked like a black body bag into the incident room. Louisa gasped. They surely weren't bringing her Stewy's corpse? Vika nodded to Lavneet, who threw a blue tarp-like cloth over the conference table. The men placed the bag on the table and the bigger man of the two unzipped it. Inch by inch Louisa's brown and tan Diane Von Furstenberg cloth suitcase came into view, along with a terrible smell of soil and excrement.

'Is this your suitcase?' said Vika.

Louisa swallowed. It was her case. No doubt. The tartan

ribbon was still tied to the handle. It looked as if it had been kicked about a football pitch. Breathing through her mouth to avoid the pungent smell she said, 'Where did you find it?'

'Go closer. Check the inside. You must be sure.'

'I can see clearly from here.' Louisa had no intention of getting any closer to the case. The germs on it had to be in the millions.

DI Vika nodded to the officer and unzipped the case and opened the lid. The smell of putrefaction was overwhelming. Louisa took a step backwards. It was her case. No doubt. The blue lining was besmirched with dried blood and mud and who knew what else, but she recognised it.

'It's definitely mine.' She asked for a second time. 'Where did you find it?'

'It was buried–' said Makereta before Vika could stop her.

'Buried?' said Louisa, looking from Vika to Makereta to Lavneet. 'Where?'

'We can't tell you where we found it,' said Vika, nodding to the men to take it away. 'Is this the first time you've seen the case since you left Tarawa?'

'You know it is. I explained it was lost. And you were with me at the hotel when I was asking about it. And Makereta was with me when we arrived at Rick's and it wasn't there.' Louisa watched the men zip the case back in the black body bag and carry it out of the room.

'You could have had two suitcases. The one that got lost and this one,' she nodded to the case. 'You could have killed Stewart Norris before you left The Garlands and hidden his body in your suitcase.'

'What was Rick doing while I was slaughtering his friend?'

'He could have helped you. Or maybe you helped him?'

'I'd never met Rick, or Edwin or Stewy, until Tuesday evening.' Louisa was incredulous. 'I had no reason to kill any of the men or help any of them kill the other!'

'We only have your word for it that you didn't know the men,' said Vika.

'When I last saw Stewy he was in the centre of town with Edwin and a shoeshine lad called Wame. I was with Rick, who stopped to talk to them. I have told you all this already but in case you've forgotten, Rick argued with Stewy and told him to meet him back at the house and we left. This was about eight thirty. Rick then dropped me off at the hotel. He must have gone straight back to The Garlands because less than three quarters of an hour later Makereta and I found his body. If you don't believe me, talk to Edwin or the boy called Wame. They'll both confirm the men were alive at that time.'

'I would but they've disappeared.'

Louisa groaned. 'You cannot seriously believe I'm involved with these two killings?'

Vika raised her eyebrows in a look of disbelief. 'You said yourself you thought the mysterious break-ins into your room were linked to Rick's death. And while two men you met are very dead you are very much alive. I must warn you that until we find either the man called Edwin or the shoeshine boy called Wame, you must remain in Fiji.'

'No,' said Louisa indignantly, 'I have a flight on Tuesday to Brisbane, the first leg of my return trip to Scotland. I'm not missing that.'

Vika laughed. 'This is a double murder investigation

and finding one of the deceased in your suitcase means a romantic trip with your boyfriend is not a priority. Do not leave the hotel without permission and talk to as few people as possible. Under no circumstances tell anyone what you have seen in this room, and under no circumstances involve yourself with any aspect of the investigation.'

29

Once again no one answered the phone in the house on Tarawa when Louisa called from reception. Where was Mataio? Could he have had an accident? Was that why had he'd not phoned back, he was in hospital? No, Reteta would have told her if Mataio was in hospital. So where was he then? Unless he was deliberately avoiding her? But why would he not want to speak to her? They'd been getting on fine right up until he went to visit his mum on her island. Louisa wished she could remember what she'd said to Makereta about Mataio. But she could not, so that was that.

Louisa waited while the phone continued to ring. She really wanted to talk to Mataio. Hear a friendly voice. Have him reassure her that everything would be fine. His was always the voice of reason. The idea that she could have killed Stewy was so ludicrous Louisa couldn't believe Vika believed it. Yes, two people were dead and she was indirectly linked to both killings, but no one in their right mind could believe she was the murderer. Was someone trying to set her up? But why? And where had Edwin and the shoeshine lad disappeared to? She hoped they were alive. Could she be in any danger? Louisa gave herself a shake. No, if someone had wanted her dead they could have bumped up her off while she'd slept at Rick's, which suggested the attack in the car park yesterday was a mugging gone wrong. Or the shoeshine boss getting his own back. She shivered.

Still no answer. Louisa put the phone down and headed for her room. She hoped Makereta with her blabber mouth had moved out and taken all her stuff with her. What had possessed Louisa to tell Makereta anything about her relationship with Mataio, especially their big trip together? Louisa pressed the lift button and waited. Well, she wouldn't trust her again, that was for sure. As for Stewy, she should have realised he was dead when no one could find him. She shook her head wearily. She was losing her skills. She needed to get back to proper detective work again and soon, before it was too late. Poor Stewy and Rick. They'd seemed nice enough people. Someone must have really hated them to butcher them the way they had. But, she'd been told in no uncertain terms, it was nothing to do with her. And she didn't want anything to do with it. She was sick of Suva and Fiji. At least Mataio was arriving on Monday. So, even if she did have to stay longer, he would be with her. She suddenly remembered her mum. Shit! If she had to stay longer, who would "top and tail" her?

Ahead. Down the corridor. It was Makereta and Lavneet. They stood side by side engrossed in conversation. Louisa frowned. So much for Makereta not liking Lavneet. From where Louisa stood they looked like BOMAS. Clearly, Makereta had been invited to be part of Vika's "team", after all. Well, good for her. Louisa for one would not make the mistake of trusting her again. Louisa abandoned the lift and nipped down the corridor to the kitchens. No way was she going to let Vika's lackeys watch her as if she were a child or prisoner.

The kitchen staff in their kitchen whites didn't bat an eyelid when Louisa nipped between the stainless steel cookers and sinks and out into the hotel car park. Within five minutes Louisa was in Albert Park in the town centre. "Park" was too grand a word for what it was, a patch of scrubby ground with a bandstand in the middle of it. It was where she'd seen the police officers line dancing the morning Rick had dropped her off – at least, the police officers had been doing something that had very much looked like line dancing. Had that only been a couple of days ago?

Louisa wandered across the grass, heading nowhere. The last time she'd been in town, she'd got coshed. Was her assailant still around? She glanced in all directions. A group of teenagers in school uniform picnicked by the bandstand, couples meandered along the path and a bunch of scruffy men hugged beer cans and hogged the only bench. It seemed safe enough. Louisa stopped at the edge of the road. What to do? The traffic was heavy. Taxis tooted. Lorries rumbled between buses and cars, petrol fumes spewing from their badly tuned exhausts. Louisa covered her nose and mouth with her hand. Opposite a row of shops sold mobile phones, shoes, bread, linen and sports clothes. The street was packed with people. The thought of pushing her way through the throng did not appeal. Maybe she should go back to the hotel and read a book? She turned back into the park in time to see the lad duck behind the trunk of a breadfruit tree. It was the younger of the two shoeshine youths from the day before, the one with the good teeth. Louisa marched up to the tree and looked round the back. 'Are you following me?'

The boy's skinny cheeks turned a rich mahogany colour. 'Yes.'

'Why?'

The shoeshine lad looked at his feet. 'My boss sent me to find you. He wants to hurt you.'

30

The cafe was around the corner from the shopping mall. It was all polished tables and swish counters and smoked glass picture windows and spotlessly clean. Louisa felt hungry suddenly and thought she might risk eating something. The boy's name was Malaki. Louisa had insisted they go somewhere to talk. Malaki had been reluctant at first, but Louisa had persuaded him with the promise of a chocolate milk shake.

'The boss never comes here,' said Malaki, waiting by the counter to give his order.

'Why is that?' said Louisa, looking around.

'He hates homos,' said Malaki, nodding towards the barista, who was a bulky über gay young man in tight jeans, a tight bright yellow T-shirt, bouffant hair, swept onto the middle of his head in a blond wave, and make up. Camp with a capital C.

Louisa ordered a cheese toastie and a blueberry and raspberry smoothie, she was hungry. Malaki got a strawberry milkshake and a chunk of homemade chocolate brownie and two slices of carrot cake. At first the barista pouted and huffed and puffed, as if he couldn't make up his mind if he was going to be helpful or bitchy to them. In the end he was almost polite.

Louisa followed Malaki to a table at the back. The cafe was quietly busy. Two single foreign men separately worked on their laptops and a young Fijian couple by the window shared a giant slice of chocolate cake.

'So, tell me, how did you find me?'

'I went to hotels where foreigners stay,' said Malaki, greedily slurping his milkshake. 'The Holiday Inn was the third hotel I came to. I waited and saw you leave and followed you.'

It was that easy. 'And why exactly does your boss want to know where I am?'

'He wants to hurt you,' he said matter of factly.

'He's done that already.' Louisa pointed to the dressing at the back of her head. 'I was attacked yesterday. Wasn't that him?'

The boy looked surprised. 'Oh no. He didn't make that little bump. He says when he finds you he is going to do very terrible things to you and you will be awake when he does them so you know it is him hurting you.'

'Ah.' Louisa pushed her plate away. Suddenly she wasn't hungry. 'Are you going to tell him you've found me?'

'I will not tell on you!' said Malaki, his little hands bunched into fists. 'God says you must repay kindness with kindness. You were kind to me yesterday and I want to repay you. But even if I don't tell him where you are, he will send someone else to look. You must leave Suva before it is too late.'

'I'll be leaving in a few days,' she hoped, 'I'll be fine. Thank you for the warning, though.' Louisa shivered. She was implicated in two killings and now a mobster was looking for her. Great! But had she really expected the shoeshine boss to do nothing? Would she never learn?

'He will find you,' said Malaki, shaking his head. 'You must be vigilant.'

'I'll be careful, I promise. Besides, not everyone will be able to find me as quickly as you have done. How long did that take you, half a day? Not bad detective work. You could have a job with the police one day.'

The boy blushed. 'I am sorry he is angry with you because you were kind to me.'

'Why do you work for him when he's so horrible?'

Malaki wriggled in his chair. 'It is very expensive to be a shoeshine boy. First, we need police clearance to prove we are not a tramp or thief or conman, that costs twenty-two dollars, and then we need a shoeshine licence, which costs another five dollars, and both the licence and the clearance have to be renewed every year, and then the Suva council charges us five dollars for being in the street.'

'How do you afford it?'

'The big boss pays for everything.'

'And you pay him back with interest?'

Malaki scrunched his lips. 'It is very difficult to get a clearance letter from the police but he makes sure we always get it, and he pays for our food and rent.'

'Our?'

'We city centre boys live together in a house. We have our own volleyball team.' He beamed. 'We were runners-up last year in the annual competition.'

Louisa knew better than to judge but it didn't seem much of a life to her. 'Do you know where the other shoeshine lad is, the one called Wame?'

Apprehension creased Malaki's face. 'Why?'

'The police want to ask him some questions about Wednesday morning. They can't find him.'

Malaki pushed away his empty plate. 'He has gone away.'

'Where?

'I don't know. I got back to the boss house after work yesterday and all his things were gone.'

'He's disappeared?'

Malaki nodded. He looked tearful. 'I miss him. He always told me where he was going but not this time. I am scared he is in trouble.'

'Have you asked his family or friends?'

'He has no friends or family here.' Malaki's his eyes lit up. 'Wait. I have remembered. There is one place he used to go to all the time. It is called the Y.'

He was kidding her. 'The Young Men's Christian Association Centre?'

'That's it.'

'Okay,' said Louisa, getting to her feet. 'Why don't we go and see if he's there now?' Malaki had gone out of his way to help her, the least she could do was help him find his friend.

'Now?'

'Why not?'

'But what about the big boss?' said Malaki looking shocked. 'He could see you.'

'He won't see me if I see him first. He's not easy to miss.'

Malaki didn't look convinced.

'I'll be vigilant. I promise.' And if Wame was at the Y, she could ask him a couple of questions of her own, like why he lied to her about being with Edwin and Stewy on Wednesday morning. And there was still the possibility that he knew Edwin's whereabouts. It was a coincidence that Edwin and Wame were missing and Louisa didn't believe in coincidences. Only after she'd talked to Wame would she consider letting Vika know where he was.

31

The Y was a giant ramshackle hall, with a corrugated iron roof and walls of wooden louvre windows on three sides. It sat at the end of a makeshift car park and next to a rugby pitch. Louisa counted at least six different groups of burly men practising rugby on the pitch. They charged and rucked and ran and kicked and roared under the noon day sun. Every square inch of grass was used.

Malaki nodded at the vehicles in the packed car park.

'It's lunchtime aerobics. That's why it is so busy,' said Malaki.

Aerobics inside in this heat? He was having her on. Louisa followed Malaki into the YMCA building, silently balking at the dust and grime everywhere. Malaki nodded a hello to a skinny Indo-Fijian man behind a scratched counter inside the entrance. The man looked at Louisa suspiciously but said nothing.

Malaki said, 'As long as we are only watching we don't have to pay.'

'Pay?' Now he really was joking.

To the left an open door revealed a small changing room and the pee smell from it suggested the toilets were there too. To the right, a short corridor took them to a large hall. Louisa could hear music. As they approached the hall the music got louder and louder and Louisa got hotter and hotter.

Inside a lithe blond woman dressed in a purple lycra body suit ran on the spot on a small stage at the end of the hall. Her hair was swept up on her head into a ball of candy floss. No matter how much she bounced her hair remained perfect, like her make-up. In front of her rows of sweltering women dressed in misshapen shorts and baggy T-shirts struggled to copy her. Thudding garage music exploded from a ghetto blaster on the floor next to the stage.

'That's Renu,' shouted Malaki, pointing to the thin woman, his voice full of admiration. 'She is the aerobics teacher.'

'But where's Wame?' Louisa shouted back.

'Maybe out the back. I will go and ask around.'

'I'll come with you.' The hall was filthy. The dirt was creeping her out.

'No. I will come back,' said Malaki. 'If Wame sees you he may run away. He didn't like you. He said you were pushy.'

'So, he does remember me, even though he couldn't remember Stewy and Edwin?'

'I will come quickly back,' said Malaki, ignoring her last remark.

Louisa focussed on the marching. She hoped it would take her mind off the dirt in the hall. Her obsessing about dirt and germs had started after her father had walked out on the family when she was ten. At least that's what her therapist had said. His abandoning the family had left Louisa with "a feeling of loss and being out of control, compounded by her having to adapt to a new way of life in Edinburgh after living in Tarawa for the first eight years of her life." He said her obsessive compulsion to clean and be clean was her way of trying to take control. At the time Louisa thought it was a load of crap. She still did. And it didn't really explain the voices, although to be fair she'd not told the therapist about them. When he'd suggested she take some pills to help manage her compulsive behaviour she'd been furious. Loony pills? No way! Why was it so crazy to want to be clean? But she'd recognised she had to do something about her germ thing, even the kids at school had started to call her weird.

That was when she became fastidious about washing everything, especially herself. She'd started carrying her own soap and tissues, and alcohol gel and antibacterial wet wipes when she could get them. Whenever possible, even sometimes in her own home, she'd wipe an item clean before she handled it. And then there was the rule of four. It was a simple rule really. If for some reason she could not immediately clean her hands after touching something that was dirty, as soon as she could afterwards, she would wash and dry her hands four times. Even better, was to shower four times. It almost always worked. If she didn't use these strategies, and others like them, the voices in her head would start, telling her over and over again that she was so disgustingly dirty and contaminated with germs that her mother would become sick and die a terrible death.

She'd never discussed the voices with anyone. Ever. It embarrassed her that she took such rubbish seriously. She knew it was impossible and ridiculous that her mother, at the other side of the world, could get ill because she'd not washed her hands properly. Common sense told her the voices were not real, just her thoughts getting twisted. But it made no difference. They felt very real. And once they started, they consumed her. The weird thing was, six months after being on Tarawa, they'd vanished. She thought she was cured. But then, six months later they came back with bells on. This time they focussed on her clothes. Telling her what she was wearing was a problem. She'd begun changing four, five, six times a day. It was out of control. So she'd developed new strategies to get back in control. The strategies were more like rituals. They made no sense but they worked. Her underwear had to match, and she only wore the same two colours, black and white, and only on certain days: black on Mondays, Wednesdays and Saturdays and white on Tuesdays, Thursdays, Fridays and Sundays. And never black and white together. Not negotiable. Her coat hangers always had to face the same way. She always hand washed her underwear. She dressed from top to bottom, never bottom to top, and she always folded her clothes in the same way. As long as she stuck to them she could wear her clothes for a whole day without ripping them off and throwing them in the wash. She'd nearly talked about them to Mataio but she'd not wanted him thinking she was mad.

A roar! Louisa jumped. A herd of chunky rugby players, wide as they were tall, charged past her and into the hall, leaving a trail of soil behind them. One by one they scrambled behind the rows of women. Louisa stood agog as she watched the massive rugby players copy Renu, who was now doing burpees.

32

The rugby men were like hippos next to the exercising

women. Louisa thought of the Disney cartoon Fantasia. Renu smiled at the men and the women, and started doing star jumps. The keep-fitters promptly copied her. The noise of the men's boots clattering against the floor, coupled with the loud music, was almost deafening. It amazed Louisa that no one bumped into each other. As for the heat, it was stifling. Everyone was sweating, except for Renu, who somehow remained cool looking. Louisa couldn't work out her nationality. Her lithe body was more Indo-Fijian but her blond skin and hair suggested European. There was a pause in the music and an older Asian man hopped onto the stage and Renu hopped off.

'The rugby men join us for the cool down,' said Renu, standing next to Louisa and dabbing her forehead with a white cotton hand towel.

Louisa laughed. 'They don't look very cool.'

'I have trainers if you want to join in?'

'I could never keep up.'

Renu shrugged. 'You're new, aren't you? Why are you here if you don't want to do the class?'

Louisa was surprised by her abruptness. 'I'm looking for someone.'

'Who?'

Louisa started. There was no harm in asking her. 'A boy call Wame. Late teens. Not very tall. I was told he used to come to the Y.'

Renu nodded. 'Wame, yes he was often here.'

'You know him?' Louisa tried not to sound surprised. She'd half believed Malaki had brought her to the hall under false pretences.

'Everyone knows Wame. He used to go to the gym round the back. It's poorly equipped, though. I told him he could join the aerobics class if he wanted, free of charge, like the rugby men.' She nodded to where the men sat on the ground twisting and turning their legs trying to copy the older man on the stage who sat, yoga style, with his legs around this neck. 'But he never came.' Someone in the hall farted. Someone else began to laugh. Renu shouted to the keep-fitters, 'Better out than in!' She faced Louisa. 'What's Wame doing these days?'

'Apart from shining shoes, you mean?'

Renu's pretty face frowned. 'He's back doing that.'

'So what did he do when you knew him?'

'He was at school getting excellent grades. He was supposed to go to Australia to study but it fell through.'

'Are we talking about the same Wame?' said Louisa. He'd not struck her as the academic type.

'The Wame I knew was bright, polite, courteous and very clever. It's a great pity he never got the chance he deserved. And what shocking news about his sponsor, that man he used to live with.'

'What man?' said Louisa, feeling a tingling sensation in her arms.

'The one who was murdered. It was in all the papers.'

'Wame lived with Rick?' Louisa was astounded. 'Are you sure?'

'Rick, yes, that was his name. I'm sure. Such a horrible death. He had all that security and for what? No one is safe in Suva any more. No one. Excuse me, I have to get back.'

'Wait!'

Too late. Renu was back on the stage. Louisa struggled to take in what she had just heard. Wame had lived with Rick? How? Why? Could the stories about Rick enticing young men back to the house be true, after all? Louisa wanted answers from Malaki and she wanted them now.

33

Malaki leaned against a gleaming black Cherokee Jeep. He looked dejected. When he saw Louisa approach he said, 'No one has seen Wame since last week.'

Louisa marched Malaki away from the hall to a shaded spot under a breadfruit tree at the edge of the rugby pitch. 'You know the man, Rick, who was murdered on Wednesday and whose picture is all over the papers, yes?'

Malaki screwed up his face. 'Why are you asking about Rick?'

'Because,' said Louisa, trying not to shout. 'Wame lived with Rick.'

'That was a long time ago.'

'Wame knew Rick and now Rick is dead and Wame is missing. Do you not think these two things could be connected?'

'No,' said Malaki, looking surprised. 'Wame did not know Rick and Stewy any more.'

'Not true. I saw Wame talk to Stewart and Rick on Wednesday morning. But when I asked Wame about it he lied and said he had not seen Stewy. Why would he do that?'

'I don't know,' said Malaki, kicking the ground with his foot.

'Listen to me and listen good. I want you to tell me all you know about Wame and his relationship with Rick and Stewy. If you don't, I'll take you to the nearest police station and tell them to arrest you for withholding evidence in a murder enquiry! Have you got that?'

Malaki nodded reluctantly.

'Right then.' Louisa was furious. 'On you go.' All this time Malaki knew Wame had lived with Rick and he'd said nothing. What was he hiding? What were they hiding?'

'Wame used to clean Rick's shoes,' said Malaki, looking at the ground. 'Rick used to talk to him about many things. Rick told Wame he was clever. And one day he said to Wame he was wasting his talents and offered to pay for him to go back to school. A private school. Wame said yes. He was so happy to go back to school. When he was younger he'd done well but had met some bad boys and did silly things and had got thrown out. And while he was at school Rick and Stewy looked after him in their house. He had his own room and even had a play station and a television and his own toothbrush. Rick said Wame was so clever he was going to send him to university in Australia. And for a long time everyone knew that Wame was going to Australia to study. But one day, before he was supposed to leave, Wame turned up at the boys' house and asked for his old shoeshine spot back. It was a big surprise to everyone.'

'Had he changed his mind?'

'Rick had changed his mind.'

'Why?'

'I don't know.'

'Wame must have been angry to have lost that chance?'

'Oh yes, he was very angry about not going.'

'He must have hated Rick and Stewy.'

Malaki shook his head. 'He never said anything bad about Rick, or Rick's friend Stewy. He said they were good men. They went to church even though they were gay.'

'It's hard to believe he wasn't angry with them, though?'
Louisa tried to gather her thoughts. Wame knew Rick
and Stewy, not just casually as she had assumed, he had
lived with them. Had there been a price to pay for his new
education. Could Rick and Stewy have been grooming
boys, after all? Ugh! What a thought. It gave Wame a
motive for murder.

'Wame liked Rick. He was very upset when he heard
Rick had been killed. It was after he found out about Rick's
death he had the argument with the big boss and left.'

'Do you think Wame knows who killed Rick?'

Malaki looked shocked. 'How would he know that? He
had not been to their house for a long long time.'

'What about your boss?'

'The boss?' Malaki said, genuinely puzzled. 'Rick was
nothing to him.'

'But the boss must have been cross when Wame went
to live with them.'

Malaki made a sour face. 'We are not prisoners. We can
leave when we want. As long as we pay what we owe him
he doesn't care. If we leave he says it is one less mouth to
feed. And new boys arrive every day wanting to take our
place. The boss has started building a second house we are
so many. I don't like some of the new boys. They are rough.
They don't go to church. They take drugs all the time. The
boss isn't worried about such things. As long as we do our
jobs and pay our way, that is all he cares about.'

Louisa frowned. 'I need to talk to Wame more than
ever. Even if he's not involved directly with Rick's death, he
may know something.'

'He does not know anything about the killings!' said
Malaki, scrunching up his little fists in anger. 'He liked Rick

and Stewy. He would tell the police if he knew anything.'

'So why has he disappeared?'

Malaki looked sad. 'I don't know.' He looked around furtively then leaned forward and whispered, 'He told me he was going to get a lot of money and then we would leave and never have to work for the boss again.'

'And where was the money coming from?'

'I don't know.' Malaki made a sad face. 'He was going to take me with him and now he has vanished.'

A coughing sound. It came from behind them. A lad nodded to Malaki and whispered something in his in ear.

'My friend here,' said Malaki, 'knows where Wame is.'

'Where?' said Louisa.

Malaki blushed. 'He wants some money first.'

Louisa looked the boy up and down. She addressed Malaki. 'Can you believe him?'

'Yes. We have to give him ten dollars but I have no money.'

Louisa handed the boy, who looked like a thinner, unwashed version of Malaki, a ten dollar note. In British money it was only about three pounds, still, she hated paying for information.

The boy slipped the note into the pocket of his shorts then whispered something into Malaki's ear and sloped off.

'Well?' said Louisa. She was unimpressed with all the cloak and dagger crap.

'He says he saw Wame earlier today with a boy called Api.'

'But we want to know where he is now, not earlier on. And who the hell is Api?' said Louisa looking around for the boy, who had vanished.

'Api is a friend of Wame's. He'll know where we can find

Wame but we have to hurry.'

'What are we waiting for?' said Louisa.

34

Louisa stood next to Malaki at the corner of Princess Road and Edinburgh Drive. Louisa imagined the street names were as a result of some colonial connection between Edinburgh and Suva but she couldn't think what. Yes. Suva was by the sea, so was Edinburgh. Yes, there were hills surrounding Suva and there were hills surrounding Edinburgh. And yes, lots of people lived in both places. And, yes, it rained a lot, although it wasn't raining now, which was something. The comparison was over.

Malaki pointed to a towering concrete built church on the corner of the junction. Its giant spire loomed skywards. 'Api is in there.'

'The church?' said Louisa.

'Yes,' said Malaki, running up the dozen steps to the entrance. 'The lunch time service is not over. We are in time!'

Louisa followed him, all the while, keeping her eyes peeled for his boss. She did not want to meet him again. Ever. It was very disconcerting knowing he was looking for her. But she wasn't going to hide in the hotel because of him either. She'd been vigilant all the way to the church. As long as she stayed alert, it should be fine. She hoped.

Malaki stopped outside a massive arched double door. 'Shall we go in?' said Louisa, aware for the first time of the glorious singing coming from inside.

Malaki shook his head. 'We must wait for them to come out.'

'Why?'

'I am not dressed smartly enough to go in.'

'I don't think God cares about clothes, or appearances generally,' said Louisa.

Malaki shook his head. 'I am not going inside a house of God dressed as I am.' Malaki plonked himself down on the top step and stared ahead.

Louisa sighed, took her lava-lava from her bag, spread it out on the step next to Malaki and sat on it. The evangelical singing crescendoed in her ears. 'Probably better to talk to Api without all that singing going on, anyway. Are you sure he's in there?'

'He is a good church boy and this is his church.'

'Ah,' said Louisa. She may as well have thrown away her ten dollars. A gentle breeze danced across her face. After the intense heat and noise of the YMCA hall, it was deliciously cool. 'You and Wame must be good friends for you to be so concerned for him, yes?'

Malaki chewed his bottom lip. 'When I first came to Suva I was very young and I didn't know anyone. He looked after me.'

Louisa stifled a laugh. Malaki was still very young. 'Are you sure you don't know why Wame has run away?'

Malaki shook his head wearily. 'He tells me nothing. None of the boys do. I told you, they think I am a child.'

'How old are you?'

'Thirteen. Fourteen.'

'You don't know?'

'No.'

Why was she surprised? Lots of people on Tarawa didn't

know their exact age. It cost money to register a birth, so if there wasn't much money around, it wasn't done. With no record of the birth the exact date was forgotten. Generally, birthdays weren't a big deal. Not like back home. On Tarawa if you made it to your first birthday, they threw a party and that had to do you for the rest of your life.

'Either way, surely you should be at school?'

Malaki's mouth slipped downwards. 'Mum had no money so she got me a job cutting sugar cane. There are lots of cane fields near my village.'

'This was before you came to Suva, so you were what, eleven or twelve?' Louisa was shocked. That was way too young to be working.

He nodded. 'I didn't like the grown up world. The man in charge was very strict. I was scared.'

'Didn't you tell your mother you were unhappy?' What kind of mother did that to their kid?

'We needed the money.'

'Were there any other young boys cutting sugar cane?'

'There was one other boy my age. They put us together but I didn't like him. He was always eating sweets and drinking fizzy drinks and saying ugly things. He lived with his uncles. I don't know how he had money for sweets but he did.'

'Why did you leave?'

'My mum got a new boyfriend. He took all my wages for himself. When I complained he beat me. The next time I got paid I got on the bus and came here. Everyone knows there is more work in Suva. Even for young boys like me. The very first day I met Wame. He looked after me. And I am glad I came. I would do anything for him–'

Dong! Dong! Dang! Ding! The church bells clattered to

116

life above their heads. The noise was deafening. Louisa put her hands over her ears. It did little to block out the racket, which, the longer she heard it, sounded more and more like a recording. Malaki jumped up and said he was going to look for Api. Louisa watched him disappear into the throng of people cascading out of the church and spilling down the steps. If she didn't want to get trampled, she was going to have to move. She got to her feet, picked up her lava-lava, carefully folded it and stood to one side. She imagined the service was a special advent service, or maybe lunch services were popular in Suva. She scoured the crowd to see if she could see where Malaki had disappeared to. Everyone was dressed in their Sunday best despite it being a Friday. Hats and sunshades jostled with bibles and prayer books. Just as Louisa was beginning to wonder where Malaki was, she found herself looking straight into Vika's glinting black eyes.

35

Vika towered over Louisa. She seemed taller than ever, with even bigger hair than ever.

'I gave orders to stay at the hotel. What are you doing here?'

'I'm to be denied coming to church?' said Louisa, feigning indignation but sensing Vika wouldn't be fooled.

'You don't believe in our Lord God,' said Vika, furiously looking around. 'Who are you with?'

'No one.' Louisa hoped Malaki would be sensible enough not to approach her while she was talking to someone as officious looking as Vika. 'You know, I'd welcome the opportunity to help with the case. I'm sure I could make a contribution if you let me.'

Vika laughed. 'Clearly the sermon fell on deaf ears. It was about humility and you still have none. I suggest,' she said, turning to leave, 'that you return to the hotel immediately.'

Louisa watched Vika and her entourage, half a dozen young women and men, swoop down the steps and climb into a convoy of Rav4s and Prados and drive away. Louisa had considered telling Vika about Wame's relationship with Stewy and Rick. It was of obvious significance to the murder investigation. But she also had a feeling Vika would construe her contribution as interfering and it would probably be career suicide on Louisa's part. No. Until Louisa had actual solid evidence that could point to the person who was breaking into her room and/or the killer or killers, she would say nothing. Besides, if the Renu woman knew about Wame living with Rick, there was every chance Vika knew too.

Malaki was back beside her. He pointed to a group of young men at the top of the stairs. 'Api is the tall one. Can you ask him about Wame? He will not take me seriously.'

'No problem,' said Louisa, heading up the steps towards the group.

Api was tall and unapologetic looking, in designer denim jeans, a black T-shirt and expensive trainers. His short hair had a quiff at the front, reminding Louisa of Hergé's Tintin.

'Hey,' said Api, ruffling his hand through Malaki's hair before Malaki pulled himself away. 'He looked at Louisa. 'Young Malaki says you want to talk to me.'

Louisa had no intention of wasting time. Vika could be back at any time. 'We're looking for Wame. Do you know where he is?'

Api looked surprised. 'I've not seen Wame for months.'

'Oh?' said Louisa. She should have known the toerag who'd taken her ten dollars was lying! 'You're sure you haven't seen him?'

'What's this about?' Api looked concerned. 'Is something wrong?'

Louisa smiled. She hoped she sounded convincing. 'No, please don't worry. We just need to talk to him.'

Api shrugged. 'I've just arrived in the country. As I said, I've not seem him for months.'

'Have you been on holiday?' said Louisa.

He tutted. 'I'm halfway through my second year of a BSc in Artificial Intelligence at Monash University in Melbourne. On my Christmas break.'

'Impressive! Well, if you do see Wame, can you tell him to get in touch with Malaki.'

'To be honest, it's unlikely he'll be in touch with me.'

'Aren't you friends?' said Louisa.

'We were but we've not been in contact since I first went to Australia.'

'Oh?' said Louisa. 'Why not?

Api put his hands in his jeans and shrugged. 'My going to Australia made it awkward between us. He's a clever guy, could have studied overseas too, if only he'd kept away from the drugs.'

'He doesn't do drugs!' blurted Malaki, who'd not said a word until then.

Api tried to ruffle Malaki's hair a second time. Malaki shook him off. 'You're a liar!' he yelled and ran into the crowd.

'Malaki!' shouted Louisa. Too late. He'd gone.

'The little guy likes Wame,' said Api. 'Can't blame him. Wame can be very charming. He had me fooled. But when he stuffed up his chances to go overseas he got bitter and became envious of anyone else who was doing well. To be honest, even if he wanted to talk to me I'd avoid him. He has a nasty side to him. Sorry, I can't be of more help. Have to go. I've got friends waiting for me.'

'Thanks anyway,' said Louisa, watching Api saunter down the steps and wander towards a group of young men waiting at the junction of the two roads.

'If you want my advice?' Api shouted back. 'Find someone selling drugs and you'll find Wame.'

At that precise moment a police car stopped at the bottom of the steps. Makereta got out of the driver's side of the vehicle.

'I've been told you need a lift,' said Makereta, walking round to the passenger side of the car.

'That's very kind,' said Louisa, still scouring the streets for Malaki. 'But I think I'd prefer to walk.'

'You don't have the luxury of that option,' said Makereta, opening the passenger door of the vehicle.

36

Louisa started when she saw the mess in her room. Then she remembered. It was Makereta's stuff. Bangles. Bags. Belts. Brushes. Combs. Dresses. Shoes. Wet towels. Stuff everywhere.

'Why are your things still here?' said Louisa. 'I'm in no danger of concussion now.'

'But you are in danger of getting arrested,' said Makereta, standing behind her. 'Until told otherwise, I've been ordered to stay with you.'

'And if I object?'

'This is way preferable to what Vika wanted to do, which was lock you up and throw away the key.'

'House arrest, is it?'

'You shouldn't have sneaked off.'

'I didn't sneak off!' said Louisa.

Makereta smiled. 'You ran out of the hotel through the kitchens.'

'Ah.' Louisa cleared her throat. She should have known they would find out. They were detectives, after all. 'I'd just seen my suitcase covered in blood and been told it had been used to hide Stewy's body. I felt sick. I wanted to be by myself. Is that so much to ask?'

'You're a suspect in a murder investigation,' said Makereta. 'So, yes it is.'

Now Louisa laughed. 'How many times do I have to say, I saw Edwin getting his shoes polished next to the market. Stewy was with him. Rick stopped to talk to Stewy. They were both alive and well at that point. It's a physical impossibility that I could be involved in either of their deaths. And if you must know, that's what I was doing at the church, trying to find the lad who'd polished Edwin's shoes that morning, ask him to confirm being with them.'

Makereta swept her thick hair behind her ears and frowned. 'Of all people, you must know we can't let you carry out your own investigation.'

'It's "We" now, is it?' Louisa nodded. 'You've swapped

sides.'

Makereta eyed Louisa carefully. 'Yes, I was invited to join the team. The discovery of Stewy's body meant Vika needed more hands on deck. It is my job, after all. However,' she said, hand on her hips. 'As I let you "get away", I have since been uninvited.'

'Ah,' said Louisa. Now she knew why Makereta had given her the silent treatment in the car on the way back to the hotel from the church. 'I didn't mean to get you into trouble.'

Makereta flopped onto her bed. 'You were out of the hotel before I could blink. According to Vika, I "failed at the first hurdle" for not being able to keep you in my sights. Had I realised you would sneak away I would have watched you more carefully, but I trusted you. I foolishly thought we were friends."

Louisa sat on her bed and faced Makereta. 'I trusted you too yet you told Vika and Lavneet about my relationship with Mataio. What possible relevance can that have on the investigation?'

Makereta looked surprised. 'You never said it was a secret.'

'I have this funny quirk, Makereta, I prefer my business to stay just that, my business.'

'You'd been assaulted. Lavneet needed to know why I was staying with you overnight. In the morning she enquired about you. I told her what I knew. She must have repeated what I said to Vika.' Makereta wriggled up her bed, leaned her back against the wooden headboard and crossed her legs. 'But why are you so cross? I'm the one who's got into trouble for not knowing where you were, and I'm the one who's had to move my things from room to room. All you have to do is carry on much the same as before for a few days. You'll be gone soon enough and Fiji will be a vague memory. Meanwhile, I'll still be here, stuck working with Lavneet and Vika.'

'I said I'm sorry and I am. I didn't think you'd get into trouble.'

Makereta sighed. 'It could have been worse, I could have lost my job. Please, don't go anywhere without telling me. I'm on my last chance.'

'Of course, I won't. Anyway, I have nowhere to go.'

The hotel bedroom was in darkness and eerily silent. Louisa had spent longer in the shower than she'd intended. It took a second to realise the air conditioning was off and the curtains were drawn. By the light coming from the shower room she could see Makereta lying on her side on top of her bed, facing the wall. Was that gentle snoring? Yes, it was. Louisa quietly closed the shower room door behind her and sat down on her bed. She took off her indoor flip-flops, placed them neatly by the side of the bed, pulled back the top cover, slid under the sheets and closed her eyes.

It was a weakness of hers to go off on one. She always regretted it later. Makereta had only been doing her job and Louisa was the last person to criticise a police officer for doing what was asked of them. But it was maddening that she was now under what amounted to house arrest. And she still couldn't remember what she'd told Makereta about Mataio. Not that there was anything to hide but like any relationship they'd had their ups and downs.

In the quiet of the room Makereta's soft breathing sounded remarkably loud. Louisa knew if she let it, it would distract her from sleeping and she wanted to sleep. She felt exhausted. An afternoon nap would help get her back on track. If Louisa was still awake after five minutes, she'd get up and find her earplugs. For now she needed to empty her mind and drift. Put the events of the past few days out of her mind. She would be positive. Vika would find Wame and Edwin alive and well. They would testify to the fact that Stewy and Rick had been outside the market on the morning of the killings and therefore it was impossible that Louisa could have had anything to do with their deaths. She would be off the hook and be able to leave with Mataio on Tuesday.

A noise. Muffled sounds. Louisa opened her eyes. She'd fallen asleep, after all. In the dim light, she saw the outline of two people, struggling. 'Help!' It was Makereta. Louisa jumped out of bed. Threw herself at the shadow. Ouch! She got a punch in the stomach. She staggered. More shouts. Fists flailing. Someone ran. The door flew open. Slammed shut. Louisa chased. Opened the door. The corridor was empty.

'What way did he go?' said Makereta, panting behind her.

'I'll go left, you go right,' gasped Louisa.

They ran in opposite directions. Within minutes they were back.

Makereta shook her head. 'He's got away again.'

'Bastard!' said Louisa.

37

Vika showed no interest when Louisa told her the intruder

was back. In Vika's eyes if nothing was missing, there was no crime. Makereta checked with all the hotel staff, no one had seen anyone act suspiciously. Security did agree to keep a special watch on her floor, though. Still, Louisa got reception to change the key code to the room and when she returned to the room with Makereta, they wedged a chair against the door handle – no one was getting in again, at least not while they were in the room.

After checking the chair wedged against the room door handle was secure for the umpteenth time, Makereta flopped onto her bed, crossed her legs, pulled a carrier bag up from under the bed and brought out a packet of sour cream and onion Pringles. 'Want one?'

Louisa flinched. She hated eating any food in the bedroom, but especially crisps, they made such a mess. Now was not the time to say. 'No thanks.'

Makereta shrugged and popped a couple into her mouth and crunched.

'What exactly happened?' said Louisa, sitting down opposite her.

'I woke up and saw someone rummaging in the room. At first I thought it was you, tidying up.'

'In the dark?' said Louisa.

'I assumed you'd got so fed up with my mess you were taking the opportunity to organise stuff while I slept.'

'Oh?' Louisa was shocked Makereta had noticed her behaviour. 'What happened then?'

'I wanted to go to the toilet so I got out of bed. This startled the intruder. By the time I realised he wasn't you, he grabbed me. His hand was over my mouth. We struggled. That's when you must have woken up.'

'Wait a minute,' said Louisa. She disappeared into the

bathroom and came back with her antibacterial wet wipes. 'Hold still.' Louisa took one of the wipes and gently dabbed a bloody smear around Makereta's eye. 'You've got a small cut. There's some blood. Shouldn't need stitches, though.'

'Good. My parents will worry if I have to go to hospital, no matter what the reason.' Makereta stood up and looked in the full length mirror in the middle of the room to study her face. 'They're anxious as it is that I'm still staying in the hotel.'

'Here,' said Louisa. Makereta turned back to face her. Louisa took a fresh wipe and gently cleaned all remaining traces of blood. 'It doesn't look too bad. Does it hurt?'

She shook her head. 'Not at all.'

Louisa threw the wipes in the waste paper basket and then used alcohol gel to clean her hands. 'I can't believe we nearly had him. He must be getting desperate to break into the room while we were in it.'

'It was dark, he probably wasn't expecting to find us having afternoon naps,' said Makereta, switching off the overhead light and pulling open the curtains to let the afternoon sunlight flood into the room.

'If we could only figure out what he's looking for.'

'If he's your snooper, he's very determined,' said Makereta, getting comfortable on the bed once more.

'It has to be the same person who broke in before,' said Louisa. 'And the only connection I can see between them and me is the killings, don't you think?'

Makereta shrugged. 'But how are the incidents linked.'

'I have no idea. Did Lavneet tell you anything earlier?'

Makereta groaned. 'Lavneet swore me to secrecy. If she finds out I'm discussing the case with you, I'm for it.'

'Do we trust each other, or not?' said Louisa.

Makereta grinned. 'I suppose so.' She crossed her legs. 'You may as well know it all then. The boy you were looking for at the church, the one called Wame, he's significant because not only is he a witness but he used to live with Rick and Stewy.' She said this with a flourish.

Louisa nodded. 'I met someone at the Y who told me as much.'

'The Y?' Makereta gave Louisa a funny look. 'You've been carrying out your own investigation, haven't you?'

Louisa cleared her throat. 'Just asking around. By chance I met someone called Api and he said he used to know Wame.'

Makereta pursed her lips and dropped the Pringles back into the white plastic carrier. 'If Vika hears you've been asking the public questions, she'll ... she'll, well, I don't know what she'll do but I wouldn't like to be in your shoes when she does it.'

'All I know is that this man called Api said that Rick kicked Wame out the house for taking drugs.'

'So, you know Rick and Stewy funded wayward boys to finish their education?'

'Boys, plural?' Louisa sat up. 'I only thought it was Wame? There were more?'

'Did your Api tell you he was one of the chosen few to be funded by Rick and Stewy?'

'No. He did not! That could that make him a suspect?'

Makereta shook his head. 'He's halfway through his studies, why would he harm his benefactors?'

'Could the rumours about the men grooming boys for sex be true? Did they pay for their education with their bodies?'

'If it helps, forensics is back and Lavneet says there's no

porn of any kind anywhere – the videos are all perfectly normal home videos. Ditto the dvds.'

'Nothing?' Louisa was shocked but pleased. 'And the drugs?'

'The white stuff they took from the house?'

'Yes?'

'It was baking powder.'

'No way!' Louisa laughed. 'So the papers got it wrong?'

Makereta leaned over and grabbed her Pringles back from under the bed. 'Totally. There were no drugs in the house, not even a cigarette.'

38

'So, no drugs and no porn,' said Louisa. 'What did Vika say?'

'Oh, she's in big trouble,' said Makereta, offering Louisa a Pringle.

'Why?'

'For not finding Stewy's body in the garden on the first day. It was half buried under some bushes in the back. The Chief of Police hauled her into his office and shouted at her. He said she should have searched the garden thoroughly. He can't have the police look bad, especially with the army watching our every move. There's talk now that she may even be taken off the case.'

'Really?'

Makereta nodded. 'She has a lot of enemies, especially among the men. It's not easy for a woman to become an inspector. Sure, being from a powerful family has helped, but she worked hard. The traditionalists think a woman's place should be behind a man, not in front of him telling him what to do. They are ready at every turn to denounce her. She has to watch her back and her front.'

'Sounds just like home.' Louisa felt sorry for Vika for about a second. 'But how did my case get under the bushes and, more to the point, why was Stewy in it?'

'The evidence suggests Rick was stabbed before Stewy. Vika believes Stewy was probably coming into the house through the back garden, the front door was locked, when he bumped into the killer leaving. The killer panicked, attacked Stewy and killed him. Your suitcase was on the veranda, the driver from the airport admitted that he'd dumped it there when no one answered the front door. The killer saw the case and decided to hide Stewy's body in it. It is a very big case and Stewy was a slight man. It was a risky thing to do. But he probably hoped that if Stewy couldn't be found, it would look suspicious and the police would focus the murder investigation on finding him. He was right.'

'But what did he do with the things in the case?'

'The city dump is behind the house. Vika believes the killer dragged Stewy into the bushes, then your case. He threw the contents of the case over the back wall into the dump, knowing your things would be found by scavengers. He then squashed Stewy into the case and using his bare hands tried to bury him in the wet soil under the bushes. He was probably in the middle of doing this when we arrived at the house and he fled.'

'But we saw no sign of a fight outside?'

'The heavy rain washed away all signs of what had happened. You remember, it was very heavy?'

Louisa nodded. 'We should have searched the garden.'

'Yes, we should have.'

'So, it was an opportunistic crime. Spur of the moment. Unplanned,' said Louisa, noticing for the first time that Makereta was still wearing her shoes while sitting on the bed.

'It looks that way. The murder weapon came from a set of butcher knives in the kitchen.'

'So who is Vika looking for?'

'Other than you?'

'Very funny.' Louisa frowned suddenly. 'I'm not really a suspect, am I?'

Makereta shook her head. 'Just a pain in Vika's side. She doesn't like people who won't do what they're told. It's obviously different in Tarawa but here, if a superior officer tells you to do something, you do it.'

'Vika isn't my superior officer.'

'She can lock you up. Seriously.'

'I get it,' said Louisa, standing up and picking a crumpled green skirt off the floor and placing it over the chair next to Makereta's bed. 'But she must have someone in the frame for the killings? No person of interest?'

'She wants to talk to Wame and Edwin but they've disappeared.'

'Does she think they're dead?'

'I don't think so.' Makereta scrunched her soft cheeks. 'Edwin isn't a suspect. He arrived at the hotel shortly after we left. It's impossible for him to have got to The Garlands, killed the men and got back to the hotel by that time. But Vika thinks he may know something. On the other hand, Wame, the boy you saw in the market, he has a strong motive for disliking the men. They reneged on their promise to support him in his studies. He's Vika's prime suspect.' She paused, leaned forward and said quietly. 'Someone has told the press she's looking for him. They're calling him the Shoeshine Killer.'

Louisa groaned. 'If it is him, he'll never get a fair trial.'

Makereta nodded in agreement.

'You know, I saw Wame at eight-thirty that morning. He would have needed to have been very quick to get to Rick's and kill both men by nine – and he doesn't look strong enough to overpower them. Rick and Stewy were both fit and healthy men.'

'It's possible though.'

'Well, I hope Vika finds either Edwin or Wame soon, then they can testify to the fact that Stewy was alive at eight thirty and put me in the clear, then I can leave on Tuesday with Mataio.'

Makereta paused for a second. 'Do you and Mataio really live together on Tarawa?'

'Yes.'

'Does no one object?'

'No.'

'So no one goes to church then on Tarawa?'

'I think almost all the people on Tarawa go to church.'

Makereta looked serious. 'In my church it's a sin to live together when you are not married. What kind of church do you have on Tarawa?'

'All the same churches you have here but I do know a lot of Kiribati people can't afford the marriage licence fee so they don't bother. The churches don't seem to mind.'

Makereta frowned. 'It's a bit primitive in Kiribati, though, isn't it? They say the people still use the beach for a toilet, is that true?'

Louisa sighed, even here they judged a whole people by how they did the toilet. 'Yes, it's true but not everyone has that particular habit and things are changing.'

'Tell me about you and Mataio.'

Louisa laughed. 'There's nothing to tell. What about you? No secret lover hidden away somewhere?'

Makereta blushed. 'No. There was someone but Fijian men don't want to go out with girls who have their own opinions.'

'They sound just like Scottish men. Makereta, can you please take your shoes off the bed.'

'It's okay, they're not dirty. By the way, what did Mataio, want?'

Louisa looked at Makereta curiously. 'What do you mean?

'Don't you know? While you were at the church, he called to talk to you. At least three times. Jyoti was looking for you everywhere. There's a message for you.'

39

Jyoti was at reception. Mataio had left a message. It was brief. Just two words: Call me. So Louisa did.

'Hello?' It was Reteta. On the other end of the phone.

'It's me,' said Louisa. 'Is Mataio there?'

'He's gone!' shouted Reteta.

'Gone where?' said Louisa trying not to shout. Reteta always shouted on the phone. It drove Louisa nuts and always made her want to shout back.

'To the new maneaba. He's helping get everything ready

for the celebrations this weekend,' said Reteta.

'I can't believe I've missed him again. When will he be back?'

'I don't know,' shouted Reteta.

'He left a message asking me to call him. Do you know what that's about?'

'Oh, yes,' said Reteta, 'he said to tell you he's not coming to Fiji.'

'He's what?' Louisa's blood froze in her veins.

'Yes,' said Reteta matter of factly, 'he's staying here.'

'But he has to come, we're leaving the next day for Scotland. He'll miss the flight–'

'Oh, yes, that is another thing, he is not going to Scotland either–' There was a click and the line went dead.

'Hello?' said Louisa. 'Hello?'

Louisa got Jyoti to call Reteta straight back. The line was still dead. And stayed dead. Louisa was in shock. Mataio wasn't coming to Fiji or going to Scotland with her. It didn't make any sense? It had to be a mistake. Reteta was always getting things wrong. Louisa had to talk to him. A noise. Angry shouting. Coming from outside. It sounded like a fight. Louisa didn't care. She needed to think. The shouting got louder. She couldn't ignore it. In the car park Malaki was on the ground in a crunched up heap. The doorman towered over him, with his foot raised, as if to kick Malaki.

'Hey!' yelled Louisa. 'Stop right there!'

'Excuse me,' said the doorman, jumping to attention. 'The chef caught him eating the scraps for the dogs.'

'Tell him you're my friend!' sobbed Malaki. 'He won't believe me!'

'I know this young man,' said Louisa. 'I asked him to visit me. Let him go. And, by the way, since when is it a crime to eat discarded dog scraps?'

The doorman shook his head. 'He's a thief.'

'I am not a thief!' yelled Malaki.

'I'll vouch for him,' said Louisa, indicating Malaki should stand up.

'He's not getting in the hotel,' said the doorman, squaring up to Louisa.

'That's fine,' said Louisa. She had no intention of arguing the point. She nodded to a shaded picnic table to the side of the car park. 'Let's go over there.'

Malaki swiped grubby tears from his face, drew himself upright and followed her.

They sat down at the table. Louisa couldn't imagine anyone wanting to have a picnic next to a hotel car park, but what did she know? She'd thought Mataio was coming with her to Scotland and she'd got that wrong.

'Why does he keep looking at us?' said Malaki, glowering at the doorman, who was making a point of staring at them from where he'd planted himself in the middle of the car park.

'Ignore him. Firstly, did you really eat the dog scraps?'

Malaki looked down at his knees. 'I was hungry.'

'You told me the big boss fed you. What's up, you didn't like his menu?'

'I'm not staying there any more,' said Malaki, blushing.

'Oh?' said Louisa. 'Why not?'

'One of the other boys saw me with you on the church steps earlier. He told the boss. When I got back to the house the boss knew I had been with you. He said I had to tell him where you were. I would not tell him and he tried to hit me so I ran away.'

'Thank you for not giving me up,' said Louisa, meaning

it, while looking around to check the bad mad boss had not followed him. 'Are you homeless now?'

He looked down at his hands and nodded.

'But what are you going to do?' Bending the boss man's arm like that had been a mistake. And it had only made matters worse for Malaki. Would she never learn?

'I am going to find Wame,' said Malaki, looking back up at her. 'Will you help me?'

'You know where he is?' said Louisa.

'I think so. Wame has an aunty who lives a squatter settlement the other side of Suva. One of the other boys said Wame told him he was going to ask her for money.'

'When did Wame say this?'

'Yesterday.'

'Do you know why he wanted the money?' said Louisa. 'Was it to buy drugs?'

'Api is a liar!' Malaki jumped to his feet. 'I don't know why he said Wame took drugs but it is not true!'

'But why would Api lie?'

His small face fell and he sat back down on the bench. 'I don't know. But Wame is a good person. And when I find him he will help me.'

Louisa sighed silently. 'You know the police are also looking for Wame, don't you? They want to ask him some questions to do with Rick and Stewy.'

Malaki scowled. 'One of the boys said the newspapers are saying Wame is the killer. They are calling him the Shoeshine Killer. Why do they say such horrible things? Wame will never go to the police when people are saying such terrible things about him.'

'Ignore the papers. He needs to be eliminated from the police enquiries and so do I. He can prove Stewy was alive after I left the house the morning of the killings.'

Malaki looked surprised. 'You're a suspect?'

'It's procedure to eliminate anyone who knew the victims. When you find Wame, you must tell him to go to a police station and volunteer to make a statement.'

'He will not listen to me. You will have to come with me and talk to him.'

'No,' said Louisa, standing up. 'I'm busy.' She was going to go straight back in the hotel and phone Tarawa. Stay on the phone until she'd talked to Mataio and found out what was going on. 'Besides, why would he do anything I ask, you said he didn't like me?'

Malaki shrugged. 'He said you were pushy, it's not the same.' Malaki made a face. 'Why can't you come with me?'

'I have urgent stuff to do.' She would sit on the phone all day, if she had to, until she talked to Mataio and got the truth. 'You must explain to Wame the importance of going to the police.'

'I told you, he will not listen to me. I can't go to see him, anyway, I have no money for the bus fare.'

'Here,' Louisa took out her purse and handed Malaki a ten dollar note. 'That should cover your fares and have something left over for breakfast.'

'You're not giving him money, are you?' said Makereta, appearing behind them.

'A few dollars,' said Louisa. Where had she come from? 'Malaki thinks he knows where Wame is. Tell her what you told me about the aunty.'

'I'm not telling Constable Makereta anything!' said Malaki viciously.

Louisa was shocked. 'You know Makereta?'

40

'Malaki and me, we go way back, don't we?' said Makereta. 'How do you know him?'

'We met yesterday, when Malaki polished my shoes.' Louisa should have known everyone would know everyone. It was the Pacific. 'We bumped into each other again earlier today. He was looking for Wame. I offered to go with him. I thought I could find out something that might help the investigation. That's how we ended up at the church.' As long as Malaki said nothing about the incident with the shoeshine boss, she wouldn't.

Makereta frowned. 'And even though Malaki is Wame's brother, you didn't think it important to tell me, or Vika, that you were with him?'

'Brother?' said Louisa, eyes widening with shock.

'Stepbrother. Didn't he tell you that?' said Makereta,

Louisa looked at Malaki. 'What's going on?'

Malaki shifted on the bench. 'I thought you wouldn't help me if you knew he was related to me.'

'Exactly how much did you give him?' demanded Makereta, sitting down next to Louisa.

'Eating dog scraps is unacceptable. I gave him ten dollars to cover his breakfast and the bus fares to the aunty's village.'

Makereta shook her head wearily. 'Our very own little Malaki has tricked the mighty foreigner. Shame on you Malaki!'

Malaki scowled.

'He has not tricked me,' said Louisa, sitting down at the table. 'Why are you saying that?'

'Because young Malaki here...' She gripped Malaki by

the arm, preventing him from wriggling free. '...and his older stepbrother made a habit of conning unsuspecting foreigners out of their cash. Their modus operandi was to ask visitors for money for fares to get home to help their very ill mother, or granny, or for milk for a sick baby brother they don't have. You know the sort of thing, I'm sure.'

Louisa threw Malaki a suspicious look. 'Is this true?'

'We may have done some small tricks in the past but this is not a trick, not this time. Wame is lost and I have no money to find him.' He looked as if he was about to burst into tears.

'I believe him,' said Louisa.

Makereta raised her eyebrows in disbelief. 'You are willing to take the word of a common thief?'

Louisa shrugged. 'Wame has disappeared. His brother here wants to know he's safe. I have a brother. What doesn't make sense?' Telling Makereta about the boss being after her and Malaki warning her off was definitely not an option.

'Wame is a vital witness in a murder enquiry. If you have any idea of his whereabouts you need to tell me,' said Makereta, addressing both Malaki and Louisa.

'I know what the papers are saying about him! You think he killed Rick and Stewy!' yelled Malaki. 'You want to lock him up! I'm not telling you anything!'

'Calm down,' said Louisa. 'You have to tell her where he is,' said Louisa. 'It's the only way his name can be cleared.'

Malaki crossed his arms and looked away.

Louisa sighed. 'Malaki thinks Wame could be with his aunty in a village the other side of Suva. I thought ten dollars was a small price to pay to help him find him.

And before you ask, I advised Malaki to tell Wame to take himself to the nearest police station and make a statement.'

Makereta puckered her lips. 'This is what is happening, we're all going to go to the aunty's village. If Wame is there and he can prove he has a good reason for being there, I'll not arrest Malaki. But if he's in hiding so Malaki can con you out of money–'

'All this fuss over a few dollars!' said Louisa, indignantly.

'If Wame is hiding so Malaki can con you, and who knows who else, out of money, I'll arrest both of them.'

41

It was get in the car with Makereta and Malaki or Makereta was arresting them for withholding evidence. Louisa didn't believe she would do it but didn't want to put her to the test. Makereta was as angry as Louisa had ever seen her. Of course, in hindsight, Louisa should have told Makereta about meeting Malaki and Wame. She didn't know why she hadn't, because as Louisa was rapidly discovering, Makereta was no dummy. One thing was certain, they weren't BOMAS now. Louisa wiped her hands on a fresh wet wipe. The air conditioning was switched off and the heat in the car was unbearable.

Makereta said if she found Wame laid low, safe and well, she would nick both brothers on the grounds of employing dishonesty to deprive another of money, because that's what she thought was going on – Louisa had balked again at that, an arrest over a measly ten dollars, really? If they could not find Wame, or he was there and it appeared he had genuine reason for lying low, other than to con people out of money, Makereta would let Malaki go but not before she took the brothers' statements. It seemed back to front logic to Louisa but Malaki was all for it. As far as he was concerned, Makereta was going to help him find Wame, and that was a good thing.

If Louisa was honest, she didn't care one way or another what happened, not any more. If Wame was at his aunt's, well and good. At least he would verify Stewy had been alive at eight thirty on the morning he was killed, proving categorically she couldn't have had anything to do with the deaths. If he wasn't, bad luck. But if Mataio wasn't coming with her to Scotland, what did it matter, anyway? She had to talk to Mataio and find out what the hell was going on. The sooner they got to the aunty's, the sooner she could get back to the hotel and phone. For all she knew, Reteta could have got the message wrong?

The car rumbled past a row of swanky houses before winding down a steep road, pulling up outside a patch of swamp ground in a dank valley smothered in shoulder high greenery. Makereta got out and Louisa and Malaki followed her. She led them along a muddy path in the overgrown foliage to a clearing and a higgledy-piggledy mess of what looked like container sized corrugated iron and plasterboard box houses. Wame's aunty's village.

Narrow wooden walkways connected the houses to each other. Wet clothes draped the sills of square gaps where windows should have been. Between the dwellings sat colourful plastic basins, and miscellaneous crate boxes, stripy bags, sandals, shoes, pots and pans, and rusty bicycles and car tyres and parts of cars, and a twin tub washing machine. Chickens pecked at the wet ground and mangy dogs slept in muddy puddles. It reminded Louisa of a local village in Tarawa, except it was wetter, and dingier, and more squashed together and there were no straw roofs here or coconut spine floors. It was as if someone had dumped a bunch of containers over the top of the hill and left them where they had landed, in a mess.

'The squatter village is illegal, of course,' said Makereta, 'but it's been here for years.'

'It looks pretty temporary to me,' said Louisa.

'You,' said Makereta to Malaki, who was skulking behind them, 'go find Aunty and ask if Wame is here.'

Louisa watched Malaki scurry away. 'What if Wame isn't here and she doesn't want to talk to us?'

'She will. I know her and have helped her on many occasions.'

'Ah. Then we just have to be sure Malaki doesn't run away. You seem hard on him, he's only a boy.'

'You think he would have been happy with taking just ten dollars from you? That was the start. Who knows where it would have ended up?'

Louisa laughed. 'I'm not an idiot!'

'Time and time again I let them off with warnings. I wanted to give Malaki a chance. He's so young. I should have known Wame couldn't change.'

'Aren't you jumping to conclusions?'

'He's had chance after chance, and not just by me, by Rick and Stewy too. He blew them all.'

'What about sewage?' said Louisa, changing the subject.

'Pit toilets and rain water showers. This is one of the better squatter settlements. They're not all this organised.'

Somewhere not too far away Louisa thought she heard singing and then it stopped. 'Was that singing?'

'Songs go well with the kava.'

'Kava?'

'It's a drink made from a plant. You bash the roots with a metal post, add to water and strain. It takes a long time.'

'Does it taste nice?'

'Not particularly. It's a relaxant. A kind of mild drug. The church says we shouldn't drink it.'

'So you don't take it?'

Makereta smiled wearily 'I didn't say that. It's a traditional part of our way of life. Everyone does it. It connects communities. And when we take kava, we sing.'

Malaki was back with an older, gaunt woman. She looked harassed. Anxious. Malaki's face was white with fear. He said, 'Wame is not here but the boss is. He is looking for me, Wame and for you,' he pointed to Louisa, 'the Scottish detective lady!'

42

'You must hide,' said the aunty, quickly leading the group towards the first house. 'If the boss sees you here he will think I am your friend and he will make big trouble for me. Come!'

'But you're police!' said Louisa to Makereta. 'You have the authority to stop him.'

'No,' said Makereta, hurrying after the woman. 'We have no back up. If Aunty thinks we should hide, we hide.'

Louisa followed Makereta and Malaki, who had already darted ahead, into the house. She did not want to go into the dark and dingy hovel but she wanted to be battered to death less. She would scrub thoroughly later.

It was unbearably warm inside and dark. As Louisa's eyes got used to the dim light, she saw a dozen local men and women sitting cross-legged in a circle around a medium sized, pink plastic basin half full of a muddy brown liquid.

The aunty said something in Fijian to the seated people before skirting around them, heading towards a doorway at the back of the room, draped with an old, grey blanket. 'Hurry! Hurry!'

One of the women in the group dipped an enamel cup into the bowl, scooped up some of the muddy liquid and passed it to the woman next to her. Before taking the cup, the new woman clapped once, downed the liquid in a oner, said 'Bula' and everyone else clapped three times and started singing. It was as if Louisa and Makereta and Malaki were invisible.

'They're drinking kava,' whispered Makereta.

Louisa was glad she didn't live in Suva. They were big on communal eating on Tarawa, and while she had just about mastered eating cooked fish and rice taken from a communal washing basin-cum-food bowl with her fingers, she knew she would never be able to drink anything that looked as disgusting as dirty dish water, scooped from a communal basin that looked like it had never been cleaned.

Behind the dirty grey blanket was a smaller room, even warmer than the first one, and darker. The aunty told them to go inside and wait for her to come and get them. The room smelled of old clothes and cockroaches. Louisa grimaced. This was not good. Trickles of light seeped through gaps in the corrugated iron roof above their heads. There was just enough to see by. The floor was covered with bulging blue and white and red nylon stripy bags, rolled up straw mats, cardboard boxes and round plastic basins packed with stuff. It seemed to be a store room of sorts. The singing from the main room was reassuring. In the corner of the room Makereta pushed some bags to one side and unfurled a mat in the space left.

'We may as well get comfortable,' whispered Makereta, sitting crossed legged on the mat. 'We could be here a while.'

Louisa took out her lava-lava and placed it on the mat next to Makereta and sat down. Makereta eyed the lava-lava curiously but said nothing. Malaki sat between the two women. The singing in the first room stopped. Louisa held her breath. The warm stifling silence seemed deafening. Then came the muffled voices. Angry and deep and mean. They grew louder. The boss was really there. In the next room. Was he coming closer? Shit and bloody shit! Louisa glanced at Makereta next to her. From the worry in her eyes she was clearly as anxious as Louisa. A shout. Malaki jumped. Makereta took his little hand in hers. He left it there.

Louisa closed her eyes. Why had she let Makereta drag her to the aunty's village? She'd wanted to stay at the hotel. Phone the house on Tarawa until Mataio answered. She didn't care who'd killed Rick and Stewy. Or if Wame and Edwin were alive or dead. Yes, she did feel sorry for Malaki, she opened her eyes to look at him, was he trembling? Louisa closed her eyes again. Malaki wasn't her problem. All she wanted was for things to be as they were before she came to Fiji. She'd been planning the trip to Scotland for over six months. Mataio had never said he didn't want to go with her. They'd even talked about her applying for her old job and moving back there.

Makereta touched Louisa on the arm. 'I think he's gone.'

Louisa strained to listen. The angry voices had stopped and the singing had started again. Louisa sighed with relief.

'Better wait for the aunty to come get us, though,' said Makereta. 'To be sure.'

'Okay,' whispered Louisa. 'I'm in no hurry to meet that obnoxious man again.'

'How are you?' Makereta said to Malaki. He nodded, although his eyes stayed fearful. Then Makereta turned to Louisa and said with quiet anger, 'Why is the shoeshine boss looking for you?'

43

Louisa knew she was blushing but couldn't do anything about it.

'He was hitting me, and she stopped him,' whispered Malaki.

'How?' demanded Makereta.

'She hurt his arm.'

'Oh?' said Makereta, eyeing flashing with anger.

'I know it was a foolish thing to twist his arm,' said Louisa quietly. She should have known Makereta would be cross. 'I reacted emotionally but he was being such a bully.'

'I'm glad you hurt him,' said Malaki. 'He was always horrible to us.'

'Oh boy,' hissed Makereta. 'I am so ticked off. I mean, really, really ticked off! In fact, I have never been so ticked off! When were you going to tell me about this?'

'I didn't tell you about it because I was angry with myself for losing control. It could have ended up very badly and it would have been my own fault. The fewer people who knew what happened, the better.'

'You talk about me trusting you but it seems for you trust is a one way thing, where you feel no need to reciprocate.'

Louisa shifted uncomfortably. 'I told you Wame lied to me about seeing Stewy and Edwin on Wednesday morning. I was simply trying to find out why when the boss challenged what I was doing and started on Malaki.'

'And you didn't think to pass on what had happened?' said Makereta, stone-faced.

'I didn't know he would start looking for me or that Wame would be a person of interest in the investigation,' whispered Louisa. 'I was looking for Edwin. I thought Wame might know where he was. I never expected Wame to lie to me.'

'You are so sure he is not truthful,' said Malaki suddenly, his face scrunched into a tight ball. 'But what if you are the one who is wrong?'

'I saw him talk to Edwin and Stewy with my own eyes. It was him.'

Makereta addressed Malaki. 'Did your brother say anything to you about meeting Stewy and his friend, Edwin?'

Malaki's mouth drooped into a slouch. 'He tells me nothing.'

'The last time you saw him, what kind of mood was he in?' said Makereta. 'Was he sad, or angry, or crazy. Maybe he was happy?'

'Why are you asking such a silly question?' said Malaki, raising his voice.

'Sh!' said Louisa.

'Everyone is saying Wame killed those men,' mumbled Malaki. 'It is not true. He liked them. He is not the Shoeshine Killer.'

'If Detective Louisa says she saw Wame talk with the men, then she did.'

'How often did Stewy come and see Wame?' said Louisa.

Malaki shook his head. 'He didn't. After Rick and Stewy asked Wame to leave their house, Wame never saw them again.'

'So, why did Stewy come to see him that Wednesday, suddenly, out of the blue?'

Malaki put his head in his hands. 'I don't know.'

'We have to find Wame and ask him what he knows. If he is innocent he has nothing to fear,' said Makereta.

'Why is the boss looking for him?' said Louisa.

Malaki brought his knees into his chest and hugged himself. 'Wame was doing bad things.'

Makereta gave Louisa a look as if to say 'told you so'.

'What kind of bad things?' said Louisa.

'Sh!' said Makereta, 'someone's coming.'

44

They waited in the claustrophobic heat of the stifling store room for someone to appear but no one came. Trickles of sweat ran down Louisa's neck and into her blouse. She dabbed herself with a clean hanky. At least the singing hadn't stopped. The soft melodic tunes coming from the other room were comforting. Louisa looked at Makereta.

Makereta turned to Malaki, still hugging his knees. 'If you want us to help you find Wame, you must tell us what bad things Wame did?'

'Some foreign men come to Fiji to have sex with young men for money,' said Malaki quietly.

'Rent boys?' said Louisa.

Malaki shrugged.

'Wame slept with foreign men for money, yes? Where?' said Makereta.

'He stayed with them in hotel rooms. If they wanted company for a lot of days they used holiday flats. When he didn't turn up yesterday I thought he was with a foreign man. But the others told me that Wame was not with a man. They said he had argued with the boss and run away. He was always arguing with the boss but he never ran away before.'

'You know what they argued about, don't you?' said Louisa.

Malaki blushed. 'They said it was about me. The boss told Wame he was too old to sleep with the old foreign men, the men want young boys. The boss told Wame I had to take his place. Wame said he wouldn't let me do that and ran away. The boss said Wame owed him money and I had to pay it for him by sleeping with the old men. So that is why I ran away too.'

'I thought you ran away from the boss because you wouldn't tell him which hotel I was staying in?' said Louisa.

'It was that too. But also because I don't want to sleep with a man. The church says it is a sin for a man to sleep with a man.' Malaki was close to tears. 'That's why I know something must have happened to Wame, he would never leave me alone, not to do that. He always said he would take me with him when he left but now I am all alone and have nowhere to stay. He must be in trouble.'

'It's against the law for anyone to force anyone, let alone a young man who is under eighteen, to sleep with another man,' said Makereta. 'The boss is breaking the law. We can arrest him if you agree to testify against him.'

Malaki looked petrified. 'No. I will not do anything like that. All the other boys will be in trouble if I do that. You said you would help me. This isn't helping me.'

'Okay,' said Makereta. 'Let's find Wame first and take it from there. You are sure he is not with a foreign man in a holiday apartment somewhere?'

'No. He would have told me,' said Malaki, wiping away his tears with the back of his hand. 'He knows I will be worried for him.'

'How do the foreign men make contact if they want sex?' said Louisa suddenly.

Malaki blushed. 'They tell us shoeshine boys. We take their details and pass them to the boss and then he contacts the men directly to find out what they want and plans it.'

'Are all the shoeshine boys prostituting themselves like Wame?' said Louisa.

'I only know what happens in our group.'

'Did Stewy bring Edwin to the city centre in Wednesday morning, to pick up a boy?' said Makereta.

'Wame said Rick and Stewy were good men. He liked them. He did not like the men he had to sleep with.'

'But Wame was cross with them for not sending him to Australia, yes? You could say he felt let down by them, yes?' said Makereta. 'It made him angry, yes?'

'You'd be angry too if your dreams had been taken from you!' whispered Malaki, furious tears falling down his thin cheeks.

45

When Makereta dropped Louisa off at the Holiday Inn it was almost dusk and the hotel was eerily quiet. Jyoti confirmed the closing conference speeches had been at 3pm and everyone had since checked out. Louisa called Tarawa. No answer. She tried four more times. Still no answer. She did not want to give up but she needed a shower. One boiling forty minute deep quadrupole scrub later Louisa lay on her bed and gathered her thoughts.

When they'd left the village, the aunty had said Wame had been there earlier and told her he was going to Nadi. Malaki had been visibly dismayed at the news. It looked as if his brother had abandoned him, after all. Makereta had asked the aunty if Malaki could stay with her; she'd refused. It was too dangerous with the shoeshine boss still looking for him. Determined that Malaki should not wander the streets, if only for that night, Makereta was taking Malaki to a hostel she knew of. She promised Louisa she'd be back within the hour. Louisa was glad Makereta was helping out Malaki, she liked the feisty wee waif, but she was even more glad she'd been left alone. An hour wasn't long but it gave her time to think. And she needed it. She didn't care who had murdered who any more, or why, all she wanted to know was why Mataio was not coming to Fiji. The most obvious reason for Mataio staying on Tarawa was another woman. In fact, it was the only reason as far as she was concerned.

When Louisa was about nine and her brother Euin was five, not that long after they'd returned to Scotland from Tarawa, they'd lived with their Scottish granny in her wee bungalow. At some point Dad had gone away for work. Mum had suddenly got sick and needed to go into hospital for a few weeks. Scottish Granny said she was too old to look after Louisa and her brother by herself. Mum wrote to Dad to tell him to come home to look after the children. Three days later the letter was returned unopened. Her mum had grabbed the envelope and Louisa by the hand, left Euin with Granny, and took Louisa on a bus to a strange part of town.

They'd got off the bus in a street of towering stone tenements. It the afternoon sun the buildings looked orange. Mum stopped at a stair with five steps leading to the main entrance. She rang one of the bells and rang and rang. Louisa was embarrassed. Her mum was acting like a crazy lady. Then Louisa's dad had looked out of a window above their heads. At the sight of him Louisa's heart had lifted. That was until a strange woman had popped her head out the window behind him. The woman shouted at them to go away. Her mum had shouted right back at the woman. Other people looked out their windows. A crowd gathered. Soon everyone was shouting at everyone. Louisa wanted to die with shame. Eventually, her dad threw a scrappy piece of paper out of the window, letting it float down rather than make the effort to come down and give it to her. Her dad had agreed to look after Louisa and Euin while Mum was the three weeks in hospital. Until then Louisa hadn't even realised her dad had left them.

It had been three weeks of unwashed clothes, forgotten meal times, missed days at school and hours of being left alone. Luckily, Louisa could remember how to get to Granny's bungalow, so when it was really bad and they were really hungry, she took Euin by the hand and walked him there. Granny would feed them Tunnock's caramel wafers and give them cups of sweet tea until Dad came to get them, which he did, eventually. The only good thing Louisa could remember about the awful three weeks was the other woman wasn't anywhere to be seen and the visits to Mum in hospital. On hospital visit days Dad gave them flowers and chocolates to give to Mum and made sure they were scrubbed and in their best clothes. When Mum finally came out of hospital instead of going back to live with Scottish Granny, they stayed at Dad's. At first it was good being together. But it didn't last. The drinking started, followed by the arguments. Then one day he was gone forever.

There was a knock on the door. 'Hey, can you let me in?' It was Makereta.

Louisa got up, moved the chair she'd wedged under the door handle earlier and let her in.

'Thanks,' said Makereta tight-lipped.

'Everything okay?' said Louisa. Was Makereta still ticked off at her?

'No.' She kicked off her shoes and flopped on her bed.

'Oh?'

'The hostel was full.'

'That's a shame, so where is Malaki now?'

'I left him at my parents.'

46

Louisa sat on her bed and faced Makereta. 'Malaki is staying with your parents? Is that wise?'

Makereta shrugged. 'I couldn't leave him homeless, not with the boss looking for him. Besides, they insisted.'

'What if the boss tracks Malaki down to your house, your parents could be at risk?'

'It's unlikely but even if he does my dad is big. I mean, really big and he used to be a police officer. He can easily take care of himself and Mum and Malaki. But I warned Malaki: no peeing in the garden; no back chat; no eating without a knife and fork; no bare feet – and he has to always wash his hands.' She shook her head wearily. 'My folks always wanted a son. This is giving them a taster for the weekend. Lets see how they like it.'

'The weekend? That's very kind of them. I don't know if I could do that.'

'They are very unselfish, Christian people.' She sighed. 'Besides, as far as they're concerned the more the merrier. They wanted me to bring you back to the house too, said we should all stay there with them.'

'One big happy family.' Louisa didn't want to stay with anyone's parents, no matter how kind. But she wished Makereta would go. 'Would Vika allow it?'

'Oh yes, especially as Dad is an ex-cop. Plus she'd be saving money on my hotel costs.' Makereta made a face. 'But I'd rather stay here. I love my parents but I live with them all the time. Nothing ever happens. Sharing a room with you is an adventure.'

'Yes, right. You must get out even less than me. But your parents and Malaki, a street boy? Are you sure?'

'Nope,' said Makereta seriously. 'But without his big brother to look after him there's every chance Malaki will end up either beaten or forced into prostitution or both. I don't want that on my conscience. Wame may be a bad influence on Malaki but he's not as bad as the boss.'

'Even if he's a murder suspect?'

'I agree Wame may know something about the killings but –' Makereta paused to sweep her hair out of her eye '– I can't believe someone who cares for his brother the way Wame cares for Malaki could be a murderer.'

'We only have Malaki's word that his brother cares for him,' said Louisa. 'If he loves his younger brother so much, why has he buggered off and left him?'

'If he has,' said Makereta. 'At least for the time being Malaki is safe and until it's proved Wame is the killer I'm reserving judgement.' Makereta dragged herself off the bed and headed for the shower. 'I could have been too hasty in judging him before. I won't do it again. I just hope he's not in danger.'

Louisa stayed where she was. She was moved that Makereta and her parents cared so much for Malaki, and had such faith in Wame. In less than a day Makereta had totally reassessed her opinion of the two brothers. It was good that she was open-minded, prepared to change her mind. It was a refreshing change from the blinkered attitude of many people back home, where no one much cared for anyone else, especially the homeless and destitute. Prostitutes weren't much loved either. The council were constantly petitioned by the public into closing the sex saunas in Edinburgh. When they did, the prostitutes then moved into flats. Flats were less safe for them, though better than being on the streets. The council didn't care.

What mattered was they were out of sight. Not that Louisa necessarily wanted to live in a street where there was a sex sauna, but prostitutes had rights like any other workers. The most basic right was to be safe in their workplace. End of. And it wasn't as if men were suddenly going to start ignoring their cocks. On Tarawa, the problem was even worse.

Before she'd returned to Tarawa she'd had memories of an idyllic, remote paradise, populated with nature's gentlemen and women, who were innocent, untouched and untainted by western influences. How could she have been that naive? Sure, she had met some lovely people, no doubt about that. But she'd quickly discovered that no matter how remote you were, the human beings were the same the world over. If you let them, they could behave very badly indeed. On Tarawa prostitution was a serious problem. Worse, over seventy percent of the sex workers on Tarawa were under eighteen. The police service had a continuous serious ongoing issue with child prostitutes working the Korean fishing boats harboured in Betio Port. Made worse because there was no actual law in Kiribati against prostitution, underage or otherwise. The best her colleagues could do was to enforce a custom law which prohibited anyone going on to a ship without permission from the custom office. As a law to prevent underage prostitution it was useless. But Fiji had laws to stop young people being abused. Why weren't they using them?

'Are you okay?' said Makereta, coming out the shower room with her hair wrapped in a white towel and dressed in a white towelling dressing gown.

'Pardon?' said Louisa, from where she still lay on the bed.

'You seem different. Disinterested. Yesterday you couldn't be stopped sleuthing, even after you were told to stop, and today you don't seem to care.'

Louisa cleared her throat. 'Maybe I know when I'm beat.'

Makereta sat down on her bed and eyed Louisa carefully. 'What's going on?'

Louisa felt her cheeks blush deeper. 'What do you mean?'

'You've changed. What is it?'

'Nothing.'

Makereta lay back on the bed and looked at the ceiling. 'So much for trust.'

'I'm sorry. I'm not good at sharing. It's a weakness of mine.' Louisa licked her lips. 'If you must know, Mataio isn't coming on holiday with me. That was his message earlier.'

'He's what?' Makereta sat bolt upright.

Louisa nodded. 'Not coming to Scotland with me.'

'But why not?'

'I don't know. Reteta gave me the message. I've not talked to him yet.'

'But you must!' said Makereta already on her feet. 'You must!'

'I've tried. He won't come to the phone.'

'If he won't come to the phone, then you must go to him.'

Louisa laughed. 'Sure.'

'I mean it!' Makereta began to pace the room. 'There's a flight to Tarawa first thing tomorrow. You can return on the Monday flight.'

'Are you serious'

'Is it the money?'

'I can afford the tickets. But it's a four hour flight.'

'Do you want to talk to him or not?'

'Of course I do, but he obviously doesn't want to talk with me.'

'That's it? You're just going to give up on the only true love of your life?'

'I didn't say that.' Louisa groaned silently. Had she actually told Makereta that Mataio was her only true love? 'But what about Vika?'

Makereta stopped pacing. She frowned. 'She's preoccupied trying to save her job. If she asks where you are, I'll say you're staying with me at my parents', I'll have to move back with them when you leave.'

'It's a crazy idea,' said Louisa, sitting up. 'If I leave after Vika's specifically told me to stay, she really will try and lock me up when I come back.'

'When it comes to true love, you shouldn't let anyone or anything stand in your way, especially not Vika!'

47

As the big plane approached the only runway on Tarawa, children playing football scattered, scaring the chickens and pigs they shared it with. Louisa smiled. Where else would the runway for an international airport be a football pitch? She couldn't believe she was here. It was probably the most rash decision she had ever made. Makereta had taken her to the airport as soon as the morning curfew had lifted. Louisa had got the first flight to Nadi. One hour later she'd caught the international connection to Tarawa.

No stopovers. No delays. No time to phone ahead and say she was on her way. It had cost her a small fortune for the last minute tickets but so what? One thousand and four hundred miles later and she was home.

As Makereta saw it Louisa had no choice. She needed to talk to Mataio and if Mataio wasn't coming to see her, she had to go to him. If for no other reason, Louisa had to be sure Reteta had not made a mistake. And Louisa acknowledged Makereta was right. But deep down, Louisa was worried. What if Mataio had simply fallen out of love with her and into love with someone else? She knew from her mother and father's relationship that it happened. But Mataio was the only man she'd ever imagined walking into the sunset with. She needed an explanation. But was she ready for the worst?

Louisa gave herself a shake. As long as she was freshly showered, wearing clean clothes and had her lippy on, she could cope with anything. Well, almost anything. And she was glad Makereta was a romantic and had persuaded her to come back. She just hoped Vika didn't come looking for Louisa at Makereta's parents' house. She didn't want Makereta to get into trouble on her account, but more than that, she didn't want to totally stuff up the only other important thing in her life, her career.

Louisa stood at the open door of the plane and let the heat of the early afternoon sun melt around her. The dry hot air tasted delicious. It had none of the extreme humidity of Fiji and it was clean. In fact, the cleanest air in the world, according to the researcher sitting next to her on the plane. He travelled the world with a suitcase of flasks, collecting air samples from everywhere he went. Tarawa was so far from land, he said, by the time the air got there it was super pure. Pity you couldn't say the same about the water.

Bonriki International terminal was a shed. One room for both arrivals and departures. It had an overhead fan, a check-in desk, one member of staff from Air Pacific, a customs official and a passport control official. Sometimes they were one and the same person. Today they were all there. Taking their time. Making the long line of passengers wait under the overhead fans. There was no hurry, their luggage still had to be off loaded and dumped onto the tarmac, ready to be collected.

Louisa glanced at the waiting people. They were mostly Pacific Islanders, a handful of foreigners. Were they here on business? What business did people do on South Tarawa? It was a tiny island with a population of thirty something thousand. Maybe they were visiting relatives for Christmas? She kept forgetting it was that time of year. Christmas wasn't the same without the cold, dark wintery nights.

Louisa's colleagues in passport control and customs looked surprised to see her. They'd not expected her back until the end of January. She blamed the coup for her change of plan. Said it had muddled everything. All smiles, they waved her through but she saw the look of sympathy in their eyes. The one that said they knew what was going on when she didn't.

She got a lift in the back of a lorry belonging to her neighbour. He had come to pick up an uncle with half a dozen members of his family. The trip in the back of the truck was chilly, even with the sun beating down and her lava-lava round her shoulders. By the time he dropped her in front of her house, she was tired and dusty and in desperate need of a change of clothes and a hot shower. She hurried past her orange Beetle, still parked in the driveway where she'd left it. She'd bought the car from an Air Pacific pilot who was going back home to New Zealand. When necessary he would send her parts to keep it going.

The front door was locked. Louisa went round the side of the house to the back. She heard the sea first. Crunching against the shore out of sight. Then she heard the singing. A single voice, growing louder and louder. Reteta stood in the middle of the back veranda, her arms stretched out at either side of her plump body. Her face glistened with sweat. Her eyes stared ahead in rigid concentration, trance like. Her long black hair softly swished from side to side as she turned her head to the right then to the left in sharp, short movements. Her hands, palms facing down, tips of fingers raised skywards, swept one way then the other. She made each movement to the beat of the song Kana, Reteta's mother-in-law, sang from where she sat, cross-legged on the ground with her back to Louisa.

Louisa recognised the dance moves. They were part of a traditional dance to do with love and leaving. How ironic! The hand movements mimicked the movements of birds. Daisy, Reteta's dog, snoozed in the sandy soil next to the verandah. He was a male dog, despite his name. He came with Reteta. And was by far the ugliest dog Louisa had seen: white with brown patches, skinny, mangy, sad eyes and big, sticking out ears. He lifted his head. Growled for second. Saw it was Louisa, barked gleefully and hobbled towards her, his tale wagging wildly. Reteta lost concentration. Her trance broken she now saw Louisa. A broad grin swept across her round face.

'Lulu! You are back!'

Louisa nodded. 'I got a chance to come back early.'

48

Reteta plonked herself next to Kana on the ground. She patted the straw mat covering the concrete area where Kana sat and said to Louisa, 'Teka teka! Sit! Sit!'

Kana shuffled over and made a space for Louisa to sit. Kana appeared to have grown even thinner in the few days Louisa had been away.

'Your head?' said Kana. 'What has happened. Did you have an accident?'

'Someone hit me.' Louisa sat cross-legged between the two women. She patted Daisy behind the ears, despite herself. She'd have to use the rule of four later.

'The coup in Fiji. Is it very bad? Is that how you got hurt?' said Reteta, frowning.

'No, nothing like that. Fiji was fine. The army are in charge, but everything seems to be carrying on as normal.'

'We have some tea, yes?' Reteta leaned over and threw a handful of coconut husks onto the glowing red embers of the camp fire in front of her.

Louisa nodded even though she didn't much like sweet tea, but it was how tea came on Tarawa, sweetened with condensed milk and directly from the kettle.

'Okay,' said Reteta, placing a big blackened kettle on the embers. 'Now you tell us all about the killing of the gay man, the one you found.'

'You heard about that?' The news had already travelled this far. 'Does everyone know, even Mataio?'

'Oh yes, it was on the radio. Have they found the killer?'

'No, not yet.' Louisa looked around. 'Is Mataio here?'

Reteta swiftly raised her eyebrows and then lowered them. The action momentarily made her look wide-eyed with disbelief. It was a local gesture, which Louisa knew from experience meant either I don't know or I do know. Or even, who knows? It was the equivalent of shrugging your shoulders.

'Ah,' said Louisa, listening to the ocean wash against the sandy shore ahead. She'd missed that noise. Had she only been away five days? Surely not? It seemed like months. 'Where is everyone?'

'The old men are fishing. The children are at the church group dance practice. We are having a big celebration for the opening of the new maneaba tomorrow. You can come now you are here,' Reteta leaned back and took three enamel cups from out of a pink washing up basin sitting on the ground behind her.

'Why doesn't Mataio want to come to see me in Fiji?' said Louisa.

'You must ask Mataio,' said Reteta flatly.

'But I'm asking you?' said Louisa. Reteta was like a sister she'd never wanted but had come to accept and like, although maybe not love. They had too many differences to be really close, to do with religion, cultural identity and sense of humour, none of which Louisa had. 'You do know, don't you?'

Reteta did the thing with her eyebrows again, then looked away.

Louisa turned to Kana. 'Do you know why he's not coming?'

Kana shook her head. 'He tells me nothing.'

'Reteta, what exactly did he say?' said Louisa.

Reteta shrugged again. 'That he was not going to Fiji.'

'That's it? Nothing else about why? Does he realise the new tickets are there, paid for? Did he not see them?'

'Yes, yes, he saw the tickets.'

'So what's the problem?'

'I am sure there is no problem,' said Reteta beaming.

'He's not coming with me to Scotland, of course there's a problem!'

Reteta shrugged. 'He is very busy.'

Louisa felt suddenly squeamish. Mataio didn't do busy. She didn't want to ask any more but she had to know. 'Busy doing what?'

'You know, he is helping with the church preparations for Sunday.'

Louisa shifted her position, she still found sitting crossed legged for too long uncomfortable. 'So busy he can't find time to call me, not once?'

Reteta said. 'The opening of the new maneaba is a big day, there is a lot of work involved.'

'Kana,' she turned to Reteta's mother-in-law. 'Is that where he is now, helping with the preparations?'

Kana did the thing with her eyebrows.

Louisa assumed that she meant yes. At least she hoped it did.

'Let us have some tea,' said Reteta. 'Mataio will be back later. You talk to him then. You wait and see all will be good.'

'But I still don't understand what helping with the opening has to do with his not coming to Fiji on Monday?'

Kana and Reteta looked blank. Louisa felt suddenly sick. This was not good. Not good at all.

Reteta smiled. 'Here!' She handed Louisa an enamel cup, filled with milky tea.

'I'm not thirsty,' said Louisa.

49

Louisa watched the red embers from the burning coconut husks in the campfire hiss and glow. She loved the smokey smell from the open fire, even if it did make her clothes stink and in need of an immediate wash. The fire had become a feature of her sandy back garden from the day Reteta had come to Louisa's door and offered to do some cleaning for her. Louisa hadn't wanted or needed a cleaner – there was only herself in the house at that time – but Reteta wouldn't go away. Eventually, Louisa gave in, but only because Reteta was her cousin. Louisa and Reteta had played together when they were wee. It had seemed a good way for Louisa to get to know her cousin again. But by offering Reteta a few hours work a week, she'd unwittingly gave permission for Reteta and her family to camp out in her garden. The family were now a permanent feature, just like the camp fire.

The longer Reteta had stayed, the more her belongings had multiplied. They now mushroomed out from the veranda and across the sandy scrubby garden, right up to the line of coconut trees, which marked the end of Louisa's garden and the beginning of the beach. Reteta used the trees to string up a washing line. Before Reteta arrived, the vista from the living room window was of the magnificent Pacific Ocean thrashing onto the beach. Now the view was of an assortment of rainbow coloured T-shirts and shorts, strung between the trees, flapping and flailing like headless scarecrows.

Louisa thought of the back of her house as a cross between a squatter's camp and a busy jumble sale: it was covered with blue and red and white stripy nylon bags, of all sizes; rolled up sleeping mats; pillows; basins of utensils; tea chests; bags; boxes; mosquito nets; the pig, which was tethered to the pandanus tree in a makeshift pen, and her piglets, all seven of them, which hugged her teats at every opportunity. The pen reeked of animal. Where had the bicycle wheel come from? The rusty roller skate, just the one? A giant inflated tyre – she'd seen the kids playing with that in the sea. The cat (for the mice?). And not forgetting Daisy the male dog.

'I have to talk to Mataio,' said Louisa, finally, getting to her feet. If she stayed any longer she would lose her momentum. 'I've upped and left Fiji, costing me a small fortune, and maybe my job, to talk to him. So, where is this new maneaba?'

Reteta nodded. 'I'll show you.'

'Thanks.' Louisa didn't want to jump to conclusions, but in her book, there was only one thing that kept someone from being with the person they loved and that was someone else.

The new maneaba community hall sat in a clearing in the middle of the traditional village. The vast roof was made of corrugated iron sheets and held up by eight sturdy concrete pillars. The modern materials looked out of place surrounded by the local huts. Louisa had imagined the new building would be made from traditional thatch and natural wood, like the old one. Reteta explained that building a maneaba the old fashioned way was much harder work and took much longer than building one with modern materials. Plus, she'd explained, with all the old men dying off, fewer and fewer of the young men had the skills to build a maneaba the old way. Reteta thought the new style maneaba looked smart. Louisa wondered how long the corrugated iron sheets would last in a high wind.

Mataio sat crossed legged inside the big maneaba hall, deep in conversation with some other men. They were all neatly dressed in clean T-shirts and lava-lavas. Louisa's first reaction was relief. He was alive. He was well. He was not with a woman. Although, she did think he looked different. Smart. But unlike Louisa, Mataio didn't do smart. He didn't give a shit about how he looked or what people thought of him. That was one of the reasons she liked him so much. He was her opposite. His disregard for rules and authority made Louisa mindful of her obsessive behaviour and that it was okay to be less controlling.

Louisa and Reteta kicked off their shoes outside the hall, as was the rule, ducked under the eaves of the giant roof and entered the maneaba. Louisa wanted to go straight over to Mataio but Reteta insisted she waited. The men were clearly having a meeting. She said it would be rude to interrupt. So, instead, Louisa took a clean lava-lava from her bag, spread it out on the concrete floor and sat down with Reteta and waited. A breeze danced in from outside and fluttered over them.

'The man in the middle,' whispered Reteta, 'He is our pastor.'

'But I still don't understand what Mataio is doing here?'

'He is the curate. He has to be here.'

'He's a curate for real?' Louisa was surprised. Everyone used to call Mataio The Curate or TC for short. When she asked him about it, he said he was not so much the curate of the church as an odd job man who helped out occasionally. 'When did this happen?'

'I don't know but we are very proud of Mataio. He

got aid money to buy the modern material to make the maneaba.'

'Really?' Louisa had had no idea Mataio had been so involved in the project.

Just then Mataio saw her. He looked surprised. Then smiled. That look. She could forgive those eyes anything.

50

'Hey,' said Louisa, leaning up to meet Mataio's lips, as he sat down next to her.

'I felt terrible about not being able to get to Fiji but now you're here, it's wonderful!' He sat down just far enough away so she couldn't kiss him.

'I was worried,' she said, trying to ignore the feeling of a giant spider crawling over her insides. Why no kiss? Any sign of affection in public was not culturally done on Tarawa, but Mataio never bothered about doing the right anything. He was a rebel. They always had some kind of physical contact when they met, even if it was only a squeeze of hands.

'Worried?' said Mataio? 'About what?'

'You're pleased to see me then?' she said.

He laughed. 'Of course, I am!'

'Lulu was hurt, see,' said Reteta, pointing to Louisa's head, as if Mataio wouldn't have been able to see the dressing without her help.

'That looks bad, is it?' His voice was full of concern.

'Not really.' She smiled while her guts flip-flopped like a beached flounder. He looked like the same Mataio. But his body language, his new smart look, his lack of obvious affection, were all wrong.

'May I?' One of the other men from the group joined them.

'Of course,' said Mataio. 'This is Pastor Johan. This is my friend Louisa.'

'Hello,' said Louisa. Did he just say friend, not girlfriend?

Pastor Johan sat down cross-legged next to Mataio. 'We are so grateful to Mataio for his contribution to the maneaba. He works tirelessly.'

'So I've been hearing,' said Louisa.

'I can see you two want to talk but I've come to ask if you'll let us keep Mataio for a few more hours yet. We have so much to discuss and we can't do it without him.'

Louisa smiled. 'I'd rather like to talk to Mataio myself.'

'Of course, of course,' said Pastor Johan, a broad smile stretching from ear to ear. 'We'll be finished by five, can you wait a few hours for the benefit of the children's dancing groups?'

Louisa wanted to smack his silly, supercilious grin off his face. 'That's up to Mataio, isn't it?'

Mataio took her hands in his and gave them a squeeze. 'I am so happy you came. We'll talk later. I'll explain all, I promise.' He dropped her hands and stood up.

'We'll not keep him any longer than we have to,' said Pastor Johan, leaning over and patting her on the head.

'I am not a dog!' said Louisa, furiously.

The pastor chuckled, put his arm through Mataio's and took him back to where they'd been sitting.

'If he touches my head like that again, I'll punch his lights out,' growled Louisa.

Reteta burst out laughing. 'You are so funny.'

'I'm serious!' Louisa got up. Whether she liked it or not, she was going to have to wait till later to talk to Mataio. The good news was he seemed genuinely happy to see her. And even though there was no kiss, maybe that was a maneaba rule, he had given gave her hands a squeeze, which was their thing. Plus, there was no obvious sign of another woman. What she didn't get was why he acted as if there was nothing amiss with him choosing, without discussion, not to go on their big trip. No two ways about it, something was still seriously wrong.

51

Louisa always showered after being in a maneaba, new or otherwise. She would never get used to the custom of removing her shoes as she went in and only coped with doing so by following a visit with a long shower. Now feeling fresh and clean, she put on her sexiest underwear. She was going to think positively. Mataio would have a good reason for not going on holiday with her. She would be understanding and forgive him for a) letting her down and b) not telling her about it until now. They could go to bed and make up for three weeks of lost time together. She grinned. A night in bed with Mataio would well compensate for leaving Fiji the way she did and the backlash that might be heading her way as a consequence.

The receipt was in the bin. Louisa only took it out because she hated untidiness, including discarded bits of random scrunched up paper. Her intention was to put the offending item in the main rubbish bin outside. As she headed for the kitchen door, curiosity made her unravel the ball of paper – she was sure she'd emptied the waste paper before she'd left on Tuesday. It was a receipt for the amount of $13,666.00. A cash refund from Air Pacific for the cancellation of one business class round the world trip. It was dated five days ago. Tuesday, the day she'd left and Mataio had arrived back. It took Louisa less than a nano second to realise what it meant: Mataio was not only not coming with her on the trip, he'd cashed in the round the world ticket she'd bought him. It was as if she'd been punched. Wham! In the guts. Her heart sank to her knees. The bastard! The travel agency was open on Saturdays. A brief conversation with the agency confirmed Mataio had indeed cashed in his ticket. Louisa gripped the dining table and sat down. She couldn't believe it. Didn't want to believe it. The day she had left for Fiji, Mataio had returned from his mum's island, got to the house, read her letter and instead of looking forward with excitement to their big trip together, had walked into town and cashed in his airline tickets. Had she paid by credit card instead of cheque the money would have come to her. But she had not. His tickets were in his name. In that sense, legally he had done nothing wrong. But that didn't make it right. Morally, he'd betrayed her. Unless, he intended to give her the money back? Louisa searched the house for the $13,666.00. Twice. She didn't find so much as a cent. She wanted to weep. She never once imagined Mataio was a thief. Was this the real reason why he'd not wanted to talk to her?

A voice came from outside. It was Mataio. Louisa checked her watch. She frowned. It was late but she knew he'd come eventually. He'd want to justify his actions. No doubt he thought of himself as one big justified sinner.

'Hello?' Mataio called again.

'Come in.' She called, not moving from where she sat in the middle of the living room.

'No lights?' he said, when he spotted her in the shadows.

'I don't want to disturb Reteta and the others,' she said, nodding towards the back verandah. 'They've gone to bed. There's enough light to see with just the small back light on, isn't there?'

'Sure.' He slipped out of his "outside" flip flops and slipped into his "indoor" flip flops, which were at the side of the kitchen door. He sat down opposite her. He smiled. 'By the way, what did happen to your head?' He seemed genuinely worried for her.

'A random mugging.' That seemed such a long time ago now.

'I thought you were at a conference?'

'And I thought you were coming to Fiji.' She promised herself she would stay calm but her heart was struggling to agree with her head. 'I phoned the house and left message after message for you to call me at the hotel in Fiji. Why didn't you?'

'I told you. I was busy with the maneaba stuff. I only got back from my mum's on Tuesday myself, remember? There's been a lot to do since then, far more than I could have imagined.'

'Since when have you been concerned about the maneaba?'

'I've always helped the church, you know that.'

Louisa had had enough. 'Why are you not coming to Scotland?'

'I've made commitments to the maneaba project.' He

sounded serious. 'I can't leave. It's too important, I'm sorry.'

Louisa burst out laughing. 'The maneaba project? Important? That hall is a monstrosity.' Even in the half light she could see him flinch.

'What do you mean?

'Concrete posts and sheet metal, really?' said Louisa. 'I thought you were more of a traditionalist than that?'

'There's nothing wrong with that building.' His voice sounded tense. 'I'm proud of my part in its construction.'

'You've changed your tune. You were the one who told me that the old way of building a maneaba involved the whole village. Quote "building a maneaba is as much about making villagers feel connected to one another and their village as building a village hall" unquote.'

'It's the church that will make people feel connected,' he said, half shouting.

'Sh! You'll wake the others,' she said quietly. She'd really pissed him off now. Mataio never raised his voice. 'Let's not argue. Just tell me the real reason you're not coming with me to Scotland? You owe me an explanation. You know you do.'

Mataio got up. Walked to the window and looked out over the dusky vista.

Louisa waited. The overhead fan whirred. Outside the Pacific Ocean crashed against the sandy shore. There wasn't as much as a peep from Reteta and her family. Everyone had gone to bed but them.

Mataio finally said. 'When I was at Mum's I started drinking again.'

Louisa felt her body collapse inwards. Not that. Even stealing was better than that.

52

Mataio had not touched alcohol for months and months. Louisa hadn't even considered it could still be an issue for him. 'Why?' she groaned.

'Why do you think?' he said bitterly. 'I'm weak.'

'But you're not drinking now, are you?' said Louisa, her fear subsiding a notch. He looked very sober.

Mataio came up to Louisa, knelt down and took her hands. 'It's like a miracle. Pastor Johan happened to be on the island too. He found me and sobered me up. He showed me that my drinking was my way of avoiding facing my fears.'

'What fears?' In the half light his eyes sparkled. She caught a glimpse of the old Mataio. Was there a chance for them, after all?

Mataio smiled. 'Fears to do with my mother dying. Fears to do with you.'

Louisa pulled her hands out of his. 'I can understand your mother being ill is difficult for you but how am I responsible for you going on the booze again?'

'I didn't say you were.' He smiled and took her hands back. 'Pastor Johan made me see that I'd agreed to go to Scotland even though I didn't want to go.'

'Pastor Johan obviously doesn't know you if he thinks anyone can make you do anything you don't want to.'

Mataio removed his hands from Louisa's and sat back in the armchair opposite her. 'This is why I didn't want to talk about it with you, I knew you wouldn't understand.'

Louisa frowned. 'If you didn't want to come to Scotland with me why didn't you just tell me?'

'I did try to tell you but you wouldn't listen.'

'When?' said Louisa.

'Many times. You kept saying it would be fine. But it will not be fine.'

'I didn't realise it would be so awful for you to spend a few weeks with me in my home country,' said Louisa, trying not to shout. She absolutely didn't want Reteta outside to hear them.

'A few weeks is one thing but you talked about living there with you permanently.'

'You said you'd be happy to live in Scotland.'

'I lied,' said Mataio flatly. 'I would be a stranger in a strange land with no job, no chance of a job and no family and no friends.'

'You don't know you won't find work.'

Mataio shook his head. 'I am thirty-six. Apart from my marine college qualification, which I got when I was eighteen, I have no skills. What job would I get? Sweeping streets?'

'You could retrain, you're clever.'

He shook his head. 'It is not what I want to do.'

Louisa made a face. 'You told me so many times there was nothing for you here on Tarawa, that you wanted more from life.'

Mataio shrugged. 'I didn't want to hurt you so I said what you wanted to hear.'

'In all the time I've known you, you've never said anything you didn't mean!'

'You can't believe I didn't want to hurt you?'

Louisa's head began to ache. 'I don't want to argue. I just want to understand.'

'Then let me explain. The closer it got to us leaving for Scotland the less I wanted to go and the less I knew how to tell you. Pastor Johan explained it. He said that's why I went to Mum's, I was running away. And once I was there I was too scared to come back and face you so I started drinking to avoid facing my problems.'

'I didn't realise I was a problem.'

'You're putting words into my mouth. I'm sorry. I never wanted to hurt you but I can't go with you to Scotland. I should have been honest from the start.'

'Are you telling me we're over?'

'No, I'm not saying that. But I've changed. I'm not the same person I was. Pastor Johan has helped me see I was looking at myself in the wrong way. He's shown me how to feel good about myself. Look I have to go again. I'm sorry but there's so much to do before tomorrow. We'll talk later. I promise.'

'No.' Louisa stood up. 'You're not going anywhere until you explain this.' She handed him the receipt for the refund of his air travel.

Mataio suddenly scowled. 'I was disgusted when I saw how much the trip cost.'

'I can't help it if the EU insist on calling Tarawa a "hardship post" and pay for me to travel business class. It's part of the package. And I was happy to use my own money to buy your business class tickets so you could travel with me.'

'So much money wasted in the name of aid. It's wrong. A sin. And I didn't want to be part of it.'

Louisa didn't know whether to laugh or cry. She whispered, 'You were meeting my mum! I was going to show you where I'm from. We were having a holiday! You said you wanted to come.'

'That was the old Mataio. The one who was lost. But

now I am found.'

'You weren't lost.' She wanted to pull her hair out. His holier than thou attitude was too much to take in. 'You know what? I don't care any more. You're not coming with me. Fine. But I want my money back. The tickets were only a gift if you came with me.'

'The money's been spent.'

Louisa was incredulous. 'All $13,666.00 gone in five days and on Tarawa, a place where there's nothing to spend money on? Impossible.'

'The church was in debt.'

'What debt?'

'They needed money to pay for the maneaba roof.'

'Thirteen thousands dollars for a shite corrugated iron roof? You were had!'

'It's the best thing I've ever done.'

'But it wasn't your money to give!' she hissed.

'I did love you,' said Mataio seriously. 'But I see now the kind of love we had was egotistical bad love. Polluted. Unpure. Now the only love I have is for God.'

'Is it?' she said, unable to control herself any longer, 'Well, see you, you thieving toerag bastard, and see your God? You can both fuck right off!'

53

The festivities to celebrate the opening of the new maneaba started at nine in the morning with traditional dancing. By the time Louisa and Kana arrived outside the maneaba it was eight thirty and most villagers had already taken their places on the concrete floor inside. That's my roof, thought Louisa, looking at the vast covering of metal sheets overhead. My bloody roof! She had been so angry with Mataio she'd not been able to sleep. She'd bought him that business class return air ticket to Scotland so he could come home with her! As far as she was concerned, cashing in the ticket and keeping the money without her permission was theft. Her first reaction, after wanting to smash a sheet of his fucking roofing over his head, was to arrest him. Bang him up and throw away the key. And she would have arrested him if she hadn't thought it would made her look a fool. And it would make her look a fool. The locals would lap it up. What a hoot! The fancy foreigner being tricked by the clever native!

Why had she bought the ticket with a draft cheque and not her credit card? Thinking about it, that had been his idea. Or was she imagining things now? Didn't matter. No one would think Mataio had done anything wrong. They'd see him as a modern day Robin Hood, cheer him on for robbing from one of the rich, greedy expatriates and giving to the poor of the parish – not that she thought the evangelical church was poor!

Even Reteta had had a smile hovering around her lips when she'd told her about the ticket. The thing was, if Mataio had just asked her, she'd have probably given him the money. The old Mataio could have had anything he wanted. But this new sanctimonious holy roller was a total shite and creep. She should have arrested him. Then and there. As soon as he told her. But she'd not. The fewer people who knew about what had happened the better, especially Nakibae, who still didn't know she was back. She didn't want people laughing at her behind her back.

It was probably a mistake to tell Reteta. She had a big mouth. Couldn't keep anything to herself. Louisa stopped in her tracks. Suddenly she got it. Reteta had known! The way she'd reacted to the news, or didn't react, more like, gave her way. Smiling sympathetically but saying nothing. Not like Reteta, who had an opinion on everything. And then Louisa realised. The whole of the island had probably known that Mataio had cashed in his tickets. In fact, there was a good chance she was the only person who had not.

Kana slipped out of her sandals and left them outside the maneaba with all the others. Louisa copied her. She hoped she'd find them again. It wasn't something she wanted to do, walk bare-feet onto a concrete floor where scores of others walked, but it was what you did. As long as she scrubbed herself when she got back, she would cope. She'd only come because Reteta was dancing and she'd promised. It was Sunday. The big day. The kids were dancing too. Besides staying alone in the house with her thoughts wasn't a great alternative.

Louisa ducked into the maneaba behind Kana. It was much hotter inside the hall than the day before. The place was packed. Young people, children, older people, all sat in groups on straw mats around the edges of the floor, leaving a space in the centre for the dancers. Louisa sat cross-legged on a mat next to Kana, squashed between the villagers. Some faces were familiar. Some unfamiliar. Was everyone looking at her? She gave herself a telling off. Get a grip! Who gave a monkey's about her? People had clearly come from all over to celebrate the opening of the new maneaba. It was not about her. She glanced up. But they're sitting under my roof, she thought. My bloody roof!

54

It was sweltering inside the maneaba. Louisa took a deep breath. It was going to be a long day. She had to stop thinking about Mataio. It was not the end of the world, after all, just her relationship. So what if she was thirty-six? Maybe getting on a bit for kids, but she didn't want kids, did she? No, she did not. Not that she was going to let him get away with it, though. No way. It wasn't so much his swapping his plane ticket for cash, bloody cheek, as his total disregard for her feelings. Not one attempt to talk to her directly to let her know he wasn't coming to Fiji, let alone Scotland. If she had not come to Tarawa, she could still be in Suva waiting for him to call.

No, she would get him. For now, though, she had to concentrate on the dancing. She was too emotional to think straight about Mataio. In time, an idea would present itself. That is how these things worked. And when it did she would act. But for now she needed to calm down. Put Mataio out of her mind. Worst thing of all, though, despite his holy roller act, she still had the hots for him. Couldn't shift the image of his glorious naked body on top of her. Inside her. She groaned silently. Oh how her mum would lap up this latest development. Proof, if proof were needed, that Louisa was a lost cause in the boyfriend department and attracted to life's losers. At thirty-six both an old maid and a bampot. Was there really any point in her going to Scotland by herself?

Kana nudged her. A group of four men wandered into the maneaba. Louisa started. Mataio was with them. Since when was he a church leader? Clone-like, the men wore matching long sleeved, white shirts and dark blue lava-lavas and white knee-length socks with leather Jesus sandals. They wandered towards the centre of the hall and sat on straw mats already placed there for them. They smiled the same inane, cheesy smile. Louisa nodded to herself. Of course, with the money Mataio had brought to the table, or should she say, roof, he had become a bigwig. She wanted to scratch his smug eyes out and feed them to the chickens outside!

Kana tutted next to Louisa. 'Everyone has come today as if this is real maneaba. But this is not the real maneaba and those men are not real unamani leaders. They are church leaders. It is not the same.'

'Isn't it?' said Louisa, trying not to look at Mataio.

Kana scowled. 'The village maneaba may be falling down but it still a maneaba. Now we have two maneabas. The real one and the church one. It is confusing for everyone. Who do we go to for advice on village matters? This church maneaba or the real one? We should have repaired the proper maneaba and not built this church one. And this church is not even my church. What if my church want to build a maneaba too? Then we will have three maneabas. I don't understand.'

'Is it really such a problem to have more than one?' said Louisa.

'A maneaba has nothing to do with religion. It is the heart of village matters. A church looks after our souls. The maneaba over law and order and our daily affairs.'

Louisa thought the police and the judiciary looked after law and order, just showed you what she knew.

Thump! Thump! Thump! The drummers had begun. A hush fell over the maneaba. Those villagers still on their feet quickly sat down on their mats. All talking ceased. The thumping continued. Thump, thump! Thump, thump! The drummers sat, cross-legged to one side of the body of the floor. About twenty men. Around a square wooden drum, like a giant coffee table. A ring of women sat behind them. Singing. The flat palms of the drummers thumped. One man, the conductor, moved between the drummers and singers, waving to them as if they were rowers in a boat. Two lines of teenage boys and girls swished into the maneaba. Bare feet. Grass skirts for the girls. Red lava-lavas for the boys. They all wore white T-shirts. Arms outstretched. Fingers poised upwards. Arms and hands decorated in straps of fine straw made from coconut or pandanus. Oil glistening on their skin. Swaying. Stepping. Gliding. Soft voices singing. Lilting. One by one they began slapping their hands on their arms and their bodies to the rhythm of the beat. The grass skirts swirled higher and higher. Swish. Swoosh. Swish.

The hall was packed. Not even standing room left. Louisa glimpsed a bunch of pale foreign faces towards the back, eyes glued on the grass skirts. Tourists? A maneaba opening was a day out, something to do on an island that had no cinema, or theatre, or museum, or parks. One head. Behind everyone. Sticking out above the rest. Blond. Louisa blinked. It was Edwin.

55

Edwin was on Tarawa? How was that possible? Louisa touched the dressing on the back of her head. For reasons as yet still unknown, someone in Suva had broken into where she was staying three times and had physically attacked her once, and had tried to hurt Makereta once. Edwin was her number one suspect for all the incidents. Had he followed her to Tarawa? If he had, he would regret it. Louisa was on home territory now. She had authority and she wanted answers to questions, not just about what had happened to her, but about Edwin's relationship with Stewy and Rick. If he knew anything, she would find out what it was.

Louisa got to her feet. Someone tutted. She ignored it. She would haul Edwin outside and interrogate him in the brilliant daylight. If he didn't feel like answering her questions, she'd take him to Betio station. See how he liked that? But the dancers were in full swing, literally, and Louisa knew the rules: you did not cross the dance area once the dancers had started. To go round the hall was equally impossible. Too crowded. Louisa sat back down, ignoring more tutting from behind her. She kept her eye on him, though, which wasn't difficult, in a sea of dark heads his very blond one stuck out. And on the plus side, he didn't appear to have seen her. She preferred it that way. Didn't want to give him the chance to think up some lies or worse still, slope away.

Louisa watched the dancing. Watched Edwin. Watched the dancing. Watched Edwin. The dancing grew more intense. The atmosphere grew more charged. For the dancers, men and women who would normally refuse to look at you in the eye in the village, it was their chance to take centre stage, dance and shine. Their fifteen minutes of fame. Especially for the women. Sweat dripped from Louisa's neck and arms. She used a tissue to wipe it up. The metal roof was not as cool as a thatch roof that's for sure. The dance was reaching its finale. The singing grew louder and louder. The drumming became more and more frenetic. Some of the sitting singers jumped up and wailed and then swooned. Finally the group stopped in an explosion of singing and drumming. Everyone cheered. Louisa got to her feet a second time. Edwin was still the other side of the hall. She went to cross. Reteta's group came into the hall and everyone sat down again. Louisa sighed and sat back down. Next time she was crossing the hall, dancers or not.

Reteta was with five other women. They wore white T-shirts and huge, heavy hipped straw skirts, like haystacks. Louisa had seen the big skirt dance many times. The women swished their hips in a swaying movement that made the coconut grass swirl and twirl. It reminded Louisa of waves breaking against the shore. All the time the women's hips swished and swirled, their bodies had to remain still, with only their arms moving.

Women from the audience got up, approached the row of dancers. Some had perfume bottles, while others had body spray. One by one they sprayed deodorant or perfume over the dancers' chests and backs. A heady mixture of musk and lemon scent filled the maneaba. Louisa wasn't sure where the tradition of spraying the dancers stemmed from; no one had properly explained it to her. It was a form of complimenting the dancing, that much she knew. As was tucking money into their costumes, which no one was doing yet. Reteta would be disappointed Louisa had not got up and sprayed her and the dancers, Louisa had brought body spray with her especially to do so, but if she got up now Edwin might see her and she wanted to avoid that. Suddenly, the drummers thwump, thwump, thwumped. A new hush descended. The dancing women raised their arms to shoulder height and held them in mid air, perfectly still. Concentration metamorphosed the contours of the women's soft generous faces into hardened steel. Very slowly, as if by magic, the giant grass skirts began to swirl left and then right, whoosh, whoosh, whoosh. Each swish bigger than the last.

56

The swaying haystack skirts shuddered to an explosive stop. The hall erupted with appreciation. Everyone got to their feet, including the singers and drummers. Children hared across the hall. Everyone else followed. Within seconds the floor was swamped. Louisa pushed through the throng. She could still see Edwin. Just. All around her people laughed and cried. Slapped backs. Talked. Mingled. Moved. Reteta waved from the opposite side of the hall. Louisa smiled and nodded back. Clearly, there was some kind of interval in the dancing programme. It was her chance to catch Edwin. His blond head was still there, sticking out above the rest. For the first time she realised he was chatting to someone. A man. His back was towards Louisa. She couldn't see who it was. He was small. Wiry. Foreign looking. Louisa thrust forward. A tap. On her shoulder. It was Mataio. Smiling.

'When today is over we must talk.'

She wanted to say yes but said instead, 'About what?'

Mataio's smile curdled. 'Us, of course.'

'There is no us. Not until you give me back what you owe me.'

'I can understand you being angry. I didn't explain myself very well. The church had debts. Crippling debts.

How could I travel across the world business class when I could save my church?'

'It wasn't your money to give.'

'I see that now. But you told me the ticket was a present to me. As a present, I thought I could do with it as I liked?'

Louisa cleared her throat. 'The corrugated iron above our heads is not a gift I would have given.'

He took her hand in his. 'Sometimes, don't you agree, we have to make sacrifices for the greater good?'

'You didn't even discuss it with me!'

'There was nothing to discuss.'

She snatched her hand back. 'We'd been planning the trip for over six months!'

'No. You'd been planning it, not me,' he said, his smile all but gone. 'But I agree, I should have told you what I was doing.' He sighed. 'It was a last minute decision and you weren't here–'

'You could have phoned me. You had the hotel number.'

'I only got back this week, remember? But you are back now and the celebrations will be over with by this evening.' He clasped her hands. 'I want us to talk. There's so much to discuss.'

Louisa left her hands in his. 'Maybe.'

'Good. I'll see you later.' He squeezed her hands, let them go, turned and waved to Pastor Johan at the other side of the hall.

Louisa looked at her fingers. They were trembling. Should she have said no? Was he right? Had she been unreasonable? Was she foolish to say she would see him again? Would Mataio stay the night this time? She'd waited up all night hoping he'd come back after their argument but he'd not. Edwin? Shit! She'd forgotten about him. She scanned the hall. He'd disappeared.

Louisa thrust her way outside. A mangy dog. Scrub. Children chasing scrawny chickens. A bright blue sky. But no Edwin. Shit! Shit! Shit! She wanted answers and Edwin could have given them to her. Where was he? Wait a minute. She took a deep breath. She was on home territory (well, it had been home for the last two years!). If anyone could find out where Edwin was staying, Louisa could.

57

On Tarawa getting information was only a matter of asking the right questions and Louisa had learnt by trial and error what the right questions were. In fact, she was very good at asking the right questions on Tarawa. It took her almost the rest of the day but she found out what she needed to know. Edwin had arrived in the country on Thursday the day after Rick and Stewy had been killed. He was staying at the Otintaai Hotel at the other end of the island.

He sat in the open plan dining restaurant of the Otintaai Hotel. A second man sat opposite him. Another foreigner. He was older than Edwin. Middle-aged. Pasty skin. Red face. Dark hair. Blue slacks. Shiny black shoes. White shirt. Business wear.

'Mauri! Mauri!' said Louisa, pulling up a chair next to Edwin.

'You?' Edwin's face squished into a knot.

'Yes, me,' beamed Louisa. She'd decided a friendly, naïve approach was better than a confrontational one. Confrontational would probably work, Edwin was a coward, but if she was too heavy handed he could complain. She didn't want to run the risk of getting into trouble with Nakibae. 'I didn't know you were coming to Tarawa?'

'I was not but the homophobia in Suva after the tragedy of Rick's death was frightening. Did you see the papers? I felt it was not safe to stay. Freddy agreed.' He nodded to his friend, who smiled.

'Rick's death was terrible and the reports in the papers were shocking,' said Freddy, offering his hand to Louisa. 'Frederick Hatcher at your service.'

Louisa disliked him on sight. Smart in a sleazy way. Eyes calculating slivers of ice. She ignored his hand. That was never happening. She nodded. 'Detective Sergeant Louisa Townsend.'

'A police officer?' said Freddy, letting his hand fall, his smile still glued on his face.

'We both stayed in the murder victims' house the night before they were killed,' said Edwin, dropping his knife and fork onto his plate and pushing his plate of half eaten grilled tuna and chips away.

'Terrible business,' said Freddy, tutting. 'Two killings.'

'You know about Stewy's death?' said Louisa. So much for secrecy.

'It was on the radio. Imagine squashing him into a suitcase. Ugh! Have they found the killer?'

Louisa shook her head. 'Not so far.' When would she learn that everyone knew everything in the Pacific? 'The police are looking for you, though.'

'I had nothing to do with it,' said Edwin horrified.

'The police want to question you about Stewy's movements before he died. You have to make a statement.'

'The papers said homosexuals are rapists and killers.'

His voice high with tension. 'I'm not sure I want to go back to Fiji ever.'

'The Fijian people are a very tolerant people normally,' said Freddy. 'I've done business there before, this new homophobia is shocking. It will die down though.'

'Let's hope so,' said Louisa. Was Freddy gay? She'd not pegged him as being homosexual even though he was keeping Edwin company. 'You will have to go back.'

'And what if I don't want to?' His eyes trailed three young Kiribati men as they walked into the restaurant. 'As it happens I like it here on Tarawa.'

'If you don't want to find yourself with an international warrant for your arrest and deported, I suggest you call into Betio Police Station first thing tomorrow, tell them I sent you. Say who you are and that you want to make a statement for DI Vika. In it say exactly what happened Tuesday evening and Wednesday morning when you were with Stewy getting your shoes shined.'

Edwin's button eyes narrowed into two tiny glassy orbs. 'What difference is it to you if I do this or not?'

'I'm a police officer. I want to see people do the right thing. They'll also ask you about the shoeshine boy who polished your shoes.'

'What about him?'

'He's missing.'

Edwin gasped. 'Has he been murdered too?'

Louisa shook her head. 'We don't know. I hope not. But he may be in trouble and your statement could help.'

Edwin puckered his lips, as if to think. 'Okay, I'll go to the police station but I'm not returning to Fiji until I'm sure it is safe.'

Freddy stood up. 'If you excuse me, I have things to do.

I'll see you at dinner, Edwin.'

Edwin nodded.

'How do you know him?' Louisa watched Freddy walk out of the restaurant.

'How does one know anyone?' said Edwin blushing.

Louisa frowned. What was that supposed to mean?

58

Louisa ordered a bottle of Coke, no ice. After the waiter brought it she asked Edwin more questions, she wasn't letting him off that easily. 'Why did you and Stewy leave without saying goodbye to Rick that morning? He'd prepared breakfast for you both.'

Edwin squirmed in his chair. 'I didn't want to sneak away like that but Stewy was still angry with Rick because of the argument the night before.'

'What argument?' said Louisa. This was the first she'd heard there'd been a row.

'After we had gone to bed. You didn't hear it? Impossible!'

'I heard nothing!'

'It was horrible.' He shivered. 'There was a lot of shouting and doors banging. I was most distressed.'

'Shit!' She'd missed it all. Her bloody ear plugs. 'Have you any idea what it was about?'

Edwin pinched his lips. 'Despite the terrible noise from Rick and Stewy I eventually fell asleep but I woke up very early the next day. Someone was moving in the kitchen. I went to see who it was. It was Stewy. He said he couldn't sleep. I asked if everything was okay. He told me he'd had a very big argument with Rick the night before. Someone they had treated like a son had stolen from them. Stewy wanted to go to the police but Rick wanted to give the person a second chance.'

'Was it the shoeshine boy called Wame?' said Louisa. Were they getting to the truth at last?

'He did not mention any names. But I do not think it could have been the boy called Wame because Stewy liked him.'

'How do you know that? Never mind. You have no idea what they were arguing about?'

'All I know is Stewy said he'd accused Rick of being gullible and foolish and called him other words he preferred not to repeat. He felt ashamed in the morning and didn't want to see Rick. He was going for a jog. I offered to accompany him. But the jogging was horrible. I did not enjoy it. So we came back and Stewy offered to take me to the Holiday Inn.'

'Stewy brought you to the hotel? I didn't realise that.'

Edwin shook his head. 'Stewy said he would show me around the centre. We stopped at the shoeshine stop, as you know, then we wandered around the market. Then, within ten minutes, Rick called Stewy on his mobile. Stewy left immediately, abandoning me in the centre.'

'Did he say what Rick said?'

'No, I did not feel like being a "tourist" any more, so I caught a taxi and went to the hotel.'

'Do you think this person who let them down could have killed them?'

'I have no idea. Stewy told me nothing else.' Edwin sniffed. 'It was the last time I saw him. It is horrible. Very horrible. By the way, what happened to your head?'

'I was attacked.'

'Here?' said Edwin, aghast, looking around anxiously.

She shook her head. 'In Suva, by the market.' Sometimes honesty was the best policy. 'It wasn't you, was it?'

Edwin looked shocked. 'If you are joking, it is in very bad taste.'

'I saw someone who looked very much like you just before it happened.'

'Why would I would do such a thing, I hardly know you?'

'There's something else. The night we were staying at Rick's someone broke into my room.'

'Impossible! The Garlands is like the Fijian Fort Knox.'

'I know. Which means it had to be someone who was already inside the house, like Stewy or Rick.'

Edwin looked bewildered. 'But why would they want anything from you, you had nothing, not even your suitcase? Besides, they were very rich men indeed.'

'Someone also broke into my hotel room at the Holiday Inn. I believe it was the same person.'

'I am confused, Stewy and Rick were dead by then so they could not be your burglar.'

'Which leaves you.'

'Me? Why would I want to steal anything from you?'

'The person didn't take anything, he simply touched my things.'

'What things?'

'My underwear to be precise.'

Edwin began nodding. 'I see, I see. Gay men must have fetishes, such as sniffing underwear of ladies, yes?' A smile danced across Edwin's lips. He began to laugh. Louder and louder, as if he'd heard the best joke ever. 'Why would a gay man want to touch a straight woman's underwear?'

59

When Louisa left Edwin at the Otintaai Hotel it was later than she thought and dark. She put her foot down and the VW Beetle rattled into full speed. She hoped pigs, dogs and drunks would hear her before they saw her and make sure they were off the road before she got close enough to knock them down. She needed to get back to the house. Mataio could be waiting for her and she didn't want him to think she wasn't coming and leave before she got back.

Despite everything, she absolutely wanted to talk to Mataio. Maybe he was sorry for what he had done? Maybe he'd be his old self and not religious. So what he'd cashed in the ticket she had bought him? She could have done the same thing. It was a hell of lot of money for a plane ticket, even if it did get you across the world and back. She sighed. But why hadn't he talked to her about it? Why say nothing?

A flash of light behind her. Headlights of another car. Way behind. She ignored it. She'd stayed longer than she intended with Edwin. He'd thought it hilarious she could have believed he, or Rick or Stewy, could have been interested in touching her clothes. When he'd finally stopped laughing, he'd started talking. Louisa had let him prattle on because she hoped she might learn something new about Stewy and Rick.

He'd said, yes, Stewy and Rick had been a couple. They'd had a lot to put up with recently. Apart from being let down by the mysterious young man they had befriended, there had been a lot of bad publicity about The Garlands being a "gay" guest house. Louisa took one hand off the steering wheel and gingerly touched the back of her head. As soon as she got to the house that dressing was going in the bin. All it was doing was harbouring germs.

The light again. Dazzling her from behind. Some arse with his full beam on. 'Idiot!' she yelled at the rear view mirror before slipping the mirror upwards to stop the reflection of the light blinding her. She was halfway home. Fifteen minutes to go. But if Edwin was not her snooper – she wouldn't put a bit of snooping past sleaze ball Freddy though – who was? And who had thumped her? She'd wished she'd overheard the quarrel in The Garlands between Rick and Stewy, she could have picked up on stuff Edwin had missed. But she had not. The thing was, the majority of killings are committed by people close to the victim. For her money, the shoeshine lad Wame was high up on her list. Not that it mattered, it was unlikely she'd go back to Fiji now.

Another flash of light. From behind. Dazzling. In her eyes. She groaned and re-angled the rear view mirror to see the idiot trying to blind her? A big car. Speeding towards her. Coming closer. Closer! Too close! Shit! She put her foot down! Made no difference. The vehicle was almost on top of her. Lights flashing. Shit! Shit! A drunk! She looked ahead. She approached the Ambo causeway. The light flish-flashed in her eyes. The car overtook her. Screeched to a halt in front of her. Louisa braked. In the half light a man got out of the car. Walked towards her. Who the fuck was this? She glanced around. The place was deserted. To the left shadowy palms and the liquid blackness of the crashing Pacific. To the right, the dark lagoon.

'Stay where you are!' She jumped out the car and grabbed her body spray from her bag – a squoosh of that in the eyes of whoever it was would sort him out. 'I'm a police officer!'

'So am I!'

Louisa jumped. It was Nakibae. Tall. Dark. Forbidding. The boss.

'Why didn't you stop when I flashed you?' He demanded, face full of anger.

'Sorry, sir. I didn't know it was you.' What the hell was he doing chasing her anyway?

'Why aren't you in Fiji?'

Uh ho. 'I returned for personal reasons,' she said. It was true.

He stared at her for a second. His black eyes burying into hers. 'DI Vika called me today.'

'Ah,' said Louisa, clearing her throat.

'It appears that despite being a suspect in Vika's double murder investigation, you fled the country.'

'It's a mistake!'

'What? You're not here?'

Louisa blushed. 'I mean I'm not a suspect. Not really.'

'DI Vika is lying?'

'Sir, I've just come from the Otintaai where I met a man called Edwin. Vika wants him to answer some questions. He has agreed to go into Betio station and make a statement that will prove beyond a shadow of a doubt that Stewy was alive after I left The Garlands guest house and that I could not possibly have killed him.'

Nakibae held out his hand to stop her. 'I never for one minute believed you killed anyone. However, in case you misunderstand, you are returning to Fiji on the first flight tomorrow.'

'But –'

'You do whatever DI Vika wants. You do not let me down.'

'But there's no point–'

'Am I speaking in a foreign language?'

She blushed. 'No, sir.'

'When you are back from your trip to Scotland we will talk about this matter further.' He thrust a plane ticket in her hand, turned and walked away.

60

Mataio appeared around ten o' clock. It was pitch black outside. Reteta and Kana and the rest of the family had gone to bed and were sleeping under their mosquito nets out the back. Louisa had almost given up on Mataio. Her heart had skipped a beat when she saw him at the side kitchen door. Then she saw Pastor Johan hovering behind him and her heart sank. In hindsight she shouldn't have let Pastor Johan in the house. They'd caught her off guard.

She sat down at the big dining table. They sat opposite her. So that was how it was going to be: them and her.

Pastor Johan spoke first. 'Mataio has asked me to come with him to help explain his position.'

'I'd rather Mataio spoke for himself,' said Louisa, giving Pastor Johan a filthy look and facing Mataio.

'Pastor Johan can explain so much better than me,' said Mataio.

'But this has nothing to do with him,' said Louisa, 'this

is about us.'

'If I may,' said Pastor Johan, still smiling.

'No you may not.'

He laughed. 'You are very funny.'

'I'm not joking.' What she would give to wipe that smug smile off his face with a fat slap.

'Mataio has told me about your life together,' said Pastor Johan, ignoring her last remark. 'He explained how you have been living in sin.'

It was Louisa's turn to laugh now. 'Who says "living in sin" any more?'

'I do,' said Pastor Johan seriously. 'Mataio has seen the light of God and is now a believer. He does not want to continue in his bad ways. He cannot live with you any more.'

'I'd lost my way, Louisa,' said Mataio, earnestly. 'But despite all the bad things I have done The Lord God has forgiven me and I'm never going to let him down again.'

'What bad things?' demanded Louisa.

'My drinking, but I have stopped that,' said Mataio seriously. 'And us sleeping together out of wedlock.'

Louisa wanted to scream. Another ridiculous outdated phrase from Pastor Johan no doubt. 'You're confusing me. Are you saying you want us to get married?'

'Yes.'

'Really?' She was stunned. As far as marriage proposals went, it was not the most romantic but still it was a proposal. 'Yes. I'll marry you.'

Mataio beamed. 'Pastor Jonah will show you how to ask for God's forgiveness for all the bad things you have done in your life. By His good grace we can have a long and fulfilling life together in His service.'

'I'm not asking Pastor Jonah for anything,' said Louisa. 'I've not done anything wrong.'

Pastor Jonah nodded knowingly. 'In your whole life you have never told a lie?'

'I may tell a white lie now and then, and certainly told some whoppers when I was small but that's normal–'

'It is not normal!' said Pastor Jonah, raising his voice. 'It is the devil at work!'

Louisa couldn't believe she was listening to this nutter in her own house. He was like something out of a Jeanette Winterson novel. She stood up. 'You should leave. Now.'

Pastor Jonah said, 'Your past is nothing to be ashamed of. We are all bad and the only way to become good is to ask God to forgive you.'

Louisa shook her head. 'I'm one of the good guys already. In fact, I lock up the bad guys.' She pointed to the door. 'Please leave. I want to talk to Mataio alone.'

Pastor Jonah smiled. 'Mataio used to think he was one of the good guys. But that was because he was blind. Now he can see. It will not be easy but if you search your soul, you will recognise the evil inside you and together we can ask God to cut it out.' He grabbed Louisa's hand in his right hand and Mataio's hand in the left and began saying the Lord's Prayer, 'Our father, which art in heaven–'

'Stop!' Louisa wrenched her hand away and stepped away from the man. 'Get out of my house!' She addressed Mataio. 'Us sleeping together was not wrong. In fact everything about it was good!'

Mataio looked pained. 'Not according to the bible.'

'If I believe in any God at all, it's a gentle, forgiving God, who had a son who suffered the little children into the Kingdom of Heaven, who looked out for the meek and the mild. Not a fanatical, evangelical God, who thought sex outside of marriage was wrong!' She threw her arms in the air in disbelief.

'It's a sin,' said Mataio quietly. 'I can't marry someone who lets evil reside in their heart.'

'You're the one with the evil in you.' Louisa swiped a tear welling in the corner of her eye. How had it come to this? 'The airline ticket was too tempting. You couldn't resist cashing it in. You're a thief and a liar. I want the money for that ticket back or will go to Commissioner Nakibae and have you arrested for theft.' An affair would have been better than this.

'Louisa,' said Pastor Johan, 'Mataio did what his conscience told him to do.'

'You shut up!' shouted Louisa. 'You took advantage of his addictive personality and his lapse into alcohol. You brain-washed a kind, thoughtful person into giving up all the things he held dear so you could get a new roof for your maneaba! Your despicable.'

Pastor Johan laughed. 'You're behaviour is typical of one who puts their ego before everything.'

'I am not egotistical!' yelled Louisa. The soft whirring of the overhead fan suddenly seemed very loud. She faced Mataio. 'You're a coward too. You owed it to me to come to Fiji and explain how you felt, you couldn't even do that.'

Mataio looked wretched. 'There was so much to do here!'

'Not even a phone call to explain?'

Pastor Jonah said. 'Thousands of dollars for one person to fly in a plane is obscene.'

'It's business class. I wanted my partner to sit next to me.' Her head was reeling. Any minute the Mataio she knew and had loved for almost two years would jump up and say 'Gotcha!' But he didn't. The hell that was unfolding before her eyes was real.

'Imagine how I felt when Pastor Jonah said the church was in huge debt and I could save them in one instant by cashing in my ticket.'

'It wasn't yours to cash in!'

Pastor Johan said, 'Come, Mataio, she needs to understand from within. We will never make her see the light if she isn't ready to embrace it.'

'I'm sorry, Louisa,' said Mataio, following Pastor Johan.

Louisa sat back down. She felt in shock. Her relationship with Mataio was over. She couldn't comprehend how it had happened. Not really. One minute they were planning a world trip together and the next, wham! He'd got religion and spent thousands of dollars of her money.

61

The flight to Fiji was straightforward. Four hours in the air. No delays. No lost suitcases. No hassles. The problem started as soon as Louisa touched down in Nadi. All connecting flights to Suva were cancelled because of technical problems. Why did that not surprise her? A message delivered via a customs official said if she waited outside someone from the Fijian police force would pick her up. She'd heard that before too.

Outside was blistering hot and dry. Nothing like wet and damp Suva. Louisa could hardly believe both places were in the same country. Louisa went back inside to the air conditioning. Nadi airport was much bigger than Suva. Sunburnt holidaymakers slip slopped about in T-shirts and shorts, dragging luggage and souvenirs behind them. At the far end of the terminal, by the arrival gates, a band of young men in colourful short-sleeved shirts and board shorts and leis of frangipanis round their necks, played ukuleles and sang cheerful songs. The only sign it was Christmas was a silver coloured Xmas tree by a tourist information desk behind the ukelele players.

Louisa sat at a plastic table and chair belonging to one of the airport's three coffee shops. A smell of toasted tea cakes and roast coffee made her feel hungry but she decided to stick to a bottle of Coke, with a straw. She faced the main terminal entrance. Whoever was picking her up, couldn't miss her – if anyone actually came.

Louisa didn't want to think about Mataio. It was over. End of story. There was no point in trying to understand the whys and wherefores. She sipped her Coke. As for coming back to Fiji for one day? What a waste of time. Especially now she'd found Edwin and he was willing to make a statement confirming Stewy had been alive after Louisa left the house on the day of the murders. But at least being ordered back meant she'd not had to fight the temptation to run after Mataio and beg him to change his mind. Not that she did begging or running after people, but she knew as soon as her anger subsided she would have struggled not to try and speak to him again. And there was also the chance her anger would not have subsided and she'd have tried to punch his lights out and been done for assault. The bastard!

An announcement asked passengers flying on the next flight for Vanuatu to go back to the check-in desk as the flight had been cancelled. Louisa sighed. The sooner she left the whole Pacific region the better. Not that she was looking forward to being at home and "topping and tailing" her mum. No! No! No! She wouldn't think about that either. One thing for sure, the bust-up with Mataio meant she definitely didn't want to go back to Tarawa. Once in Scotland she would apply for her old job, or one similar. Hopefully, most of her colleagues from the old team would have moved on. They'd been ambitious bastards, so there was a good chance they had. After she'd been back a few weeks, she'd contact Nakibae and explain her mum was ill. Say she needed to stay to look after her. She was sure Nakibae would accept her reason for not returning and give her a good reference, despite Vika's complaint. She'd done good on Tarawa. He'd told her so often enough. If there was no work in Scotland, she'd move to England. York was nice. She'd been to a couple of conferences there. And Bristol was okay too. If it came to it, she could even go to London. Take a sideways move into the new Counter Terrorism Command. That's where all the jobs were. Even this far away she knew it was the only growth area in policing in the UK. Yes, the more she thought about it, the surer she was she didn't want to return to Tarawa.

62

Makereta plonked herself down on the chair next to Louisa. 'I've been sent to bring you to Nadi!'

'You,' said Louisa, above the clamour of the Tannoy, announcing for a second time that the Vanuatu flight had been cancelled and could all passengers return to the check in desk. She was pleased to see her, of course she was. At least it wasn't Lavneet, or worse still Vika, but she wished it had been someone else. Makereta would want to know what had happened with Mataio and there was no way Louisa was going to tell her. It was way too humiliating.

'Sorry that you had to come back so soon. Someone here at Nadi airport saw you board the Tarawa flight, recognised you and told Vika.'

'My departure didn't get you into trouble, did it?'

She laughed. 'No. Vika and Lavneet assume I'm way too dumb to have helped you leave. Anyway, how did it go, then?' said Makereta eagerly.

'How did what go?'

'You and Mataio, of course?' said Makereta, looking around. 'Did he come with you?'

'I'd rather not talk about it.'

'Oh,' said Makereta, her face falling for a second then smiling again. 'Okay. By the way, Vika wants me to get your passport. You don't actually have to give it to me now, but I'll need it for when we get to Suva.'

'You're kidding!'

Makereta shook her head. 'She says she can't trust you not to abscond again.'

'But didn't she hear? I found Edwin on Tarawa and he's promised to make a statement. It will prove without doubt that Stewy was alive after I left The Garlands. I will no longer be a suspect and will not need to stay in Fiji.'

She nodded. 'Yes, your Commissioner Nakibae phoned Vika first thing this morning. Edwin made the statement and Nakibae faxed it to Vika. Lavneet called to tell me.'

'So, that's it then, isn't it?' said Louisa, leaning back into her chair and crossing her legs. 'In fact, there's no need for me to go to Suva at all, is there? I could book into a hotel nearby and take my flight home tomorrow.'

Makereta looked sympathetic. 'Vika wants to make life difficult for you. If you'd said you wanted to stay, she'd have you deported. But you want to leave, so she's going to do everything in her power to keep you here. It's a control thing. She's a bully. The only reason I'm back in her good books is because I volunteered to drive here and pick you up – the domestic terminal in Suva has been closed since early this morning. Something to do with the coup. Who knows how long it will be closed for?'

'She can't keep me in the country for no reason,' said Louisa.

'She can and she will. Pretend to agree with everything she says and if you're lucky she'll forget why she's cross with you and allow you to leave –.'

'I can't wait here indefinitely, my mum's depending on me,' said Louisa.

'We could always find the killer, you'll be able to leave then,' said Makereta, half joking, half serious.

Louisa pulled a face. 'What is the latest?'

'Vika is still looking for Wame but can't find him. Our colleagues here in Nadi haven't found him either.'

'So it doesn't look like I'll be leaving any time soon then,' said Louisa, furiously getting to her feet. She hated this country.

'Let's take it one day at a time, eh?' said Makereta getting up after her.

Louisa sighed. 'And what now? We go to Suva and I get locked up?'

Makereta smiled. 'You're not going to be locked up.

More like hotel arrest at the Holiday Inn again. But I have a little job to do first.'

'What job?' said Louisa, eyeing Makereta carefully.

'I'll tell you on the way. The car's in the car park.'

63

The airport car park was a giant rectangle of parking spaces, jam packed with gleaming vehicles, all glinting under the mid afternoon sun. Malaki was stretched out in the back of the Rav4, sleeping. Louisa was shocked. 'What's he doing here?'

'He couldn't stay at my folk's any longer.'

'Didn't it work out?' He looked different. His hair was washed and cut. His sleeping face was clean. He was also wearing brand spanking new trainers, gleaming white shorts and T-shirt and there was even a new rucksack by his feet.

Makereta laughed. 'Malaki is the son they never had and they are the parents he always wanted. They haven't stopped buying him things. If he stayed any longer he'd be dripping in diamonds and gold.'

Now Louisa laughed. 'That's good, yes?'

Makereta looked serious. 'But he's not their son. He's a minor and he can't just stay with them, especially as he has a mother. There are rules about adopting in Fiji. As we can't find Wame, I'm taking him to his mother's. She lives here.'

Louisa frowned. 'I got the impression he didn't get on with his mum?' She opened the door to the back, carefully put her suitcase inside and then gently closed the door again.

'Every mother loves her child.'

Louisa begged to differ but said nothing. 'And he came with you, just like that?'

Makereta's round cheeks flushed pink. She cleared her throat. 'I promised him we'd look for Wame while we were here.'

'We?' said Louisa. She didn't like the sound of that.

'I was coming to pick you up in Nadi anyway and Wame is supposed to be here somewhere. You're not doing anything else are you?' said Makereta before getting into the car and starting the engine.

'But how do you think we'll find him when the rest of Fijian Police Force haven't been able to?' Louisa climbed into the passenger side of the vehicle, grateful for the cold air conditioning blasting away.

'They're not actually looking for him, more keeping an eye open. It's not the same.' Makereta pulled away. 'I've only been to Nadi twice, it's not nearly as big as Suva so it shouldn't be too difficult to have a look around.'

'And does Vika know you're looking for Wame?'

'No. She doesn't.'

'And what if she finds out?'

Makereta shrugged. 'I promised Malaki I'd look for him.'

'And what if he's a killer?'

'I don't think he is.'

Louisa laughed out loud. 'You were the one who told me not to trust Wame, that he was a bad influence on his brother and that he'd take me to the cleaners!'

'But petty thieving is one thing, murder is another.' She pursed her lips. 'Mum said Malaki didn't stop talking about how wonderful his brother was. Wame more or less brought him up, did you know that?'

'I didn't but–'

Makereta interrupted her. 'And don't forget Wame stopped Malaki being forced into prostitution and in doing so lost his own job. That takes true love. I can't believe someone who could love someone else like that could take the life of another person.'

Louisa had heard everything now. 'What if he thought Malaki was going to get hurt?'

Makereta looked serious. 'Wame's love for his brother could possibly have driven him to kill someone like the boss, if the boss was out to harm Malaki. But Rick and Stewy weren't hurting Malaki, were they?'

'Not that we know of,' said Louisa.

'Malaki referred to Rick and Stewy as good men. It suggests they intended him no harm.' Makereta pulled out of the parking space and narrowly missed scraping the car parked next to them. She cleared her throat. 'I have to stop talking now and concentrate on my driving.'

Louisa nodded and looked out the window at a plane arriving overhead. She sighed. She didn't care what happened to Malaki any more or who killed who. She'd go along with whatever Makereta wanted to do. If they found Wame all well and good. Maybe it really would mean Vika would let her leave sooner rather than later. But that was assuming, of course, Wame was the killer.

64

The centre of Nadi was one long dusty street of shops made out of concrete breeze blocks. It reminded Louisa of a town in an old spaghetti western, except it was modern. Giant posters in small supermarket windows advertised boat trips to "party islands" or "beach parties". Every other person was either a tourist – bleached hair, flip flops, board shorts, T-shirt (or skimpy top, if female) – or an Indo-Fijian. Louisa had never been to Goa but she imagined it might be a bit like this: desert hot and dry with lots of tat tourist shops.

They'd been crawling along the road for the last five minutes and were now at a standstill in a line of heaving, noisy vehicles, belching out toxic fumes.

'I don't know why there is so much traffic,' said Makereta, crossly.

'Is it because there's only the one road?' said Louisa.

'Maybe,' said Makereta. 'I hope I don't stall when we start moving again. I hate that.'

'How long have you been driving?' said Louisa.

'Two weeks.'

'Fourteen days!' said Louisa, shouting. No wonder Makereta was a nervous driver.

'Sh!' said Makereta, nodding to the back of the car where Malaki slept. 'I want to let him sleep as long as possible.'

'What took you so long to learn to drive?' Louisa had learnt as soon as she could at seventeen. Being able to drive equaled independence in her books.

'I didn't really want to learn but my father was in a car accident. He hurt his leg. He struggles to drive so it seemed about time for me to become the chauffeur instead of the passenger. There are just so many things to remember.'

'It gets easier with practice,' said Louisa.

Makereta took her hands off the steering wheel, wiped them on her dress then gripped the wheel again. 'You think so?'

She nodded. 'Definitely. You're doing fine.'

'Thanks,' said Makereta, glowering at the queue of traffic ahead her.

Malaki moaned behind them. They both looked round. He shifted then fell back into snoring.

Louisa sighed. 'What if Wame is the killer? What about Malaki then?'

'I suppose he'll have to stay with his mother.'

'Did he agree to that?'

'He said he would stay with her until we found Wame.'

'That doesn't sound like a yes. You know, Edwin said that Rick and Stewy argued the night before they were killed. Apparently, they'd treated some young man like a son and this man betrayed them. Whatever he did Stewy wanted to get the police involved. Rick refused. They'd fallen out over it big time. So, there's a motive right there for the murders. Wame has to be in the frame because he knew the men and in many ways broke their trust.'

Makereta made a face. 'But you said you saw Stewy happily conversing with Wame at the market the morning of the murders. That doesn't sound like a man who is angry with someone. And, it only works if Rick and Stewy had been helping Wame out again. As far as I know, they have had nothing to do with Wame for two years. They cherry picked the very best, like Api. Wame had his chance. Sadly, he lost it. That doesn't make him a killer though.'

'Okay. Maybe he wasn't going to get funded to go overseas again. But Malaki said Wame told him he was going to get money soon,' said Louisa. 'Where was that coming from?'

'Maybe Wame got an honest job?'

Louisa shook her head. 'Why not say if the money was coming from an honest source? It sounds more like blackmail to me.'

'That's a big leap,' said Makereta.

'Stewy wanted to go to the police about this person, which tells us whatever happened it was crooked.'

'But it doesn't mean Wame was involved.'

'What if Rick and Stewy had invited him back to the house for some reason and he stole from them and got caught?'

'Why would he steal from them?'

'He takes drugs, doesn't he?'

'Malaki says he doesn't.'

'Malaki would say anything to protect his brother!' said Louisa, trying hard not to raise her voice.'

'Even if, on that fateful day, he could have got to the house from the market in time to kill Rick and Stewy before we arrived, Wame isn't a strong person. Rick and Stewy were fit and healthy men. How could he have overpowered them?'

Louisa shrugged. 'He could have taken them by surprise.'

'But we keep coming back to motive. Where is his?' demanded Makereta.

'What if Wame, forced to have sex with men for money, developed a hatred of gay men? And that hatred got compounded when he lost his funding to go study overseas. Or, what if Wame is also gay? He could have fallen in love with either Rick or Stewy while living with them. He could have killed them because one or both of them didn't reciprocate his love?'

Makereta groaned. 'It's all conjecture. And, again why wait two years?'

'If he has killed two people we'll have to be very careful.'

'So, you are going to help me find him?' said Makereta, looking at Louisa and smiling.

Louisa sighed. 'Why not, you're right, I've not got anything better to do. But we won't have much time if we've to get back to Suva before the curfew?'

Makereta looked shocked. 'I'm not driving there and back in the same day.'

'I thought it was only a hundred and twenty miles one way?'

'Exactly,' said Makereta seriously.

'Ah,' said Louisa. When they did leave for Suva it was going to be a long drive.

65

Makereta drove away from the centre of Nadi and headed along a country road. Ahead, two, giant rainbow coloured hot air balloons appeared in the sky, floating gently down from a solitary mountain in the distance. Louisa had not expected to see balloons. To the right, the green-blue sea stretched endlessly, glinting beneath a brilliant blue cloudless sky. A bunch of soldiers lounged at the side of the road to the left. A wooden barrier sat behind them.

Malaki's mother's house was in a village off the main road and up a pot-holed path. Blink and you'd miss the patch of scabby timber framed huts. No trees. No shrubs. No flowering plants. No vegetables. It was scorched and abandoned looking and surrounded by fields of wispy green sugar cane stalks. Makereta parked, leaned back and gave Malaki a shake. He looked surprised to see Louisa but said nothing.

'We're here,' said Makereta. 'Your mother will be so pleased to see you. And as soon as we find Wame we'll bring him straight to you.'

'I want to look for Wame with you,' said Malaki, his small mouth forming a determined scowl.

'Wame could be here with your mother?' said Makereta. 'Have you thought of that?'

Malaki looked up at Makereta. A frown creased his skinny forehead. 'He does like Mum. He could be here.'

'Out you get then,' said Makereta, smiling. 'Let's go and see.'

Malaki heaved his skinny little body out of the car and trailed behind Makereta. Louisa got out and followed them. She wasn't hopeful.

Ahead, a tall, emaciated woman came out of the middle hut. She wore a baggy washed-out T-shirt over an ankle length brown sarong. Her hair was black and straight and tied back in a long, grim pony tail.

'Hello,' said Malaki, not looking at her.

'Who are you?' demanded the woman, throwing Louisa and Makereta a filthy look.

Makereta showed Malaki's mother her warrant card. She nodded to Louisa. 'This is a colleague.'

'Is Malaki in trouble?' The woman scowled at Malaki

who immediately looked at the ground.

'No, nothing like that. Actually, we're looking for your other son, Wame. Is he here?'

'Why are you looking for Wame?' she demanded. 'He's a good boy. You leave him alone.'

'He's not in trouble,' said Makereta. 'We just need to find him. Have you seen him recently?'

'He lives in Suva. What's going on?' She threw Malaki a second filthy scowl. 'Have you got your step brother in trouble?'

Malaki continued to look at the ground and said nothing.

'Please don't be alarmed,' said Makereta, 'Malaki has done nothing wrong. Neither has Wame. We just need to talk to him. He's moved out from where he was staying in Suva so we thought he might be here in Nadi.'

'If he was here,' said the woman, 'he would have visited me. He's a good boy. He looks after his mother. He would not come to Nadi and not see me.'

'He may not have had time to visit you yet. Are you sure you don't know where he could be?' said Louisa.

'I told you,' said the woman, eyeing Louisa, 'if he was in Nadi he would come to see me.'

'We understand. The thing is, without his brother to look after him Malaki needs somewhere to stay.'

The woman spat on the sandy ground, just missing Malaki's new trainers. 'And how am I to feed him with no money, no work and no husband?'

'You're his mother,' insisted Makereta. 'Malaki is your responsibility.'

'Don't you tell me about responsibility. I fed him at my breast for a year. But do you think I can produce food from thin air? I'm not a magician. Or God. There are no loaves and fishes here. Do you know how hard it is to watch your own son go hungry?'

'What if we gave you some money to buy some food, would that help for now?' said Louisa.

The woman's face softened. 'How much money?'

Makereta opened her bag to get her purse.

'No. I'll get this.' Louisa held out a twenty dollar note.

'Forty,' said the woman.

Louisa took another twenty note from her purse. She passed the two notes to Malaki's mother. 'This is for food.' She did not like this woman. Not one little bit.

'He'll only have the best.' The woman snatched the money, stuffed it down the neck of her top into the side of her bra and said, 'If you want to speak to Wame so badly why don't you call him on his mobile phone?'

66

Makereta parked in the Raffles Gateway Hotel car park. The hotel was close to the airport. Makereta told Louisa she had stayed there once before when she'd been in Nadi for a police workshop. The hotel was surrounded by manicured lawns and draped in cascades of purple bougainvillea. Inside a shaded courtyard revealed a glittering rectangular ornamental pond with a delightful water fountain. More bougainvillea and various exotic plants decorated every nook and cranny. In sharp contrast to the hot dry heat of the streets, the inner courtyard was deliciously cool.

They booked a twin room. After the posh foyer, it was

not what Louisa had been expecting. Two sagging single beds sat squashed in the middle of a shabby brown room. The décor was tired looking and Louise could definitely smell the odour of cockroach. And sure enough when she opened the door to the built-in wardrobe, a flurry of baby cockroaches scuttled across the tiled floor. When she told Makereta they had to find a new hotel, Makereta said The Raffles was as good as it got in Nadi. Louisa wasn't happy about staying there, not one little bit.

'Still no answer,' said Makereta, throwing herself down on one of the beds and dropping her mobile beside her. 'It's the fifth time I've tried.'

'I don't like that woman,' said Louisa, spreading out the lava-lava from her bag over the other single bed and sitting on it. 'And I don't like leaving him there with her.'

'I don't like her much either but a mother is a mother.'

'I've seen some terrible cases of neglect back home by birth mothers,' said Louisa.

'We assume it's not for long.'

'What happens when we find Wame?'

'I will tell him his brother needs him.'

'And then what? We take both of them back to Suva to be locked up by Vika or beaten up by the big boss?' Louisa eyed Makereta. Why did she have to persist in keeping her shoes on while lying on the bed?

Makereta shrugged. 'No idea. Let's try and find him first.'

'So, where do we start? Louisa wanted to stretch out too, she suddenly felt exhausted, but there was no way she was actually going to lie down on that bedspread even with her lava-lava on top of it.

'He's young, isn't he?'

'Yes,' said Louisa.

'So we look for places where young people hang out.'

'You remember I said I met Api, the young man who also used to live with Rick and Stewy, now studying in Australia?'

Makereta opened her eyes and looked across at Louisa. 'Yes?'

'Api said Wame had drug issues. He also said that if we wanted to find him, we had to look for someone selling drugs. Are there drugs in Nadi?'

Makereta laughed out loud. 'It's the tourist capital of Fiji. Renowned for its "party islands" and "beach parties". Young people come from all over the world to "chill" here. Yes there are drugs. I could ask my colleagues, but as I'm not officially on the case that could be awkward.'

'If the shoeshine boys in Suva are associated with drugs, shouldn't we look for the shoeshine boys in Nadi?'

Makereta shook her head. 'Shoeshine boys are particular to Suva.'

'Lets follow the party then.'

67

The Croc, AKA the Crocodile Dundee hostel, was a double storey rectangular block of concrete, with half a dozen square windows carved into its sheer walls on each side. It sat behind a fenced yard, which contained a solitary rotary washing line smothered in miscellaneous swimwear. Louisa buzzed an intercom by the gate. She pitied any tourist who'd booked to stay there. The beach was miles away. You couldn't even see the sea. The view to the left was of a paint factory and to the right a field of scrub. It was a two miles beneath a blistering sun from the centre of Nadi and the nightlife. They'd been given the name almost as soon as they'd started asking around the bars to buy some weed. It became quickly clear that The Croc was the place to go to get anything you want.

Makereta rang the buzzer after Louisa. It was two thirty. They'd parked by the road. Just being in the sun for a couple of minutes was giving Louisa a headache.

'What you want?' said a voice. Male. Deep. Rough.

'We're looking for somewhere to stay,' said Louisa. 'Everywhere else is fully booked. We heard you had rooms.'

The buzzer buzzed and they pushed open the gate and were in. A concrete path took them round the building to a back yard, littered with surf boards, black Neoprene dive booties and white and blue cool boxes. There wasn't a single plant or bush or tree. A small hand painted sign next to a door said "Reception". They went inside. The biggest surprise was that it was cool. Air conditioning must have been working overtime to keep the heat at bay. The second was that it was reasonably smart. Blown up black and white photos of surfers riding giant waves decorated the cool white walls. There was even a green tree fern in a pot in the corner. Reception was a bare black shiny counter. A chunky young Fijian man sat on a stool behind it. From his jerky actions he was clearly playing a computer game on a hand held console or phone out of sight below the counter.

'What's your room rates?' said Makereta.

Without looking up the man nodded to a sign on the wall to the side of him.

'Thanks,' said Makereta, giving Louisa a look that said,

now what?

'Any twin rooms left?' said Louisa.

'Wouldn't have let you in if we hadn't.'

'Can we take a look?'

The man shrugged. 'Just up there.' He jerked his head to a small hallway. 'To the left is the kitchen and lounge. You do all your own cooking. You need to buy anything, you come and ask me. To the right is the stairs. To the left the lift. First floor. It's the room with the key in the door.' He went back to playing his game.

The hostel was incredibly quiet. Either everyone was sleeping or out. Out probably. The room was basic but clean, even by Louisa's standards. Two twin single beds. A wardrobe. Two chairs. A round table and a double glazed window and air conditioner. A door led to a simple en-suite bathroom. Everything seemed new. Louisa preferred it to the Raffles.

'Now what?' whispered Makereta.

Louisa looked out the window at the washing line below. 'I don't know. We check out the kitchen and lounge, I suppose.' She was about to turn away. Someone appeared in the yard below, coming from the reception at the back. Louisa did a double take. 'Makereta, quickly.'

'What?' said Makereta.

'There,' said Louisa, pointing to the back of a young man opening the hostel gate and leaving. 'It's Api, Wame's ex-friend. The person who got the funding over Wame, and the one who told me Wame took drugs. What's he doing here?'

Makereta shrugged. 'Looking for Wame too?

'Maybe. It's a bit of a coincidence.'

'I don't like coincidences,' said Makereta frowning.

'Me neither. Let's ask him a few questions.'

'We'd better be quick!' said Makereta. 'Look!'

Api was getting into the driver's seat of a beat up saloon car parked just outside the hostel.

68

The road took Louisa and Makereta straight back to the centre and into bumper to bumper traffic once again. They thought they'd lost Api until Louisa spied him five cars ahead. Makereta inched closer and closer, sweat dripping from her stressed face, when Api reversed into what looked like the only free parking space in the whole of the street.

'Shit!' said Louisa, looking at the side of Api's head as they rolled passed him. 'What are we going to do, there isn't another parking spot anywhere?'

'You go after him,' said Makereta. 'I'll try and park. See where he goes.'

Louisa jumped out the car and followed Api to a bustling supermarket called RB Patels. It stood on the corner of the main shopping street and a side street with no name. She followed Api inside, watched him buy a bottle of water, leave, slip up the side street and disappear into a house three blocks down.

Makereta appeared, out of breath. She licked her lips. 'I had to find a place where I could forward park, I can't do reverse parking. It's too stressful.'

Louisa pointed down the side street to the dilapidated house Api had disappeared into. 'He went in there,' said Louisa.

'Okay.'

'So, what now?'

'We could wait,' said Makereta.

'But for how long?' said Louisa.

'Or we could knock on the door and ask to talk to Api.'

Louisa ran her fingers through her unruly hair. 'He was helpful before, so there's no reason to assume he won't be helpful again.'

Makereta nodded. 'He's not the one wanted by the police.'

'Unless he has something to hide?' said Louisa.

Makereta sucked her bottom lip. 'What could he have to hide? He loses by Rick and Stewy's death, he'll not be able to finish his degree.'

'So do we go and talk to Api or stand here discussing him?' said Louisa, stepping to one side to let pass a couple coming out of the supermarket laden down with carrier bags packed with shopping.

Makereta knocked on the side of the main door. A tired looking Fijian woman answered. She looked startled when she saw Makereta and whispered something to her in Fijian. Makereta whispered something back. Louisa heard Api's name. Eventually, the woman indicated that they should come in.

'What was all that about?' said Louisa, keeping her voice low.

'I know her from Suva. I've helped her out a few times in the past. She owes me.'

Why was Louisa not surprised? 'And?'

'I said we needed to talk to Api urgently. She said we could come in providing we do not tell Api we are the police or that I know her.'

Louisa followed Makereta and the woman. She was puzzled, though. Why was it a problem, telling Api they were police? It was dark inside. It took Louisa's eyes a few seconds to adjust. A single light bulb dangled from the middle of a low ceiling. Heavy brown blankets had been draped over two picture windows on the far wall. There was no other light source. The place stank of booze and unwashed clothes. In the middle of the room a large Fijian man lay on the floor, sideways on. He looked down at playing cards which he held in one of his hands. Separate mounds of pillows propped up his head and his feet, which were draped in what looked like wet towels. He was dressed in a shapeless T-shirt and sarong. Six other men sat crossed-legged facing him. A blue-grey fug of cigarette smoke shrouded them. The men also had cards in their hands and, like the big man, were dressed casually. A pile of random dollar notes sat between them. Api was not among the card players. Louisa paused. She didn't like this.

'We should leave,' she whispered to Makereta. Too late. Makereta had already walked into the middle of the room. The big man on his side looked up from his cards, glanced at Makereta and looked back down. Louisa started. It was Malaki's boss. Malaki's fucking boss!

69

Louisa took a step back. She wanted as far out of the meagre light as possible. The door was only one more step behind her. If she were lucky, she could get to the car before they caught her. What about Makereta? Shit! Why hadn't they done a reccy first? Checked out where they were going? She was losing it. Rookie mistake after rookie mistake. No time to think about that now. Where was the woman who had let them in? She'd gone. No. She was there, sitting by the boss man's feet. She had a basin by her.

'He'll be a couple of minutes,' said the woman to Makereta while removing the wet towels from the man's feet and placing them in the basin.

Makereta nodded. 'That's okay.'

Louisa wanted to shout, run! Makereta was within a metre of the circle of men. They looked like giant slugs but who knew how fast they could move when they wanted to. What if someone had a knife, or worse still, a gun? Louisa had to stay calm. She took a further step back. She felt the wall behind her. She was in the shadows. Out of the light. Good. She just had to wait. But stay on her toes. Be ready to run for it. At any second.

The boss man slapped his cards onto the cement floor with a flourish. 'Ha!' he yelled and swept the pile of money towards him. The other men groaned and one by one they threw their cards down on the floor. All the while, the woman who had let them in squeezed the wet towels in the basin between her hands and placed them back over the big man's feet.

'What you want?' said the boss man, squinting up at Makereta, while tucking his winnings under the pillows beneath his head.

'We want to talk to Api,' said Makereta.

'Is that supposed to be funny?' said the man, glowering at the woman who was placing the freshly squeezed towels over his feet.

She shrugged.

'I need to ask him something,' said Makereta.

The man looked at the woman again. The woman looked at Makereta and said. 'This is Api.'

'Oh?' said Makereta. Even Louisa could see she was blushing. 'We're looking for a much younger man called Api. I was told he was here.'

The boss man took a tobacco tin from under his pillows and began rolling himself a cigarette between his fingers. 'Who do you think you are, you and your friend hiding in the corner there, disturbing me at my friend's home?'

Louisa looked down at the floor. Had he recognised her?

'It's a simple misunderstanding,' said Makereta, smiling. 'We were told Api was here. But you are not the same Api we are looking for.'

'Lying cow,' said the man, concentrating on his cigarette.

'I am not in the habit of telling untruths!' said Makereta, feigning indignation. 'We are visiting from Api's church and leave tomorrow to go back to Suva. We were told he needed a lift!'

The man looked up from making his cigarette. His face was puffy. His eyes were blood shot. 'I should have guessed you were church types.' His thick mouth curled in disgust. 'Young Api was here earlier. He never knows when to stay away. If you see him you remind him not go back to Suva without giving me what he owes me first.'

'And what would that be?' said Makereta.

'If you're such good friends,' said the man, sealing the thin edge of the cigarette paper around the loose tobacco with two long, slow licks. 'You should know.'

'I'll pass on your message.'

'He can run but he cannot hide,' he said, lighting his roll up with a long match, causing the tip of the cigarette to catch fire. He nodded to the woman at his feet and she jumped up and scuttled towards the door.

'I won't disturb you any longer,' said Makereta. 'Thank you for your time.'

'Don't come back.' The man, snuffed out the yellow flame coming from the tip of his cigarette paper with his thick fingers. One of the other men sniggered. The boss man gave him a filthy look. 'Are we having another game, or what?'

The woman took Louisa and Makereta outside. As they went to leave, she whispered something into Makereta's ear.

'That was Malaki's boss!' said Louisa, hurrying away from the house. 'I recognised him straight away. Bastard!'

'Do you have to swear?' said Makereta, seriously.

Louisa wanted to laugh but didn't. 'He's the one I argued over Malaki with. The one who came to the aunty's village looking for me and Wame and Malaki.'

Makereta frowned. 'You mean he's the man whose arm you twisted?' She shook her head. 'Luckily all you foreigners look alike and he didn't recognise you. He is someone I would not want to cross.'

'What did your friend say when we left?'

'She is not a friend. She thinks Api is in Denerau. It's an area at other side of Nadi. She is of the opinion he's working there in a hotel.'

'He told me he'd just arrived from Australia,' said Louisa. 'Someone is lying.'

223

70

Makereta had made an executive decision. It was too late to go to Denerau and she was hungry. She'd called it a day and taken Louisa back to the Raffles for dinner. Makereta had ordered chicken supreme with chips. Louisa a burger, but by the time it came the memory of oriental cockroaches tap dancing in the bedroom had killed her appetite – if there were cockroaches in the bedrooms, there would be cockroaches in the kitchen. Of course, cockroaches were endemic in the tropics but that didn't mean she had to be happy about putting up with them. She had to eat, though, but simply couldn't bring herself to bite into the burger.

'I thought you were hungry?' said Makereta, tucking into her food.

'I've lost my appetite,' said Louisa, putting her fork and knife down. 'Where is this Denerau place where young Api is working?'

'It's a resort, the other side of Nadi.'

'There are hotels there?'

'Of course.'

Louisa looked at her untouched burger. 'Why didn't we stay in Denerau instead of here?' Anywhere had to be better than the Raffles.

Makereta looked shocked. 'It's much too expensive. Besides what's wrong with the Raffles?'

Was she serious? 'By the way, why on earth did your friend assume we were looking for old Api and not young Api, especially as young Api was in the house only moments before we arrived?'

'She knows young Api by his middle name, Ramodi. Fijians have two or three or even four names.'

'And what is Api Ramodi's relationship with old Api?'

Makereta put her knife and fork down. Dabbed her mouth with her napkin and said. 'Young Api Ramodi owes old Api money. He was due to pay it back today. Instead of doing so he asked for a further twenty-four hours and another loan. Old Api was very cross and threw him out – there is a back entrance to the house. That is why we didn't see him leave.'

Louisa pursed her lips. 'We look for Wame and find Api instead. And young Api owes old Api, AKA the shoeshine boss, money. Maybe Wame isn't the only one into drugs?'

Makereta shook her head again. 'It's not drugs, it's gambling. Young Api has accrued huge debts. Old Api has had enough of his excuses and plans to make an example of him if he doesn't pay back what he is owed by the end of the day.'

'We should tell Vika.'

'And say what? No one will admit to any of it. But you are right about one thing, someone is telling lies. Young Api can't be in Australia and Nadi at the same time. I just hope we can find him to ask our questions before old Api does.'

Louisa frowned. 'I hope old Api hasn't made an example of Wame.'

'You think that's why we can't find him?'

'I hope not.'

'The aunty said she doesn't know Wame. He's not one of the usual gamblers she sees here. Louisa?' said Makereta, picking up her knife and fork.

'Yes?' said Louisa.

'What happened between you and Mataio?'

'Ah?' said Louisa. She was going to have to tell her. She

owed her that much. 'He got religion.'

'He's a church boy?' said Makereta, frowning. 'But why is that a problem?'

'In case you haven't noticed, I'm not a church girl.'

'But that doesn't have to preclude you from having a relationship with him, does it?'

'Well,' said Louisa, taking a deep breath. 'On top of getting religion he also cashed in the airline ticket I bought him to travel with me to Scotland. And spent the money. All 13,000 plus dollars worth–'

Makereta whistled. 'That's a lot of money. What did he want it for?'

'To pay for some corrugated iron for a church maneaba roof,' said Louisa, finally taking a bite out of her burger. 'And he wasn't in the least bit remorseful about what he'd done! Money. It's the roof of evil.'

Makereta shook her head. 'No. The love of money is the root of evil. Not money itself.'

'You know what I mean. He lied to me and he stole from me.'

'Did the airline ticket actually cost that much?'

Louisa shifted in her chair. 'It's how it is. The aid people call being on Tarawa a "hardship" post. We travel business class. I wanted Mataio to sit with me so I got him a business class ticket.'

'That's as much as I earn in a year.'

'I know it's a lot of money but it doesn't justify him helping himself to it.'

'I didn't say that it did,' said Makereta coldly.

Louisa blushed. 'Sorry, I didn't mean to suggest you did. Mataio and I had a good relationship and I can't believe it is over.'

'It couldn't have been that good, could it?' said Makereta, picking up the last chip on her plate with her fingers.

'What do you mean?' said Louisa immediately on her guard.

Makereta wiped her hands on her napkin. 'Relationships just don't stop working, do they? There's usually a reason. Maybe your relationship was in difficulties?'

'I think I would have seen signs of any problems.'

'But you're not together any more, are you?'

'Because he got all holy moly on me,' said Louisa. She didn't like the way the conversation was headed.

'Becoming a Christian doesn't usually cause people to fall out of love, in fact, if anything, it has the opposite effect.'

'Look, Makereta, I think you mean well but you're not helping.'

'There were no issues then?'

'Why do you keep talking about issues? We were very happy,' said Louisa, trying not to get angry.

Makereta shrugged. 'So, you're saying he found God not from being in despair but from being in love? It happens.'

'Are you making fun of me?' said Louisa.

'No,' said Makereta, looking surprised. 'But don't you think you are deceiving yourself just a little? After all, if you had such a trusting, wonderful relationship, why didn't Mataio talk to you about wanting to spend the money on the roof, or his interest in the church?'

'Because he's a coward and a shit!' said Louisa, getting to her feet.

'But you didn't think he was before,' said Makereta matter-of-factly. 'And must you use such ugly language?'

'Why don't you just go and read your bible or something!' said Louisa, getting up and leaving the restaurant.

71

Louisa was still awake when the fire alarm went off. It was after two in the morning. The woot wooting sound was followed by shouting, doors banging and the slip-slapping of anxious footsteps running along the corridor. Louisa was out of her bed in an instant, Makereta was just behind her. Louisa couldn't look at her. The nerve of someone who was still single and living at home advising her about relationships! Louisa threw on the white hotel dressing gown and flicked the light switch. It didn't work. In the dim greyness she scrabbled about for her handbag.

'There's no time to bring things,' said Makereta, hurrying out the door. 'We have to leave now!'

Louisa watched Makereta disappear out the room, waited a couple of seconds until she imagined Makereta had reached the stairwell – the lifts would be off limit with the fire alarm going off – then left the room. Makereta was gone. Louisa breathed a quick sigh of relief. Wherever possible she was going to avoid her.

The dirty orange emergency lighting created a murky fug in the dark stairwell. Louisa shivered and hurried down the concrete steps two at a time. The woot, wooting noise was louder here. It burst through her eardrums, piercing her subconscious. She reached the emergency exit. It wouldn't open. She pushed again. It continued to resist. She'd have to back track. Find another way out. It was a nuisance. But she didn't actually believe she was in danger. There's been no tell tale smoke smell. Obviously a false alarm. She turned to retrace her steps. What the? Someone grabbed her hair. Jerked her head backwards. She screamed. A fist of chunky fingers slammed across her mouth and silenced her. She grabbed at the hand. Wriggled. Struggled. Kicked. An arm, heavy and strong, swung across her chest, pinning her body against his. She couldn't move.

'I know he gave it to you and I want it back,' he growled into her ear, his sour breath creeping across the back of her neck.

Her heart thudded so loudly she couldn't think. But she had to think.

'It belongs to me. I wouldn't have killed him if he'd given it back. Now he's dead. It was his own fault. Where is it?' He released his hand over her mouth so she could speak.

'My bag,' she gasped. It was the killer! She was with the killer. If she could only see him. 'In the room. Upstairs.' Sweat dripped down her face. She hoped he wouldn't hear the hollow ring to her lie.

'Move!' He clamped his hand back over her mouth and dragged her backwards. Her feet slapped into the hard steps. She struggled. 'Stop that!' he snarled, thrusting his hand against her lips, ripping the skin, pressing his hand against her teeth. His waxy flesh inside her mouth made her want to throw up.

'If you are lying,' said the attacker, jerking her up and over each, cold, concrete, step. 'I'll kill you too.' She had one chance. No time to think about it. She bit hard on the skin in her mouth. He roared in pain. Released her. She stumbled downwards. Bashed her shins. Scraped her knees.

'Police! Stop what you're doing!' Makereta was at the open emergency door below. The manager of the hotel peered behind her.

Louisa's attacker bolted.

'He's getting away,' said Louisa, close to tears. 'He's

getting away.'

72

Despite her ordeal, Louisa felt oddly good. Even the dancing cockroaches in the wardrobe couldn't dent her mood. Although she'd not seen her attacker, she'd bitten his finger hard – there'd been so much blood Makereta was convinced he'd managed to stab Louisa. The thought of his blood in her mouth made her gag but it had done the trick. He'd let her go and no way was he going to be able to hide that scar. Louisa couldn't believe she'd not seen the bastard follow her. In all probability he'd set off the fire alarm. So many times now, he'd found out where she was. It gave her the creeps.

'But I can't understand what he thinks Rick gave you?' said Makereta.

Louisa opened her eyes, turned on her side and faced Makereta, who was lying on her side in her single bed. The small side light made her look jaundiced in the brown curtained room. 'I have no idea either but whatever it is he wants it back.'

'You're sure you didn't see him?'

Louisa shook her head. 'He held my back to him the whole time. And he was in the shadows when he ran.'

'You remember nothing that could help identify him?'

'Nothing, not even a body smell. But he was taller than me.'

'So, it couldn't have been Wame!' said Makereta, sounding pleased.

'No,' said Louisa, suddenly feeling tired and lying back on her back. It had to be 5am. 'This man was stronger and bigger than Wame.'

'It's my fault. I told the woman at the house in Nadi where to find us if she needed to. She must have told old Api.'

Louisa was back on her side looking at Makereta. 'It couldn't have been him either. Remember I twisted old Api's arm, I've been close to him. He's strong but he's also got a beer gut. My attacker had no beer gut.'

Makereta puckered her face into a frown. 'That only leaves young Api. What motive could he have? He's lost the most by Rick's and Stewy's deaths.'

'A friend of Malaki said he saw Wame and Api together a few days ago. Api denied it. But what if he's lying? He's big enough and strong enough to have pinned me down.'

Makereta made a face. 'But, I say again, why would he?'

Louisa shrugged, flopped onto her pillow and looked up at the ceiling which was a dirty nicotine colour. 'What if, contrary to what Api said, he's still friends with Wame?'

Makereta sat up in her bed. 'It may be nothing where you're from, but here in Fiji, it's a big deal to study overseas. With an overseas degree you are guaranteed a top job in Fiji, even a job overseas. But to study overseas costs a lot of money. Only very rich Fijian people can do that. If you're not rich, the only other way to study overseas is to be clever and win a scholarship.'

'What has this got to do with the killings?' said Louisa, only just about following what Makereta was saying.

Makereta ignored her question. 'I got the highest grades in my year. I applied for a scholarship to go to New Zealand to study law. My best friend's grades were not nearly as good as mine but her uncle was the ambassador of China and so she got the scholarship. She is part of a big powerful Fijian family. Everyone knows the people in charge of selecting the students for the scholarships are in the pockets of the most powerful Fijian families.'

'If it's so corrupt why does no one complain?'

Makereta shook her head wearily. 'In Fijian culture you do not question your superiors. It is not done. And, by the way, a scholarship is not just a passport to a higher education, it also means travelling. If you are an ordinary Fijian, or Samoan or Tongan or a person from your Kiribati, or any of the other small Pacific island countries, and you want to travel, tough. Without a scholarship, or money, or being from the right family, it's impossible to get a visa to visit a foreign country. And even when you get a visa it is no guarantee you'll get in another country.

'Last year I was to go on a week course in Australia. I had the correct visa and all the right papers, but even so, they refused to let me in the country. For a one week course! Our foreign neighbours are so worried we will stay in their precious country and not come back home, they stop us getting in at any opportunity!'

'I'm sorry,' said Louisa. It was the first time she'd seen Makereta so worked up.

'Being picked by Rick and Stewy to be supported to study in Australia was a huge thing for these boys, like winning the lottery,' said Makereta, calming down as quickly as she'd got excited. 'They got living allowances in excess of $25,000 a year, that's as good as any scholarship and more money than many of us here earn in a year, and some in a life time. You foreigners don't know how lucky you are. You take your higher education for granted along with your right to travel and work wherever you want.'

'Okay,' said Louisa. 'I'm sorry. Really. And I do get it. But from what you say that means Wame really does have a powerful motive for killing Rick and Stewy?'

Makereta laughed sarcastically. 'But an even more powerful one for killing Api. What I'm saying is Wame would have never stayed friends with Api, not after Rick and Stewy funded him.'

'Maybe they're not friends then but are still in touch.'

'Why?'

Louisa sighed. 'Who knows, but if Api has lied about being in contact with Wame, we need to know why – and, there's every chance he knows where Wame is.'

'Do we tell Vika what happened to you?' said Makereta.

'I say we talk to Api first.'

'And if Api is the killer?'

'He'll have a bloody big imprint of my teeth on his fingers!'

Makereta laughed.

Louisa took a deep breath. Makereta's prompt action earlier had probably saved her life. 'What made you come back for me?'

'When you didn't appear at the fire assembly point on the lawn I knew something was wrong. There was no reason for you not to be there. If it had been the other way around, you would have come and looked for me.'

'Of course,' said Louisa. But would she have gone back to look for Makereta? She'd been in such a strop with her she'd not noticed the killer. Too busy fuming because she didn't agree with Makereta's take on her relationship. The thought made her blush. Snoring came from Makereta's bed. It was after five in the morning. Louisa looked in her bag for her ear plugs.

73

It was already hot. Not long after eight. Makereta drove carefully along a dusty, pot-holed road surrounded by arid brown fields, direction Denerau. Far ahead the glittering turquoise sea glistened. Louisa couldn't believe it was possible for anyone to drive as slowly as Makereta, even her mum drove faster than her. Louisa checked the rear view mirror for the fourth time in as many minutes.

'Do you really think he's following us?' said Makereta, not taking her eyes off the road in front.

'This guy has always found me. How could he have done that without knowing my movements?'

'But there's not been a car behind us since we left the Raffles.'

'Hopefully, he's lying low somewhere, nursing his wound. Maybe it will give us a chance to find him before he finds us.'

'He's taking more and more risks.' Makereta shivered. 'Maybe we should call in Vika, or at least inform the local officers?'

Louisa waved her arms in the air in a gesture of bewilderment. 'But we've nothing to give them. I didn't even recognise the man's voice. And, although he said he killed Rick, that could be a lie. We have no hard evidence of anything.'

'If we only knew what this thing is that he wants back. What sort of things do people hide?'

'Money? Drugs?'

'Rick knew I was a police officer. In theory, he would not have given me drugs or dirty money to hold for him. It has to be something else.'

'Letters? A film with compromising evidence in it?'

'When I was wee my mum used to give me and my brother a pound for every A we got in our report card from school. I used to get three or four As but often ended up with nothing because she also took twenty-five pence off for every B, fifty pence off for a C and seventy five pence for a D and the whole pound for an E. I soon started to hide my report card from her. It was less humiliating. She didn't even notice the cards stopped coming.'

'What are you saying?'

Louisa pulled herself upright. 'We've assumed all this time Api's been an exemplary student because that's what he told us. But if Api is a liar, that could be bollocks. He could have been failing. And if he was, maybe Rick and Stewy could have been planning to axe his funding. There's a couple of motives right there: revenge, anger, resentment.'

'We could call the university where he studies and try find out how he's been doing.'

'He said he studies Artificial Intelligence at the University of Monash in Melbourne.'

'My phone is in my bag. You call. I have to concentrate on the road.'

Louisa got the number for university admissions from directory enquiries and waited to be connected. She glanced at Makereta. Her face was rigid with concentration. Could she have been right about her relationship with Mataio? Had there been signs things were going wrong between them? Then she remembered. Weeks ago, or even months.

They'd finished making love and were talking about moving to Scotland. He'd said he wasn't sure if he could be an alien in an alien land. She'd said that he was being ridiculous.

'What's ridiculous about not wanting to be a stranger?' he'd said.

'Being a foreigner hasn't stopped me enjoying my stay on Tarawa.'

'But you're not me,' he'd said. 'Besides, you have an extremely well paid job here on Tarawa, with a lot of status. What kind of job will I get in Scotland? A porter in a hotel carrying cases for rich people? A street cleaner? Maybe the man who washes the pots and pans in the back of a restaurant, if I'm lucky. I don't want to do any of those things. I am happy here on Tarawa. I don't want to go to a place where I'll be treated as if I am worthless and made to do something that I would hate.'

She'd insisted he was panicking about nothing and had dismissed his fears as a bit of pre-travel nerves. Had that been the beginning of the end? She should have paid him more attention. Taken what he said more seriously. Why hadn't she? Too full of herself or too frightened to face the possibility that Mataio might not want to leave Tarawa? As for Pastor Johan. There was something very sleekit, as the Scots said, about the man. She had more compassion in her big toe than he had in his entire body. Not that it was her concern now. Telling her mother it was over would be excruciating. She would wait till she was there to say. It wasn't something she was prepared to talk about over the phone. And if her trip back was delayed, as it looked like it was going to be, all the better. Someone else could top and tail her.

'We really need to talk to Api,' said Louisa, when she

finally came off the phone to Monash University.

'What did they say?' said Makereta, not taking her eyes off the road.

'There is no record of Api Ramodi, or anyone else with a similar sounding name, studying at Monash University. It's either a cock-up, or Api has lied big time. Talking to him has become a priority over finding Wame.'

74

'We've reached Denerau!' said Makereta relieved and driving over a small hump back bridge and passing a raised boon gate.

The dust vanished. The pot holes disappeared. Grass verges materialised either side of the road. Neat security guards sat in front of gleaming electronic gates, guarding massive swanky houses, bigger than Louisa had seen anywhere in Suva. Denerau was one massive luxury gated community.

'It's like *Miami Vice* meets *Desperate Housewives*,' said Louisa.

'It don't like it,' said Makereta. 'The place makes me feel uncomfortable.'

A sign with a picture of a ferry boat on it directed them to turn right at the next junction. 'There's a port?' said Louisa.

'It's where the "party boats" leave from. There are also a few shops, even a Hard Rock Café.'

A sign. Ahead. To the Westin.

'Hotel number one?' said Louisa.

Makereta nodded.

Louisa veered off the road and drove up a giant drive with lush vegetation at either side. Then Louisa saw the entrance to the hotel. 'Wow!' A profusion of purple bougainvillea, delicate white lilies and ruby red hibiscus bushes led to a magnificent sweeping entrance on top of a hill. It was huge. Striking. Glittering. Gleaming. Plush. Posh. It made the Holiday Inn in Suva look rubbish.

'Is that what the hotels are like in Scotland?' said Makereta in awe.

'None that I've ever been to.'

They followed the road round, away from the entrance, arriving at the hotel car park hidden from view behind well placed bushes and palm trees.

Louisa and Makereta walked along a snaking path they hoped would take them back to the reception of The Westin. They were agreed. The sooner they questioned Api, the sooner they could rule him out or in. Louisa hadn't liked the well-groomed young man she'd met on the steps of the church in Suva, but she'd not disliked him either. Could he be a killer? If so, he put on a good act.

A golf buggy appeared from nowhere. A smiling man in an immaculate white uniform offered to give them a lift. They hopped in. The buggy wound between perfectly trimmed lawns and glorious flower beds. Banana palms separated rows of double-storey buildings covered in cascades of pink and purple and orange bougainvillea. Louisa watched silent gardeners, dressed in dark brown, quietly trim and weed and water. It was cool and quiet and as lush and luxurious as Louisa had ever seen.

The buggy dropped them off outside reception.

Louisa reckoned the chunky intricately wooden frame entrance had to be at least ten metres high and the side posts a metre wide. A wonderfully carved wooden bridge took them across a gently murmuring stream. A massive mahogany dining table sat in the middle of the reception hall, holding the biggest vase of topical lilies Louisa had ever seen. Three gigantic chandeliers glittered overhead. The floor was polished marble. An open entrance at the back looked over three designer open air swimming pools. Two foreign women wandered across the foyer towards the pools, dressed in designer swimwear, that shouted "super rich". The overall feel was of Japanese temples, Sevilla in spring and Disneyland in summer all rolled into one.

There were three reception desks in a row, staffed by two smiling Fijian women and one smiling Fijian man. There was no queue. No sense of hurry. As Louisa and Makereta approached the man looked up, beamed and asked how he could help. He oozed hushed efficiency. Louisa let Makereta speak; she, at least, had a warrant card. They had no luck. No one called Api Ramodi or anyone like him worked at the Westin.

The Sheraton was next. It was more colourful and noisier than the Westin, with more children, which made it feel more Disneyland than Japanese temple, but it was still impressive. Then there was the Sofitel, the Hilton, the Radisson and the Wyndham. In total Louisa and Makereta checked out five five star hotels overlooking the sea – although Louisa overheard one elderly lady say the hotels were really only four star. It took them an hour to discover that no one called Api Ramodi, or Wame, worked in any of the hotels. Not on reception, not cleaning the rooms, not in the gardens, not driving the buggies, or in the shops, or handing out pool towels, or as part of the entertainment. Nowhere.

'What now?' said Louisa. They were in Denerau Tennis Club. It sat slap bang in the middle of the complex of hotels. Louisa had invited Makereta to lunch. She wasn't eating in the Raffles again, not if she could help it.

Makereta scrunched her face. 'I thought Api worked in the hotels but he could equally work in one of the big houses as a gardener or security guard. Or in one of the shops in the ferry complex.'

'It could take weeks checking out all those places,' said Louisa. 'And we still only have your friend's word for it that he works here. He might not even be in Nadi at all.' She leaned back into the plush sofa she was sitting on and overlooked a quadrangle of six, neat, deserted tennis lawns, surrounded by tidy pink rose buses.

'That's it then,' said Makereta, her voice flat. 'Api was my last hope of finding the killer and tracking down Wame. I'm not looking forward to breaking the bad news to Malaki.'

'We've still a few hours before we have to leave for Suva, don't we?'

She nodded. 'But where else is there to look?'

'If Wame knows something about the killer, he could be in hiding.'

'That makes sense but that doesn't help us find him,' said Makereta, sounding dejected. 'There's nothing else for it. We'll have to go back to his mother's village and tell Malaki.'

A waiter placed Louisa and Makereta's tropical burgers and chips on the table in front of them. He stood for a second. Then said, 'Are you the Scottish detective looking for Api?'

75

The waiter was tall and lean with a bored look about him. Louisa said, 'Who told you we're looking for Api?'

The man tucked the round silver tray he used to bring their burgers under his arm. 'Everyone is talking about the Scottish detective lady who looking for a local student.'

'Do you know where Api is?' said Makereta.

'Maybe,' said the waiter, non-committally.

Louisa took ten dollars from her purse and shoved it into his hand, she was so not in the mood for playing silly buggers. 'Will that help?'

The man tucked the note into his black apron pocket and nodded to the lawns outside. 'Api sometimes plays tennis here.'

'We are talking about Api Ramodi?' said Makereta.

The young man nodded.

'He doesn't work here then?' said Louisa.

The man looked surprised. 'He's a student in Australia, although you wouldn't know it because he's always here on holiday.'

'And how do you know him?' said Makereta.

'We went to the same school. Now he's an overseas student he's too good to speak to the likes of me. The last time he was here he ignored me. Mates shouldn't behave like that.'

'Do you also know someone called Wame?' said Louisa.

The young man looked surprised. Then he made a sad face. 'We used to be mates, me and Wame. He was at school with us. I don't see him any more though, he mixes with dangerous people now. It was bad what happened to him, though. Really bad.'

'What do you mean?' demanded Makereta.

'Everyone knows he was chosen by those rich men in Suva to go to Australia to study. Then Api's mum died. He had to leave the house he was living in. He had nowhere to live and no job. Wame persuaded Rick and Stewy to let Api stay at theirs for a while. I warned him not to do it but he wouldn't listen. I never liked Api but Api was always Wame's best mate.'

'What happened?' said Makereta.

'Almost as soon as Api got in the door he began turning the men against Wame. Oh, Api didn't come out and say Wame is a loser, pick me and ditch him, he was way more clever than that. No, he suggested Wame was taking drugs – he wasn't, by the way. Rick and Stewy were very anti drugs. It was the one thing they didn't compromise on.'

'How do you know this?" said Louisa.

'Wame told me.'

'But why didn't Wame say it was a pack of lies?' said Makereta

'By the time Wame knew what was happening it was too late.' The lad looked as if he was about to spit on the floor then thought better of it. 'I saw them the other day.'

'Who?' said Louisa.

'Api and Wame. I was coming to work. It was early in the morning – before the coup and the curfew. Maybe ten days ago.'

'Are you sure?' said Louisa, throwing Makereta a look.

He nodded. 'I was on the bus. They were at the side of the road. At first I didn't recognise Wame. He looked different. Older. They were both very serious and furtive. I thought Api was buying drugs, everyone knows Wame sells drugs now. I only had a quick look so I couldn't be sure.'

'Had you ever seen them together any other time?' said Makereta.

'No.'

'Where does Api live when he comes to Nadi, do you know?' said Louisa.

The waiter shook his head. 'He has no family but he says he has friends everywhere. Look, I have to go.'

'Thank you for your help. We really appreciate it,' said Makereta.

'It's okay,' said the young man. He turned to leave then stopped. He said, 'If you're interested in talking to Wame, I saw him a couple of hours ago.'

'Where?' said Louisa and Makereta at the same time.

'The same place I saw him arguing with Api three weeks ago. Outside the Crocodile Dundee hostel. Do you know where that is?'

76

The Croc was a fifteen minute drive from Denerau. Louisa talked while Makereta concentrated on getting them to the hostel in one piece.

'We saw Api at the Croc yesterday and Wame is there today, that cannot be a coincidence,' said Louisa.

Makereta nodded.

'And, if we can believe what our waiter at the tennis club said, Wame and Api had some kind of an argument a couple of weeks ago here in Nadi. This means Api lied when he said he hadn't seen Wame for months and that he'd just arrived in Fiji from Australia.'

'Correct. But why lie?' said Makereta, without taking her eyes of the road.

'For the same reason Wame lied when he said he'd not seen Edwin or Stewy on Wednesday morning. They both have something to hide.'

'It doesn't make them murderers, though,' said Makereta, shaking her head.

'No, but Wame and Api both lived with and were supported by Rick and Stewy for some time. In other words, they knew the victims well. And we know most murders are committed by friends or family members close to the victim. And both Wame and Api were in Suva at the time of the murders. We also know Api gambles and owes old Api money, which is the same old Api that Wame used to work for in Suva.'

'Maybe he asked Rick for money to pay off his debts and Rick said no?'

Louisa nodded. 'And Api also lied about where he's studying.'

'We've still no concrete proof of that.'

'And Wame sells drugs, –'

'Allegedly,' said Makereta without looking at her.

'Whether Wame is taking drugs or not, both Wame and Api are barefaced liars with something to hide.' Louisa wished Makereta would put her foot down, at this rate it would be dark before they got to the hostel.

'Their behaviour is certainly very suspicious.'

'Edwin said Stewy told him someone had let them down, someone Rick and Stewy had treated like a son. That sounds like Api. Maybe they found out about his gambling, or that his studies were going badly, and they challenged him?'

'Possibly. But I'm still not convinced Wame is involved in the killings.'

'Maybe not but the sooner we talk to Wame the better.' Louisa looked out the passenger window. She saw the Croc ahead. 'The place looks deserted. I hope he's here.'

'All I wanted was to unite Wame and Malaki and go home,' said Makereta out if the blue. 'I can't believe Wame is involved in the murders. Yes, he's a petty conman and thief but a killer?' Her hands gripped the steering wheel in the ten to two position. 'I just hope I did the right thing by bringing Malaki to Nadi.'

'You are not responsible for Malaki. You did your best to help him. Besides, until we have more facts we can't be definite about anything. All I know for certain is whoever attacked me this morning is Rick and Stewy's killer. He thinks I have something of his. The same thing that probably got Rick and Stewy killed. I have to stop him before he tries again because when he realises I don't have this thing, whatever it is, I have no doubt he will want to kill me. Wame might be able to help us find him.'

77

Louisa pressed the buzzer by the outside gate and they were let in. The same bored young man stood behind the counter. He barely looked up when he saw them.

'We're looking for a young man, name of Wame. He was here this morning. Could he have stayed last night?' said Makereta.

The man glanced at Louisa and Makereta then looked back at the computer screen, which they knew to be under the reception counter. 'No one that name staying here.'

'Maybe not any more, but he has been here, hasn't he?' said Makereta.

'I said no, didn't I?' said the man, without looking up.

Makereta said, 'You don't mind if we have another look about?'

'Why should I?' said the man.

Louisa followed Makereta along the corridor to the steps and lift. They pressed the lift button. As they waited for it to arrive, Louisa tiptoed back towards the reception. The man was on his mobile. He sounded anxious. Then she heard Wame's name. The bugger was warning him!

'Hey!' said Louisa. 'Who are you talking to?'

The man took one look at Louisa and shouted down the phone. 'Run man!'

A clatter. Outside. A shout, Another clatter. Front or back? Shit. She didn't know.

'What's going on?' Makereta was beside her.

'He's only gone and warned Wame. I'll go front, you go back?'

Makereta nodded and was gone.

Louisa ran outside. The bright sunlight blinded her for a second. She shielded her eyes. She listened. Silence. Then a yell. A crashing noise and another shout. 'Over here!' It was Makereta. Louisa ran round the side of the building. Makereta was on the ground, in the middle of a pile of surf boards. 'There!' She pointed away from the building. On the road outside, Wame revved up a moped and was away. 'We have to get after him!' said Makereta, scrambling to her feet.

'Are you hurt?' Louisa helped Makereta to her feet.

She shook her head. 'He pushed the shelf over. The boards slowed me down, I couldn't catch him.'

78

They lost Wame in Nadi town centre in the traffic. One minute the moped was ahead. The next it wasn't. There were only two places he could have gone. They tried the nearest first.

Makereta knocked on the door of the house where they had seen old Api. Louisa waited behind her, poised to run should old Api appear. The skinny woman opened the door. She made an ugly face when she saw Makereta.

'You go away!' she said. 'The boss is asleep in the back, he could wake up at any minute. If he sees you I will be in big trouble. He was very angry with me letting you in the house yesterday.'

'We're going nowhere until you talk to us,' said Makereta.

'Why are you so horrible to me? I told you where Api Ramodi worked and now you come back and make trouble.'

'Api doesn't work in Denarau,' said Makereta.

The woman frowned. 'He told me he did.'

'It seems he lied,' said Louisa.

She made an ugly face. 'He is from the village and should have stayed in his village. He thinks he is clever telling me stories but like all the men who come here to play cards, he is not clever.'

'We heard he's been studying in Australia, do you know anything about that?' said Louisa, while looking out for old

Api.

'Australia?' She shrugged. 'Maybe. Sometimes he is here, sometimes we don't see him for months. But always he has money and always he loses it. He thinks he is a big gambler, but he is not so big. They make fun of him behind his back.' She spat on the ground. 'His mother was stupid and so is he.'

'Do you know where he could be?'

She shook her head. 'He owes the boss money. When that happens we usually don't see him. When he came to the house yesterday whining about his problems, the boss got very cross.'

'What problems?' said Louisa.

'The usual lies. It is not his fault he has no money to pay his debts. Blah. Blah. Blah. Now you must go.' She tried to close the door.

Makereta put out her hand and held the door open. 'We are looking for a friend of Api's called Wame. I asked you about him yesterday. Are you sure you don't know him?'

'There are a lot of young men who come and play the cards but Api always comes alone and goes alone.'

'Are you sure?' said Makereta.

The woman gave her an icy look. 'I answer your questions. If you don't like the answers I give you that is your problem. Now go!'

'Why will old Api be so angry if he sees us again?' said Makereta.

'Anything makes him angry these days. His gout causes him a lot of pain. But his business is also not going well. He has land. He was going to sell it for a good price. That is why he is here in Nadi. But a rumour started that the land was going to be used to build a resort for gay men.

The people living near the beach got very angry. Their churches got involved. There was fighting. The price of the land dropped. And dropped. Now it is worth almost nothing. Only one man wants to buy it but he is offering so little money old Api doesn't want to sell it. But he needs the money. He has bad debts he must pay. You see, he is a gambler too. Now everything makes him angry, especially two interfering women.'

79

Malaki's village looked the same as yesterday, sun scorched and deserted. It was the only other place they could think of that Wame might be. Makereta wasn't expecting to find him. She'd given Malaki her mobile phone number the day before. If Wame had turned up at their mum's, she was certain Malaki would have somehow managed to let her know. Louisa wasn't so sure.

Makereta got out of the car. She looked glum. Louisa knew she wasn't looking forward to leaving Malaki with his mother. But if Wame wasn't here, she was going to have to. Even if he was there, unless he could explain his relationship with Api, he was in trouble. Very soon they were going to have to talk to Vika.

Louisa knocked on the side of Malaki's mother's hut. Nothing.

'Hello?' shouted Louisa.

'Can we come in?' said Makereta.

Still no answer. Louisa pushed open the door. It was stuffy and warm inside. A fly crawled on an abandoned dirty white enamel cup in the middle of the grime encrusted floor. A small Baby Belling enamel cooker sat in the far corner. It was ingrained with rust and old grease and grot. At first glance, Louisa thought the gloomy room was empty. Then she saw Malaki, curled up next to the cooker. He glanced at them then turned his face back to the wall.

'Malaki?' said Makereta, walking towards him. 'We need to talk to you.'

Malaki continued to stare at the wall.

'We know Wame is in Nadi but we can't find him. Did he come here?' said Louisa, crossing the room after Makereta.

'We think he may be in trouble,' said Makereta, 'We want to help him.'

'If you know where he is,' said Louisa, 'you must tell us.'

Makereta knelt next to Malaki and gently placed her hand on his shoulder. 'Anything you know could help.'

Malaki slowly turned his head towards them. Makereta gasped.

'What happened?' Even in the dim light Louisa could see his left cheek and eye was a purple pulp, twice the size it should have been.

'What do you care?' he said.

'Was it Wame? Did he come here?' said Louisa.

'You are so stupid!' said Malaki. 'Wame is the only person who cares for me.'

'Then who?' said Makereta.

He looked at her and said nothing.

'Your mother did this?' said Louisa.

Makereta groaned softly. 'I'm sorry.'

'She took the money you gave her to look after me and spent it on booze for her and her friends,' said Malaki. 'This morning she woke up with a hangover and no money.

When she is drunk she is horrible but when she has a hangover she is very horrible.'

'I shouldn't have left you here,' said Makereta.

'She asked me where my new trainers were.'

Louisa looks around for his bright shiny new trainers. 'Why?'

'She wanted to sell them for money to buy booze. There is nothing else in this house to sell. Even the cooker is broken.'

'But Louisa gave her forty dollars!' said Makereta.

Malaki gave Makereta a look that suggested contempt. 'That has all gone. It started like it always does, by calling me names.' Malaki pulled himself into a sitting position. 'She says I am a dog, a donkey, worse than a donkey. A lump of useless wood. An idiot. It is my fault she has no money. It is my fault she has no boyfriend.' He picked at his shorts. 'She shouts over and over again where are the trainers? Where? Where? Where? I make myself very, very small. She goes outside to look for the trainers but cannot find them. She comes back. She paces the room like a wild animal. Then she nips me and shouts again, calling me a stupid piece of goat shit. I still say nothing. She kicks me. Again. And again. Kick! Kick!' He touched his swollen cheek. 'I am very scared now. It will get worse. It always does. I want to run away. I know she will never catch me if I can only get a head start. But I am too scared to move. I begin to cry. I tell her I hate her. I tell her I am going to leave and stay with Wame and she will be alone. Forever. She laughs and laughs and laughs. She says Wame doesn't want to be with me. She says I am the one who will be alone. I say that is not true. She says Wame has abandoned me. She says she is not surprised. Wame is always telling her how much he hates having such a useless brother as me. She says Wame calls me a weight around his neck. I call her a liar. I don't care any more what she'll do and I make my mistake. I say Wame has not abandoned me. I know this because Wame came to see me this morning.'

Louisa looked at Makereta and then back to Malaki. 'Wame was here?'

Malaki sniffed. 'He came very early before she was awake. It was a secret. I was not to tell her or anyone else he was here. He said he had things to do and as soon as he was finished he would come and get me and take me back to Suva with him. All I had to do was wait and tell no one I saw him.'

'But how did he know you were here?' said Louisa.

Malaki shrugged. 'Wame always knows everything. But don't you see, I told her. I didn't mean to. It tumbled out that he was here and is going to take me back to Suva with him. She laughed when I told her. I hate her ugly laugh! She said Wame would never come to the house and not talk to her. Never! I say she is wrong. He did not want to see her. He came to see me. She calls me a liar. She says Wame hates me. That he will never take me to Suva with him because I am a waste of space. I say I am not a waste of space.' He began to sob softly. 'I say he will take me. I say I will tell Wame that she hits me and he will not bring her money again. She frowns. She likes Wame bringing her money.'

'Wame gives her money?' said Makereta.

'Doesn't he know she'll spend it on alcohol?' said Louisa.

Malaki takes a deep breath. 'She tells him she will stop drinking and he wants to believe her. He says it's not her fault she drinks too much. He remembers when Mum was a nice person. But that was before she met my dad.' He scowled. 'He says she is not strong. He says I am like her. I say I am not! I am strong. I have never told him that she hits me. He would be very angry and sad. I don't want him to have more reasons to be angry or sad.'

'Where is your mother?' said Makereta, looking around.

Wiping away his tears Malaki said, 'She said Wame calls me a cry baby, that he hates me because I am weak.'

Makereta put her arm around his heaving shoulders. He shook himself free.

'I am strong! I am not like her!'

'Where is she?' said Louisa.

He wiped his tears with his hand, smearing dirt across his face. 'One of her drunk friends came to the door. He said he had some beer. They don't like drinking alone. She left.'

Louisa gave Malaki one of her tissues.

He took the tissue, looking miserable. 'But Wame hasn't come back for me. She was right. He doesn't want to be with me.'

'What time did he say he would be back?' said Makereta.

'He said he would be back soon but that was hours and hours ago.' He buried his head in his hands.

'Unless something's happened to him?' said Louisa.

Malaki looked up. His eyes widened with anxiety. 'Like what?'

'I don't know. Did he tell you where he was going in Nadi?'

Malaki looked down. Said nothing.

Louisa glanced at Makereta and then back at Malaki. 'If you know where Wame was going you must tell us. His life could be in danger. We can help him.'

'I was to tell no one! He made me promise,' said Malaki, scrunching up his eyes and mouth and beginning to cry again. 'He gets angry if I don't do what he tells me. I don't want him to be angry with me!'

'If you want to help Wame, you need to tell us where he was going,' said Makereta.

'I already told Mum he was in Nadi and he'll be cross with me about that–'

'He could be in danger, real danger. Do you want to help him or not?' said Louisa.

Malaki looked down at his hands. 'He went to The Garden of the Sleeping Giant.'

'The what?' said Louisa, looking at Malaki in disbelief.

'Why?' said Makereta.

'He said he was meeting someone there.'

'Then that's where we're going,' said Makereta.

'I'm coming too!' said Malaki, scrambling to his feet.

'No,' said Louisa, 'that is not a good idea.'

'I am coming!' said Malaki, carefully opening the small door of the dirty Baby Belling cooker and taking out his Nike trainers.

80

Makereta did her best to follow Malaki's instructions to The Garden of The Sleeping Giant. They passed fields of cows, followed by scrub, followed by acres of tall, tapering green sugar cane stalks. A hooting sound out of nowhere made them jump and Makereta braked, only just stopping the car from ploughing into the side of a small steam train which appeared from the sugar cane field and crossed the road in front of them.

'What the hell?' said Louisa.

'It's the sugar cane train. It carries the cane to the factories,' said Malaki.

The old fashioned steam engine was half the size of a normal train, it almost looked cute. It pulled a dozen small carriages behind it. It had a stripy yellow and orange cow catcher on the front. For the first time Louisa noticed a very small narrow gauge railway track running across the road.

'The carriages are empty,' said Louisa, watching the train trundle in front of them and disappear into the field opposite.

'Sugar cane harvest is in June. It will be a test run,' said Malaki.

Louisa stared. Fiji was a continuous surprise. The train finally crossed the road. Makereta started the car engine and pulled away.

'What is The Garden of The Sleeping Giant?' said Louisa

'The Sleeping Giant is the name of the large hill, or small mountain outside Nadi. The garden is an orchid garden at its base, for tourists,' said Makereta. 'A famous film actor called Raymond Burr started it in 1977.'

'You're kidding me?' said Louisa.

'You've heard of Raymond Burr?' said Makereta, surprised.

'He starred in a crime series back home on TV called *A Man Called Ironside*. Oh, and another one called *Perry Mason*. My mum used to watch the shows on daytime TV, probably still does, that and *Murder She Wrote*. Did he live here in Fiji?'

Makereta shrugged. 'No idea.'

'So, Wame is going to meet someone in a quiet, out of the way place.'

'They don't want anyone to hear their conversation.'

Louisa glanced back at Malaki. He'd fallen asleep.

'I can't believe Wame is a bad person,' said Makereta, sounding miserable. 'He hasn't got a history of violence.'

'That you know of. You did hear Malaki say he didn't like it when Wame got angry, didn't you? If Wame's temper is anything like his mother's, he could well be capable of murder.'

'Wame would never hurt anyone!' shouted Malaki from the back of the car. 'He is a good person. Why are you saying such terrible things about him? He's killed no one! Never!'

Louisa turned to face a very wide awake Malaki. 'We have to consider everybody who had a motive and Wame had a good motive not to like Rick and Stewy.'

'But he didn't kill them, I know he didn't. You said you wanted to help him. You lied!'

'We only want to know the truth,' said Makereta. 'You're a Christian, you believe in telling the truth, don't you?'

Malaki looked away.

'If you know something that can help Wame, you need to tell us.'

'I don't know anything because there is nothing to know.'

'Where did Wame disappear to the morning Rick and Stewy were killed? I saw him at eight thirty, what happened after that? He has nothing to be afraid of if he's innocent,' said Louisa.

'He is innocent!'

'Are you telling us all you know?' said Louisa.

Malaki clamped his mouth shut and looked out the car window.

'We're here,' said Makereta, turning off the road into a parking area at the side of the road big enough for half a dozen cars.

81

Makereta parked next to two gleaming 4x4s. The only sign of the orchid garden was a wooden arrow nailed halfway up the fat trunk of a giant bread fruit tree, pointing to a brick path in the green growth. Makereta led the way and Louisa and Malaki trooped behind. After fifty metres of winding in intense heat, they came to a rectangular wooden bungalow on small stilts. It sat in the middle of red and yellow flowering lush vegetation. Steps took them onto a large verandah, which appeared to go round the bungalow. At the top of the steps sliding doors opened into an empty coffee area with wooden walls and wooden floor.

The room reminded Louisa of a sauna. Round tables and chairs suggested drinks and food could be on offer but Louisa couldn't see a kitchen area or even a coffee machine. It was warm and dim inside. The wooden slatted walls were covered in posters of different kinds of colourful orchids. Each poster had "The Garden of the Sleeping Giant" emblazoned across the top of it. Beyond the eating area was a long, polished counter. Leaflets and bookmarks on top of the counter mirrored the posters. They were in the right place.

'Hello?' shouted Louisa.

Silence.

'Police?' shouted Makereta. 'If there's anyone here, can you please show yourself?'

An explosion of bird chatter made all three of them jump. The twittering came from the verandah behind them. Louisa hadn't noticed the bird feeders when they'd come in. Two long pipe like contraptions with holes in them, like thin potato planters, hung from the verandah roof. A clutch of tiny green finches with red heads fought each other to get to the seeds. Louisa turned back into the room. She nodded to a door behind the counter. 'What you reckon?'

Makereta shrugged.

Louisa heard Malaki fidget behind her. She'd have preferred to have left him locked in the car but Makereta wouldn't have it. Not only would it be stifling in there without the air conditioning on, he could be at risk if left alone. A door behind the counter took them to a small office. Empty. An open door at the back of the room revealed a toilet.

'Lunch hour?' said Makereta, looking at her watch. 'The staff could be having a nap somewhere.'

'Who do the cars out there belong to?'

Makereta shrugged. 'Visitors?'

They went back into the coffee-area-cum reception. Louisa turned to Malaki. 'Are you sure this is where Wame said he was coming?'

He nodded. 'Yes, but that was hours ago.'

'And he didn't say why he was coming here?'

Malaki scowled. 'I'm Wame's little brother. He doesn't

tell me everything he does. All I know is that I was to wait for him in the village. I shouldn't have come with you. If he doesn't find me he will go back to Suva without me. He will think I don't care. I will be all alone again and it will be your fault.'

'If he's here, we've saved him a trip. If he's not here, we'll take you back to the village. If he loves you as he says he does, he'll be waiting for you there,' said Makereta.

Louisa picked up one of the leaflets from the counter. It was a map of the gardens. She nodded to the door at the back of the bungalow. 'Shall we go?'

Makereta nodded.

Louisa gently pushed Malaki in front of her. 'You keep where I can see you.'

82

The badly kept brick path meandered between hibiscus bushes and decorative man-made waterfalls. Under a blazing blue sky they saw delightful pretty orchid after orchid. Fluttering finches twittered and tweeted. They passed public toilets – one small block for gentlemen and one for women. Both empty. Gradually, the path wound upwards. The heat became unbearable.

'Are we still in the orchid park?' said Makereta, panting for breath. 'I've not seen a flower for five minutes.'

'The path seems to carry on all the way up the mountain,' said Louisa.

'But the orchids don't. Shall we go back?' said Makereta. 'Wame has either been and gone or was never here in the first place.'

'For a tourist attraction it's a very natural, un-touristy place,' said Louisa, looking around her. They were a third of the way along the path. Louisa reckoned the hill to be about as high as Arthur's Seat back home. Probably take another twenty minutes to reach the top. Grass had replaced the bushes and trees. She could already see all around, almost as far back to the visitor centre nestling in the bushes below, and ahead to the dazzling blue sea and the surrounding hills.

'We've looked everywhere. No one's here,' said Makereta. 'I think we have to go back.'

'One minute you tell me you want to help Wame and the next you don't care,' said Malaki. 'I broke my promise to Wame for no reason.'

'He's not here,' said Louisa, 'and you said he would be.'

'No. I said he was coming here this morning. That was hours ago.'

'And you have no idea why he was coming here or who was going to meet?' said Makereta.

'He said it was private.'

'It's certainly that.' They'd not seen another soul since they'd arrived. The place was beginning to give Louisa the creeps.

'Lets go back,' said Makereta. 'There's nothing to be gained by staying longer.'

'Listen!' said Malaki, raising one hand in the air as if to stop oncoming traffic.

'What?' said Louisa, looking around.

'Can't you hear it?' said Malaki.

'Hear what?' demanded Makereta.

'Shouting!' said Malaki. 'It's Wame!' He charged down

the hill.

'Wait!' Louisa hared after him. Makereta followed immediately behind. By the time they'd got to the bottom of the path Malaki had vanished.

'The bugger's disappeared!' said Louisa, looking all around.

Makereta panted behind her. 'But we were right behind him!'

'Do you think he really heard Wame?'

'No idea.' Makereta leaned on a tree fern to catch her breath. 'But I'm so ticked off with him for running away like that.'

'He has to be here somewhere,' said Louisa.

'What was that noise?' said Makereta.

'It came from inside the bushes,' said Louisa, pushing into the undergrowth.

'Wait!' shouted Makereta. 'It could be dangerous!'

'And someone could be hurt!' yelled Louisa. She could almost taste the damp soil and rotting vegetation. She came to a clearing. A body lay on the ground. It was Api. He was unconscious with a bloody gash across his forehead. Louisa knelt beside him. Checked he was breathing. 'Makereta!' she shouted. 'Call an ambulance!'

83

The twin room in the Westin was plush. There was no other word for it. Louisa loved it. She suspected Makereta quite liked it too. Everything gleamed and glistened, from the polished ash floorboards to the super silent sliding

French doors, which opened onto a balcony edged with overflowing purple bougainvillea and a vast sea vista. The twin "heavenly" double beds were divine, as was the massive tapa cloth hanging on the ivory painted wall behind them. Louisa considered opening a swish sachet of freeze dried coffee from Papua New Guinea and having one of the fancy wrapped chocolate chip cookies, or a passion fruit from a bowl of fresh fruit. Finally, she decided not to spoil her appetite and shouted to Makereta, who was in the shower, that she would head to the restaurant and meet her there.

The Westin had four restaurants and three pools. They'd agreed to meet at the steak restaurant. It overlooked the small round pool. Flickering torches placed around the pool area created a romantic atmosphere. Louisa glanced at the menu. Shit! It was expensive. Very expensive. She looked for somewhere to hide it. Louisa would, of course, pay but if Makereta saw it, it'd be another thing for her to stress over.

The Nadi police had questioned them at length about the attack on Api. For Makereta it was simple: until she'd talked to Malaki and found out why he ran away, she was not telling her Nadi colleagues anything. Not only could they jump to the wrong conclusion, they could inform Vika of what Makereta and Louisa were doing, which would not be good. The ease with which Makereta lied shocked Louisa. Makereta, in turn, was amused by Louisa's reaction. Being a Christian, said Makereta, didn't mean she was stupid.

Makereta's colleagues finally concluded the attack on Api was a mugging gone wrong, that Makereta and Louisa had disturbed the attacker or attackers, causing them to flee before they'd got what they were really after – Api had had two hundred bucks in his wallet, an expensive Blackberry mobile phone in his pocket and a fancy watch on his wrist. Louisa thought it was possible but unlikely.

A smiling waiter offered Louisa a cocktail menu, which she declined, asking for water instead. Within seconds the waiter placed a crystal glass of water, clinking with cubes, on a frilly paper coaster in front of her then silently slipped away. Louisa contemplated the ice cubes. The rule in the Pacific was never to drink water that hadn't been boiled and filtered, and to never ever have ice because ice cubes were rarely made from filtered water, never mind boiled water. But this was the Westin. Surely, ice cubes were okay here? She hesitated. She'd been sick before from taking a drink that had had ice cubes in it. She couldn't face that again. She pushed the glass away and looked around. Where was Makereta?

It had been a long afternoon. Makereta was convinced that Malaki and Wame were in danger and it was her fault. She'd refused to return to Suva without finding them. They'd spent the better part of the rest of the day looking for the brothers, without success. When it became clear they would need to stay another night in Nadi Louisa gave Makereta a choice: stay with her at the Westin, at her cost, or stay at the Raffles with the cockroaches but without her. Makereta reluctantly agreed to stay at the Westin.

Louisa wasn't convinced that Wame and Malaki were in danger. Far from it. As she saw it, there was every chance Wame had attacked Api. He had enough motive and Malaki, desperate for his brother's approval, could have helped him. It only took a second to bash someone unconscious, as she knew. Louisa sighed. Until she'd stumbled on Api lying injured in the orchid park, Louisa had been pretty sure Api had been her attacker in the stairwell in the Raffles hotel, and Rick and Stewy's killer. Now she wasn't so sure. They needed to question him urgently but the hospital staff were adamant, he was to have no visitors for twenty-four hours and Makereta's warrant card made no difference. Tomorrow would come soon enough. Louisa licked her lips. She was thirsty.

Louisa knew Makereta wanted Wame to be a good guy for Malaki's sake. But the one time Louisa had met Wame, he'd lied to her. That was not the action of someone who was innocent. And where was the evidence, other than what Malaki had told them, that Wame was a kind and considerate brother? What if Malaki had been lying? What if Wame could have been exploiting his brother? Just because you had a brother, didn't mean the brother wanted what was best for you. Her own brother was an outright shit. When they were younger he'd never missed an opportunity to get her into trouble with her mum. She wouldn't be surprised if he was still badmouthing her behind her back. He was greedy and lazy and wanted their mum's unconditional love all for himself, which he got. Louisa sighed. From what she could see, Wame had abandoned Malaki to his fate in Suva. Not the actions of a concerned family member. But even if he was a shitty brother, that didn't make him a killer, did it?

Louisa checked her watch. Nine o' clock. Where the hell was Makereta? Louisa looked around the restaurant. She started. It was Edwin. Coming directly towards her.

84

Edwin wore a crumpled white linen suit. In the light of the dancing torches and the flickering candles around the pool, he almost looked handsome.

'May I ask you for some advice?' he said.

'I thought you were in Kiribati?' said Louisa, struggling to believe he was in front of her.

'I was,' said Edwin. 'Am I permitted to sit down?'

Louisa nodded to the empty chair beside her. 'Are you back in Fiji for a while?'

'I am leaving tomorrow. May I buy you a drink?'

She shook her head.

'I have shamefully and shamelessly been taken advantage of and I don't know what to do about it,' said Edwin seriously.

'If this is a police matter, you should go to the local station for help.'

'I don't want to do that. Please, I have nowhere else to turn.'

Louisa frowned. 'I'm not sure I'll be able to help but go ahead.' She couldn't imagine what was bothering him.

'The man you saw me with on Tarawa, Frederick Hatcher?' He didn't wait for her to reply. 'He is a business associate.'

'I thought you said you came to Fiji for pleasure?'

'I did.'

'Then I don't understand.'

'If you will let me finish.' He placed his hands on his knees. The black nail varnish on his fingers was chipped. 'I met Mr Hatcher at the Holiday Inn. We made conversation. He told me of an investment opportunity, a plot of land for development. If I was interested, he would cut me in but only on the condition I tell no one else about the deal.'

'Did you give him money?' said Louisa, silently groaning, there was one born every minute,.

Edwin made a sour face. 'I am not so silly. I was, of course, suspicious. Mr Hatcher understood that. He invited me to see the land plot that afternoon. When we got there I was taken aback. It is a very lovely place and would make an excellent gay resort, which is what Mr Hatcher was wanting to do with it. However, while we were there some local people appeared. They had banners with very unpleasant writing on them, such as "No gay paedo resorts in Fiji!" and "Go home evil gay perverts!" They also shouted slogans such as "God hates gays!" and "Fiji and God want no gays!"'

Louisa was shocked. 'How did they know you would be there?'

'I do not know. But at first we tried to ignore them. But more protesters came. And more. They grew louder. And louder and became more aggressive. Mr Hatcher calmed them down but it was very unpleasant and we left.'

'Very unChristian behaviour. Did you go to the police?'

'I wanted to, but Mr Hatcher said it could get us nowhere because the police hate gays to.'

'And?'

'Mr Hatcher said I was not to worry and that we should lie low as it were. He was going to Tarawa for work for a few days and suggested I go with him. I was happy to, especially with the nasty anti gay stories in the newspapers the next day and hearing about the terrible deaths of Rick and Stewy. Mr Hatcher insisted all would be well when we came back. He promised to introduce me to the seller and told me not to worry. And, indeed, when we arrived back earlier today, everything seemed calm and we were to meet the seller at The Garden of The Sleeping Giant.'

'You were at the orchid garden?' Louisa said surprised.

'Mr Hatcher said hardly anyone goes there any more, it is a good public place that is also private. He said it was very good there for talking business.'

'Didn't you think that was suspicious?'

Edwin shrugged. 'I do not know how they do things here. But when I met the vendor I could not believe it. I knew him. He was the big mean man who employs the shoeshine boys in Suva.'

Louisa sat up. 'Are you sure?'

Edwin made a face. 'Oh yes, I am very sure. I remember people who are rude to me. He came after me on Wednesday morning, to tell me the boy who had polished my shoes had given me an "extra special" shine and I had not paid enough for it. I told him I had not asked for an "extra" anything and to go away. Stewy had left by now so I was all alone. The man shouted bad things at my back. It was very disagreeable. The poor shoeshine boy tried to stop the big man heckling me. The big man ignored the boy and stood in my way so I could go no further. He threatened to hurt me if I did not give him money. A crowd gathered around us. I was very upset but I was not going to give him any of my money. Why should I? But then a police officer appeared and the coward vanished into the crowd. The boy stayed with me. We talked to the police together. When I was calm I wanted to pay the boy for being so kind and to thank him but he didn't want any money. He only left when I said I felt better.'

'And this took place when?' said Louisa, sitting bolt

upright.

'I just said, Wednesday, the awful morning Rick was murdered.'

'What time?'

'About eight forty-five.'

'Why didn't you mention this before?'

'No one asked me. And I was glad not to talk about it. I wanted to forget about it. It was very humiliating having a mad man shout rude words at me.'

'Did you get the shoeshine boy's name?

He nodded. 'It was the one who called himself Wame. You saw him.'

'When did he leave you?' she demanded. 'Exactly.'

Edwin frowned. 'It was nearly nine o' clock. Maybe five past.'

'And a police officer can verify this?'

'Oh, yes. He recorded what happened in his notebook.'

Louisa flopped back into her chair. So, at the time Rick and Stewy were being killed, Wame was helping Edwin.

'As soon as I saw that horrible man with Frederick and realised he was the seller of the land I was very scared. The man shouted at me as soon as he saw me. I left immediately. I expected Mr Hatcher to come after me but he did not. I waited by the car and waited and when he did not come I walked back towards Nadi. Luckily, for me, a taxi came and stopped and I asked him to bring me to a good hotel and he brought me here. I like it but it is very expensive.'

Louisa frowned. 'Okay. It sounds as if you have had a very unpleasant experience but what's the problem? You said you didn't give Mr Hatcher any money?'

Edwin looked around furtively. 'I saw Mr Hatcher again. Outside this very hotel.'

'And?' said Louisa, it was like pulling teeth.

'I told Mr Hatcher I absolutely did not want to invest money building a gay resort in a country that hated gay people. Not now. Not ever. And do you know what?'

'What?' said Louisa looking around for Makereta, where the hell was she?

'He said neither did he! I was shocked. I asked him what he meant by that and he said "work it out, gay boy" and turned and left me.'

'If you do business with bad people, bad things will happen,' said Louisa.

'I didn't know Mr Hatcher was a bad person when I first met him. But now I think it was Mr Hatcher himself who told the protestors a gay resort was being planned for the land. He sabotaged his own business venture, but why?'

'There can only be one reason.'

85

Makereta still had not come to dinner. Louisa was going to have to go and find her, she was starving.

Edwin coughed. 'You said you know why Frederick sabotaged his own plans?'

Louisa took a sip of water from her glass. 'Hatcher knows Fiji. He has been here before. He is a business man and has seen other business men investing in land and making money when the land is turned into a holiday resort. He hears about some beach land for sale. It will be a good investment but it is very expensive. He can't afford it. But then he has an idea. If he can do something to make the land a bad buy it will devalue the land. He reads the outcry in the papers that a gay guest house is opening in Tamavua. He sees his opportunity. He starts spreading homophobic rumours that the land for sale is going to be used for a gay resort. There is some reaction to the rumours but not very much. Then he meets you–'

'But he did want to build a gay resort.'

'No, he just wanted to buy the land cheap.'

'I do not understand.'

'Let me explain. He sees you, an overtly gay person. He temps you to get involved with the deal of a lifetime and takes you to see the land. You think it is a bit of fun. You may invest some money. Why not? You have just arrived in Fiji and you like the country, remember you do not know Rick and Stewy have been killed yet. You go in Mr Hatcher's car to the resort. But Mr Hatcher has leaked the visit to the land to some right wing church groups. The protestors are waiting for you and when they see you, a gay man, they believe the rumours that the land is being bought to build a gay resort are true. Mr Hatcher then takes you away to Tarawa to hide you so no one can ask you about the sale. If they did, they could discover what Mr Hatcher is up to. The deaths of Rick and Stewy fuel the homophobic flames and the rumours about the gay resort spread like wildfire. Protestors mount a national campaign. They say they will never let a resort be built on the site, gay or otherwise. The seller, the boss of the shoeshine lads, sees his land lose its value before his eyes and smells a rat. But it's too late. The damage is done. Mr Hatcher will offer to buy the land at a much reduced price. If the boss needs the money badly enough, he will accept the offer. Then in six or twelve months when everything has died down, which it will, Mr

Hatcher will quietly sell the land to an overseas investor at a much hiked up price and make a killing. Mr Hatcher got you involved to be the 'patsy'. Although I don't think the boss man is an idiot. If I can work out what has happened, there is every reason he will. I wouldn't like to be in Mr Hatcher's shoes when that happens. If he has any sense he'll leave as soon as he can.'

'He has used me!'

'He's a crook and you're lucky you got away without getting hurt and losing money.'

Edwin's mouth sagged at the edges. 'Mr Hatcher said I had to trust him.'

'In my experience anyone who tells you to trust them, is the last person you should trust.'

86

When Makereta hadn't appeared at the steak restaurant by nine thirty, Louisa went to look for her. She appreciated Makereta wanted some time on her own, but the restaurant was closing at ten. They'd end up with nothing if she wasn't quick. Makereta wasn't in the hotel room. Louisa reckoned their paths must have crossed and went back to the restaurant. She still wasn't there. Louisa couldn't understand it. Unless Makereta was waiting for Louisa in one of the other restaurants? That would be it. Louisa set off to check them. She imagined Makereta would be relieved to hear that Wame had a solid alibi for Rick and Stewy's killings. Although, as far as Louisa was concerned, it didn't let him off the hook. Just because he didn't kill the men himself didn't mean he wasn't involved in their murders.

Makereta was not in any of the other three restaurants. It was as if she'd vanished. Louisa felt totally bewildered. It was well after the curfew, Makereta couldn't have gone anywhere else. Where the hell was she? Why leave without telling Louisa? Louisa suddenly felt as if she'd fallen into a deep hole and landed in a freezing cold lake. Shit! Had the killer tracked them down to the Westin? Did he have Makereta?

Louisa called Vika from Makereta's mobile, which was still in their hotel room. She knew Makereta would have preferred not to involve Vika but Louisa was desperate. People just didn't disappear. But after twenty rings and no answer Louisa threw the phone on the bed. Was Vika ignoring the call because it was from Makereta's cell phone? Maybe. Louisa couldn't decide what to do next. The local police wouldn't be able to help because of the curfew and getting the army involved didn't seem a good idea either – if Makereta had left the hotel and broken the curfew, Louisa could inadvertently get her in trouble by reporting her missing. After searching the hotel and surrounding hotels in the complex twice, Louisa tried to get some sleep but it was impossible. If anything happened to Makereta she would never forgive herself. In hindsight, they'd been foolish to interfere in a murder investigation. What had they been thinking?

At first light Louisa phoned Vika's number again. Still no answer. Next she phoned the officers who had handled Api's mugging the day before. No answer. Louisa had to do something. In any missing person case the odds of finding someone alive and well diminished the more time that passed. Louisa snatched up the car keys to the Rav4 and headed for the hospital. If Makereta had been injured, there was a possibility she was there. She would also visit Api. He had some questions to answer, namely who had knocked him out and why, and what was he doing in The Garden of The Sleeping Giant. Maybe one of his answers would help her work out what had happened to Makereta.

Louisa liked the hospital even less the second time. The crumbling Edwardian building was like something out of a 70s horror movie with its grubby green subway tiles in the corridors and mouldy covered vaulted ceilings. The smell of disinfectant did nothing to reassure her. Api's ward was on the first floor. It was heaving with visitors. Some ate rice and taro from white plastic plates, others munched on cheesy Wotsits and sipped fizzy drinks. Under almost every bed was at least one blue and red and white stripy bag, a white cool box, a couple of rolled up sleeping mats and a bundle of pillows. It was more like the hospital on Tarawa than any hospital Louisa knew in Edinburgh.

Louisa scanned two rows of eight old fashioned hospital beds. She couldn't see Api. One bed was empty. In the far corner. Was that Api's? A man stood next to the bed. He had his back to Louisa. He was too small to be Api.

'What are you doing?' demanded Louisa. The man turned. It was Wame. Louisa recognised his thin, angry face immediately.

'They said he had severe concussion. I thought he would be in hospital for days. Where is he?' he demanded.

'I don't know.'

'His clothes are gone, and his fancy phone.' He looked around. 'He's gone.'

'Why are you bothered?' said Louisa. Now she knew that Wame and Malaki were half brothers she could see the family resemblance: both were slight, with cropped, dark hair and a hungry look about them.

Wame looked at her, as if seeing her for the first time. 'You're the woman that asked me all those questions at the market in Suva.'

'You still haven't answered my question, why do you want to know where Api is?'

Wame sauntered towards Louisa, shoved his face into hers, tapped his nose three times with his index finger then turned and left.

Louisa hurried after him. He wasn't going to get away from her that easily. Not this time.

87

'You and me, we're on the same side,' said Louisa, catching up with Wame as he exited the ward.

'What side is that?' said Wame, without looking at her.

'Malaki's side. I want to help him.'

'He's got me, he doesn't need you,' said Wame, pressing the lift button and waiting to be taken to the ground floor.

'So where were you when your mum thumped him one yesterday?'

'What are you talking about?' said Wame, glancing at her, then heading for the stairs instead of waiting for the lift.

'Your mother wanted to sell his new trainers to buy booze. He wouldn't give them to her so she battered him.

Badly.'

He shook his head. 'I don't believe you.'

'She's always hit him, that's why he ran away to Suva. He doesn't want to tell you because he doesn't want to upset you.'

'You're trying to trick me.' He hurried down the steps two at a time.

'You can ask him yourself, if you can find him,' said Louisa keeping up with him.

He stopped and faced her. 'He's at our mum's. I told him to wait for me. He always does what I tell him.'

'Not this time. He came with me and a colleague to The Garden of The Sleeping Giant.'

Wame ran his tongue over his black stumpy teeth. 'Malaki was at the orchid garden yesterday?'

'He saw you. It was just before we found Api. Did you and Api have a fight? Is that how he got knocked out?'

Wame scowled. 'I've dreamed of bashing his head in a hundred times but I didn't do it. We argued, sure, but when he threatened me I ran and hid. I saw him walk into Old Api, my ex-boss. He's the one who hit him. Just my good luck, I suppose. So where's Malaki now?'

'I don't know.'

Wame's eyes flashed with concern. 'What do you mean, you don't know? You just said he was with you.'

Louisa shook her head. 'We lost him in the orchid garden. I've not seen him since.'

Wame started walking fast towards the hospital exit. 'I have to get to Mum's.'

'I told you, Malaki is not at your mum's,' said Louisa, keeping pace with him.

'He has to be there, he has nowhere else to go. And Api

knows that too.'

'What are you saying, you think Api will hurt Malaki?'

'I know he will!'

'Stop!' said Louisa standing in front of him and blocking his way. 'You tell me what's going on or I'll phone police HQ and say I know where the Shoeshine Killer is.'

Wame scowled. 'I have something belonging to Api. I gave it to Malaki yesterday morning to hide for me. I told him to put it somewhere safe, where no one would find and to wait for me.'

'What are you talking about?'

'A letter.'

'But why would Api think Malaki has this letter and how did he even know Malaki was in Nadi?'

Wame's face fell. 'Because I was an idiot, that's why. I told him. Now get out of my way. I have to get to Mum's. There's nowhere else for Malaki to go. Api will stop at nothing to get the letter. He killed Rick and Stewy for it.'

Louisa grabbed Wame's arm and stopped him. 'Are you sure Api killed them?'

'He told me himself.'

'I'm taking you to your mum's,' said Louisa, turning and heading for the exit. 'I've a car outside. We can be there in less than ten minutes.' It was suddenly obvious that Makereta was with Malaki. She was the one person Malaki would go to for help, and the only person Makereta would disappear for. Louisa didn't know why they left without telling her, or how they'd dodged the curfew, but they had and they were together and in danger.

88

Wame sat in the front passenger seat of Makereta's Rav4. Louisa hoped they wouldn't be too late.

'Can't you go any faster?' said Wame, jiggling his knee up and down.

'I'm over the speed limit as it is.'

'If Api gets to Mum's before we do, he'll hurt Malaki, I know he will.'

'My colleague Makereta went with him last night. She'll protect him.'

He laughed bitterly. 'She won't be able to do anything.'

'At least she's with him.' Louisa tried to remain calm. 'Where were you last night when Malaki was looking for help?'

Wame shifted in his seat.

'What was it? Drink or drugs or both?'

Wame cleared his throat. 'I thought Malaki was safe. I had a bad afternoon. I was expecting my money. I didn't get it. I went to chill with some friends. Is that a crime?'

'It is if you left your brother at risk. Why is this letter so important?'

Wame looked out of the passenger window.

'I can easily drive to the nearest police station if you'd rather tell someone there? Of course, that means Api has more time to get to Malaki?'

Wame shook his head wearily. 'A few months ago Stewy visited his parents in Australia. While there he decided to pay the wonderful Api a surprise visit at Monash University. Or at least, he tried to. But Api wasn't there. Stewy asked around. He'd dropped out the year before, almost as soon as he'd started.'

'Api had left?' said Louisa.

Wame nodded. 'But forgot to tell Rick and Stewy.'

'They must have been furious.' Just as Mataio had cashed in the airline ticket she'd bought him, Api had taken Rick's money given to support his studies, and wasted it on himself. 'But surely the university would have sent the fees back?'

'Api is clever with computers, that's why he was studying Artificial Intelligence. He forged letters, made up documents. He sent Rick false account details from the university and had the fees sent to himself. He fooled everyone.'

'What happened?' said Louisa.

'Rick and Stewy emailed Api and demanded he come and see them immediately to explain. Api went. He was too scared of what Rick would do if he didn't. He said he'd been enticed into gambling and got into debt and needed the money to pay off the debt, which was why he had to leave university. He said he was too ashamed to tell them and that he had stopped gambling since. It was all bullshit. I think Api had never intended to study. It was the money he was always after. Rick believed him.

'But Rick was no fool. He produced a letter-cum-confession for Api to sign. In the letter Api had to promise to pay Rick and Stewy back every cent he'd spent, including the university fees. If he signed it, Rick agreed not go to the police. Api couldn't believe his luck. He signed. Stewy was furious, though. He thought Api should be punished. He'd betrayed their trust.

'But as soon as Api left The Garlands, the reality of having to pay the money back hit him. He was furious. He thought Rick had tricked him. He believed, wrongly, that if he got the letter back, all would be as it was before. It was a fantasy. He's a crazy person.

'Api waited until Rick and Stewy had gone to bed and broke into the house to steal the letter – it was easy for him to break in, he'd set up the security systems for Rick when he'd lived in the house. He even had copies of the room keys. This was the night you and Stewy's foreign friend stayed. Room by room he looked for the letter and found nothing. Your room was the last room to check. He had only just sneaked in when he heard someone moving about in Rick's bedroom, so he fled.'

'But why didn't you go to the police?' said Louisa.

'I never thought he was a killer but I underestimated how desperate he was. Api came directly to me after he'd been interrupted from searching your room.'

'Why you?'

Wame shrugged. 'He didn't know anyone else. He told me everything and asked if I'd help him find the letter.'

'And you said you would despite all he'd done to you?' said Louisa, keeping one eye on the road and one eye on Wame.

'I was in trouble with the boss and had no money. I was desperate. Api said he had over half of his allowance for this year left.' Wame laughed. 'I believed him. You know what was really crazy? After Api came to see me that Wednesday morning, Stewy came to my shoeshine spot with his foreign friend. While his friend wandered about the market, Stewy told me what Api had done. He didn't know Api had already told me all about it, why would he?

'Stewy said he was very angry with Rick for not going to the police about Api. He said Rick was a sucker for a sob story and was worried Api would come back and persuade

Rick to tear the letter up and let him off with the debt. To make sure that couldn't happen Stewy said he'd sneaked the letter out of the house and was keeping it on him at all times. Then he apologised for believing Api over me when I lived with them. He offered to make it up to me. But before he could tell me how he would make it up, the tall man came back. Stewy didn't want to discuss Api in front of him and we agreed to talk after he'd left.

'I was so happy. In the blink of an eye my fortunes had changed. I wouldn't need to help Api now and looked forward to telling him where to stick his letter and money. Stewy's foreign friend asked me to polish his shoes. I did so very quickly because I hoped he would go away and I could talk to Stewy again. But then Rick arrived, you were with him. He started shouting and punched the pineapples out of Stewy's hands. You remember?'

Louisa nodded. 'Clearly.'

'Well, after Rick left Stewy was in no mood to talk and he left too. His foreign friend stayed a while longer and chatted with me. He was about to leave too when the boss turned up and tried to intimidate him into paying more money for his shoeshine.' Wame shook his head wearily. 'It was a very crazy morning. Finally, when I was alone at my spot, I saw Stewy's bag. It must have slipped off his shoulder when he picked up the pineapples off the ground. His wallet was in it, a newspaper and Api's letter. I was pleased he'd left the bag. It gave me an excuse to go and see him. I hoped he'd talk more about my future. Then I heard Rick was murdered and Stewy had disappeared.

'It seemed obvious, Stewy must have killed Rick, which was why he'd disappeared. I never imagined it was Api. Not once. Even when Stewy was killed I didn't think it was Api.

People said if Stewy wasn't the murderer, the killer had to be a drugged up lunatic. The men were always letting strange people into their house. Everyone knew they were too trusting.

'Now Stewy and Rick were dead Api wanted the letter more than ever. He said if it got into the wrong hands, he would be wrongly accused of having a motive for murdering them. He said he would give me even more cash if I found it. I didn't tell Api I had found the letter. I wanted to make him sweat. The longer he didn't have it, the more he might pay to get it.'

'That sounds very much like blackmail,' said Louisa, frowning, while overtaking a lorry laden down with tree trunks.

Wame shrugged. 'I encouraged him to believe Rick had given the letter to you. To convince him I pointed out you were a police officer. Someone Rick would have trusted. Api became obsessed with finding you and the letter.'

'So, until very recently, Api thought I had this letter when all along you had it?'

He nodded without looking at her.

'Did you search my rooms or was it him?'

'Him. Me. Both of us. He promised me lots of money if I helped him find the letter but whenever I asked him for some of the money he didn't have any.'

'You should have taken the letter to the police,' said Louisa, slowing down at a busy junction.

Wame looked at her. 'If you were wanted for questioning and the papers were calling you the Shoeshine Killer, would you have gone to the police?'

Louisa ignored the question. 'Why were you in Nadi?'

'Api said he was coming here to get his money. I followed

him. We met up. He still didn't have his money but he said he was getting it soon. He also said he'd seen you in the street. He couldn't believe it. It was a sign from God, he said. He followed you and found out you were staying at the Raffles hotel. He asked me to break into your room again and search for the letter, he was convinced you still had it. I agreed. But this was going to be the last time. If Api didn't have the money I was going to walk away. I'd had it with him. But Api couldn't wait for me to search your room and went to look for himself. That's when he attacked you.'

'He could have killed me,' said Louisa, beeping her horn at a taxi going five miles an hour. She hoped they wouldn't be too late.

'How many times do I have to say, I didn't know he was a killer. He came to me mad as hell that you'd got away. I told him it was okay, that I'd found the letter already. He believed me. He said he would get his money and meet me in the orchid garden. He said he didn't want anyone observing us.'

'You didn't think that was suspicious?'

'Of course I did. I didn't trust him, that's why I left the letter with Malaki. When I told him where it was and that I wanted him to bring the money to Mum's he really got angry. Screamed at me that I had tricked him. Said he had killed Rick and Stewy and would kill me too, that's when I ran and hid and saw the boss punch Api out cold.' Wame suddenly looked miserable. 'I only wanted a little bit money to get Malaki away from the bastard boss.'

89

The village was deserted apart from two scrappy dogs lazing in the sizzling morning sun. Louisa and Wame hurried into his mum's house.

Makereta lay on the floor. Her face was battered and bruised. At the sight of it Louisa wanted to be sick. But she had to stay in control. She breathed in. And out. Slowly. Deeply.

'Is she dead?' said Wame quietly.

'I hope not!' said Louisa, kneeling down and checked her for a pulse. There was one. It was strong. 'She's alive but we have to get an ambulance.'

'I'm on it' said Wame, taking out his phone.

Makereta groaned. Her eyes flickered open.

'What happened?' said Louisa, taking Makereta's hand.

'You have to stop Api. He's going to kill Malaki!' she mumbled before losing consciousness.

'The ambulance is on its way. I explained she's a police officer,' said Wame.

Louisa checked Makereta's pulse for a second time. It was still strong. A noise came from outside. Louisa replaced Makereta's hand and ran out the back. Wame's mum sat on the concrete veranda, half slumped against the wall of the hut. Eyes cold. Louisa squatted down beside the woman. Her breath stank of rotten turnip.

'Wake up?' said Louisa, giving her shake.

'Mum?' said Wame, voice anxious.

'She's drunk,' said Louisa before shouting. 'Where are Api and Malaki?'

'Mum? What happened? The woman inside, she's been hurt?' said Wame, ignoring Louisa and kneeling next to his mother.

His mother groaned.

'Wake up you stupid drunken cow!' yelled Louisa, giving her a shake. Shit! She was losing it. But Makereta had been battered to within an inch of her life and she was sure this woman had done nothing to help her.

'Leave her alone!' said Wame.

'You get her to talk!' snapped Louisa. 'I want to know where Api and Malaki went!'

'Mum,' said Wame softly, 'It's me. I've come to see you.'

The woman opened her eyes, smiled and caressed Wame's face. 'My son.'

"What happened inside?' said Wame, taking his mother's hand from his cheek and holding it in his own.

'It wasn't my fault,' she said, her words slurring.

'I know. I know.' He patted her hand. 'But what happened?'

'You couldn't get me a drink, son? I need a drink.'

'In a minute, Mum. First you need tell me what happened.'

'It's your friend's fault.'

'What friend?' said Wame.

'The one you went to school with, that boy Api. He was looking for you.' She started to whimper. 'He kept shouting, "Where's Wame? Tell me! Tell me!" But how could I tell him when I didn't know? He slapped me and slapped me. Then Malaki and that woman arrived. Malaki tried to stop Api hitting me but Api just twisted his little arm up his back and asked him about a letter. The woman told Api to let Malaki go. She said she was the police. Api laughed at that and twisted Malaki's arm harder. Malaki screamed louder and said he didn't have any letter. But you know

284

Malaki, he is not a good liar. Then, I don't know how, the woman hit Api on the side of his face. He didn't expect it. He got a fright. He let Malaki's arm go. Malaki ran out of the house,' she paused. 'Did you say you were getting me a drink, son?'

'It's coming. What happened next?'

'Api punched the woman. She tried to defend herself. She did. But he was much stronger. He punched her again and again. She fell to the ground. Now he kicked her. Malaki was back. He had a rock in his hand and hit Api hard on the back of his head. Api fell to the ground next to the woman. There was a lot of blood from his head. Malaki went to help the woman but Api wasn't knocked out. Only stunned. He started to get back up on his feet. I told Malaki to run and hide. Api was like a crazy man now. He shouted and cursed and said he was going to kill Malaki. I need a drink son. Can't you get me a drink? It wasn't my fault. It wasn't my fault...' she began sobbing.

'Why didn't you try and stop him?' demanded Louisa.

'I didn't want to be hurt,' she whimpered.

'Where's Malaki now, Mum?'

'Where he always goes when he wants to hide.' She nodded towards the sugar cane. 'Api went after him. There was nothing I could do.' She slid down and curled up on the cold concrete. 'Wake me up when my drink comes, son, I'm going to have a nap ... just a small nap ...' She closed her eyes.

'Where will Malaki go?' said Louisa.

'There's only one place,' said Wame.

90

Wame ducked and dodged through the sugar cane. Louisa struggled to keep up with him. They'd been running for almost thirty minutes. She really was getting too old for this nonsense. How had she ever run a mile and a half in twelve minutes for the police fitness test? She was so angry. The truth had been so obvious but she had failed to see it. Makereta had nearly died as a consequence. Louisa had wanted to stay with Makereta until the ambulance got there but Malaki was in danger of his life. She had to find him before Api did. Did they have a chance? She paused to catch her breath.

'We're here!' said Wame, coming to a clearing.

'Where?'

'The Garden of The Sleeping Giant.'

'What?' said Louisa seeing the lumbering mountain loom up ahead of her. 'How is that possible?'

'It's only a couple of miles away from the village through the sugar cane fields. We used to play hide and seek here when we were boys. Malaki knows the mountain better than anyone.'

'So where is he?'

'There's a place at the top, where we used to hide. Like a den. Come on. Malaki will never be able to defend himself against Api, even if Api is wounded.'

Louisa followed Wame along a narrow bush path.

'You should have gone to the police, you know. Right from the start.'

'How many times do I have to say? I didn't know Api was the killer! I thought he was a greedy bastard who had too much money, money which should have been mine.

Besides,' he said, 'the police would have never listened to me, a petty crook and shoeshine boy!'

Louisa jumped. She'd heard something. 'Sh! A noise!'

Wame froze. 'Where's it coming from?' he hissed.

'Ahead.'

Wame crept forward up the path, glancing left then right. Louisa followed behind him, body tense. Then she saw it. It appeared above the crest of the mountain. A giant bright orange orb against the brilliant blue tropical sky. 'What the?' she gasped.

'It's a hot air balloon.'

'Up here?' She watched in awe as the giant orange globe came into full view and hovered in the air just beyond the edge of the mountain slope, its basket still out of sight. 'I can hear voices!'

'Tourists,' said Wame. 'They are carried down on the warm morning currents. A place in the basket costs a lot of money.'

'Come on! Maybe someone will have seen Malaki or Api,' said Louisa, hurrying up the hill.

'It's possible,' said Wame not sounding convinced but continuing after her.

Louisa reached the crest of the hill and looked onto an undulating plateau. Ahead of her the hot air balloon bobbed quietly in the middle of the clearing. It was even bigger now she was closer to it. A number of ropes attached the balloon itself to a frame of fibre glass poles, which, in turn, attached the balloon to a straw basket beneath, which sat on the ground. Above the basket but below the opening of the balloon sat a central platform. It appeared to hold a box with two giant burners. There were more ropes and pipes. The rush basket below looked tiny under the huge orange balloon. A skinny Fijian man was already inside, fiddling with the rigging. A rush of roaring noise exploded from the burners and a yellow-blue flame darted skywards then vanished, but not before releasing a wave of hot air into the bulging balloon. Two super thick ropes, like anchor ropes, hung from either side of the orange canvas and swung downwards and across the lush grass, fixing the gigantic balloon to two jeeps, parked next to each other on the edge of the high plain.

'You can drive up here?' said Louisa surprised.

'Yes,' said Wame.

Half a dozen bronzed tourists dressed in shorts and t-shirts, sun hats, sunglasses and flip-flops stood in a huddle between the jeeps, listening intently to a tall slim Fijian man in a long sleeved T-shirt and designer sweats with sunglasses perched across the front of his bald head. She assumed he was their guide. The straw basket looked way too small to fit them all into it.

'Over there,' said Wame, nodding to a clump of bushes and trees beyond the balloon and opposite the jeeps. 'That's where we used to hang out when we were kids.'

'Hey, you for the trip?' shouted the tall Fijian man, looking in Louisa and Wame's direction.

She shook her head.

The man made a face. 'The garden isn't open till after ten, apart for balloon people. So how did you get in?'

She held up her warrant card. 'Detective Sergeant Louisa Townsend. I'd like to ask you a few questions.'

'I'm going to see if I can find Malaki,' whispered Wame and darted across the grass towards the copse of trees. Should she follow him? Too late. He'd gone. Shit!

'We're just about to get into the basket,' said the tall

man, throwing a gleaming smile at the group.

Heads nodded gleefully.

'Just one question, only take a second.' Louisa walked towards them. 'Have you seen anyone else in the garden this morning?'

The tourists looked at each other blankly. The tall man said, 'There's nobody else here but us chickens.' He looked towards the basket. The man who had been inside was outside now and made a thumbs up sign. 'That's us folks,' he said to the group. 'Your hot air balloon trip awaits!'

A piercing scream! Everyone jumped. It came from the bushes.

91

Louisa ran towards the scream. It was followed by another. Louisa reached the copse. She stopped. It was dark inside. 'Wame? Malaki?' she shouted. Silence. Louisa called out again. 'Wame, are you there?' All she could hear was her own desperate gasps. Where are they?

'What's going on?' It was the tall guide. He was right behind her.

'Are we safe?' said a male Australian voice.

'Sh!' said Louisa without looking behind her. 'Please stay back for now. If I need help, I'll call.'

'Is this part of the outing?' said another voice.

Louisa entered the wood. It felt cool. Smelled earthy.

'Wame? Are you in here?' An insect hummed in her ear. Shit. Shit. Shit. Why had she let Wame out of her sight? She crept forwards. A second scream! From behind now. Louisa ran back the way she had come. The shouting intensified. A third scream. Shit! She reached the clearing. Api and Wame were fighting. The balloon tourists stood around them in a horseshoe shape, their eyes wide with shock. Api had a knife in his hand. The blade flashed. Wame was on the ground. He gripped his side. Blood seeped through his fingers. Louisa dashed forward. Grabbed Api's left arm and twisted it back behind his back. He roared in pain. The tall guide was next to her. He grabbed the knife from Api's right hand.

'Let me go!' Api struggled to free himself.

Louisa tightened her grip. She was glad the guide had his other arm. 'Are you okay?' she yelled to Wame, who was getting up slowly. He nodded. 'Louisa twisted Api's arm further into his back. 'Where's Malaki?'

'Stop!' he yelled.

'If you've hurt Malaki,' said Wame, standing up, while gripping his bloody side. 'I'll kill you!'

'The balloon!' A voice cried. 'The basket is off the ground, it's floating away!'

Louisa looked. The basket was at least three meters in the air and climbing. Below it the anchor ropes sliced through the air, left then right. One flew straight towards Louisa and the guide. They threw themselves on the ground to avoid it. Api grabbed it and curled his arms and legs around its heavy thickness and was swept upwards and away.

'Fuck you, you crazy bitch!' he yelled above her head and out of reach.

'Oh my God!' yelled a woman's voice. 'There's someone in the basket!'

Louisa looked up. Two big brown anxious eyes peered

over the edge of the basket.

'Malaki!' screamed Wame. 'It's Malaki!'

Louisa didn't want to believe it. She looked at Api swinging beneath the basket. She said to the guide, still on the ground next to her. 'Will that bastard be able to climb up into the basket?'

The guide shook his head. 'Impossible.'

'Are you sure?'

'His arms will already be tired and his fingers will have started to tremble with fatigue. His legs will feel heavy. They will throb. His body will feel like a lead weight, pulling him downwards. He will want to change his grip but whenever he tries to move he will lose purchase of the rope. Sooner rather than later, he will let go of it.'

Louisa stared at the saffron balloon as it silently floated further and further away. 'What if the balloon lands before he lets go?'

'He'll not be able to hang on until then.'

'So, the boy inside, he'll be safe from him?'

He nodded. 'Oh, yes.'

'And the balloon will land, won't it?' said Louisa.

'It has to come down.'

'So the boy will survive?'

'If he's lucky,' said the guide.

'And if he's not?'

The man shrugged again.

'We'll have to call the police,' said Louisa.

'I thought you were the police,' said the guide, eyeing her suspiciously.

92

Nadi International airport was packed. It was Christmas Eve. Louisa was going home on one of the busiest days of the year, and probably one of the hottest. She wiped her neck with a clean wet wipe then threw it in a nearby bin. She had over three hours to wait before her flight was scheduled to leave. She didn't care. It was that or sit in her hotel room. People watching at the airport was mildly more interesting.

Every night since the balloon incident she'd dreamt of Malaki. In her dreams his anxious brown eyes stared at her from the edge of the balloon basket, growing bigger and bigger and rounder and rounder until they were the size of flying saucers and exploded and she woke up. It was guilt, of course. Had anything happened to Malaki, she'd have never forgiven herself. But Malaki had been lucky. The balloon had eventually landed in a field of cows. Other than a few bruises he was relatively fine.

Api was not so lucky. His mangled body was found in the middle of a cluster of spiny aloe vera a mile from The Garden of The Sleeping Giant. An officer said he was a tangle of broken bones. Louisa wished she'd seen him fall and hoped he'd suffered. He'd battered Makereta so badly her cheek bones and jaw bone had to be pinned and plated back together. And although she said she was much better, one half of her face was still puffy and numb and looked a bizarre yellow-purple colour.

The police found Api's letter in Malaki's left trainer, tucked beneath the insole. It was marked with dirt and stained with sweat but the writing was perfectly legible. It was worded as Wame had said. It confirmed Api's motive for wanting Rick and Stewy dead. Then, when the airport driver who'd dropped off Louisa's suitcase at Rick's remembered seeing Api approaching The Garlands guest house as he was leaving, Api was confirmed the killer.

Louisa was glad the murderer had been found before she left. It felt like closure of a sort. She had very mixed feelings about leaving Fiji. She wanted to get the hell out of Dodge, but she'd miss Makereta, who, despite her injuries had insisted on dropping Louisa off at Suva airport earlier that morning. It was the first time Makereta had left the house since she'd been attacked other than to go to the hospital. Malaki had come with them. He stayed with the family now. He was like a puppy dog. Anywhere Makereta went he went too.

Wame had also been invited to stay at Makereta's but he'd declined, much to Malaki's dismay. Eventually, he'd compromised and agreed to live in the garage-cum-den underneath the main house and, for a modest fee, to be their house guard. That way, he said, he could keep an eye on Malaki, who loved having his big brother so close, earn a bit of money and still manage the Suva Central shoeshine lads. The boss had been jailed on a drug smuggling charge and in his absence Wame offered to help the lads with their documentation – also for a modest fee.

There had been interviews with Vika, of course, which had gone reasonably well. Louisa and Makereta had, after all, identified the killer and helped Vika close the case, saving her reputation. Makereta got a promotion and Louisa a letter of thanks, copied to Commissioner Nakibae, stating how much her help had been appreciated.

Louisa chewed her bottom lip. All's well that ends well. But it could so easily have been so different. She'd made some terrible errors of judgement and seriously needed to get her shit together. And the best way to do that was to be in the thick of things again and do some proper detecting work. As soon as she got home, she'd look out for vacancies.

She wondered, for the umpteenth time, if she should buy her mother a gift from the airport shop. But, also for the umpteenth time, decided against it. Her mother had never appreciated anything she brought her in the past. Why should that have changed? Instead, she would do what she should have done years ago, and give her money.

Fortunately, because of her delay in getting to Edinburgh, her mother's care package had been reinstated. Three female carers and one male carer took it in turns to pop in four times a day and do what needed to be done, including the dreaded topping and tailing. Far from being unhappy about the situation, her mother was delighted: she had a captive audience of regular visitors for her to order about and bore to death, what was there not to like? She'd already made it clear to Louisa when they'd last talked on the phone, the carers were staying. Louisa didn't object. As if?

Louisa smiled. She was looking forward to going home, despite the cold weather, and no Mataio. She'd still not told her mother they were no longer an item. Her mum would pile on the abuse when she heard that news. According to her mum, men didn't like bossy women, especially women like Louisa who were ambitious. Maybe she was right? Clearly, Louisa was doing something wrong when it came to men. Or maybe relationships were overrated?

Louisa checked the departure board. Her international flight wasn't up yet, which was worrying. But what did it matter if she was a few more hours late? Her flight didn't get in until Boxing Day anyway. It was a pity to miss Christmas Day but at least she'd be spared her mum's cooking – Farmfoods finest – and the Queen's speech. Louisa got out a fresh wet wipe from her bag and wiped her hands a second time then dropped it in the nearby bin. She gave the contents of her bag a quick once-over. She had enough wipes and tissues and alcohol gel to last her three round the world trips, never mind one. She was taking no chances. Someone tapped her on the shoulder. She started. It was Mataio.

93

At first she thought Mataio was an hallucination. She blinked. No. He was still there, scruffy looking with his half beard and clean but crumpled T shirt and jeans. His dancing eyes full of enthusiasm and life. The old Mataio.

'What are you doing here?' she said, when she finally found her voice.

'Looking for you. Can I sit down?' he said, face deadly serious.

'If you want.' Her knees began to tremble. 'How did you find me?'

Mataio pulled up a chair and sat next to her. 'I tried your hotel so many times but you were never in.'

'How ironic.' Louisa took slow, deep breaths. She had to stay in control. She would not let Mataio upset her. Not before she was about to get on a long haul flight and be stuck with her thoughts.

'I tracked down a colleague of yours, a woman called

Makereta. She said she was your friend. I told her I needed to talk to you and she persuaded me to come and see you in person.'

'She did what?' said Louisa, louder than she intended, causing the other people in the airport café to look at her.

Mataio looked embarrassed. 'She seemed to think what I had to say was too important for a phone call.'

'That woman is a hopeless romantic,' whispered Louisa loudly. 'She had no right to tell you anything.' Louisa was shocked. Makereta had said nothing to her about Mataio being in touch.

'I'm glad she did, though, because I was right to come.'

'How could you afford it? You have no money and you said you'd given the ticket money to the church.' He was not going to trick her into forgiving him.

'My aunty works for Air Pacific –'

'What aunty?' demanded Louisa.

'She lives in New Zealand. I asked her for a favour.'

'You can get free air travel?' She'd heard everything now.

Mataio squirmed in his seat. 'Not exactly.'

Louisa leaned towards him and whispered, 'You mean it's dodgy? No, don't answer that. I don't want to know.'

Mataio brought his seat a couple of inches closer to her and said quietly. 'I wanted to see you. There was no other way.'

Louisa sat back in her chair. She couldn't think. Her hands dripped sweat. She wiped them with yet another wet wipe. 'Why didn't Makereta tell me she'd been talking to you?'

'She thought you'd refuse to see me if you knew I was coming.'

'She got that right.' He was so close to her their knees

were almost touching. His familiar scent of Lux soap and a hint of coconut made her feel lightheaded.

'I had to tell you how sorry I am about my behaviour.'

'You think I care about an apology now?'

'You have every reason to be angry. I made a very big mistake.'

'You can say that again.' She had to calm down. What was Mataio after? And she absolutely must not think of his naked body.

'I lost my sense of who I was.' Mataio blushed. 'It's not easy to explain but I want to.'

'You make the mistake of thinking I care about what you want,' she said, feigning indifference. But she did care. All her old feelings for him were back with bells on. It didn't matter that the last time she saw him he'd told her to ask God for forgiveness for being a bad person.

His face became serious. 'I know our relationship is over but I owe it to you to tell you.'

'Okay, go ahead, it will make no difference, though.' She had nothing else to do. She would listen, say goodbye, go through security, get on her flight and forget about him forever.

'I think I had some sort of midlife crisis. And whatever happens, I'll pay you back the money for the ticket.'

Now she laughed. 'Pay me back? How?'

Mataio looked serious. 'It's not impossible. The church have asked me to be their accountant, and they're going to pay me a not bad wage.' He suddenly smiled. 'It might take a few years but I'll do it.'

Louisa sighed. 'The money wasn't really the issue.' She would survive without it. 'It was the way you didn't talk to me about anything. You withdrew into your religious fervour and locked me out. Talking about religion, where is His Royal Highness Pastor Johan?' Louisa looked around as if expecting to see him.

'Ah.' Mataio cleared his throat. 'Pastor Johan was not who I thought he was.'

'Oh?' said Louisa, eyeing Mataio carefully. What was this?

'The money I gave to the church–'

'You mean my money?'

'Yes, your money.' Mataio shifted in his chair then said: 'It disappeared along with what little funds the church had.'

'How disappeared?'

'The church elders got a letter from the bank demanding they sort out their debt. They didn't understand. They should have been in the black. They checked the accounts and smelled a rat called Pastor Johan – he was in charge of finances. He'd been stealing the funds for weeks. They called him in to explain his actions and he made a run for it.'

'He left the country?' Louisa wanted to laugh but didn't.

Mataio nodded. 'At least, he tried to. My cousin saw him getting on a mini bus heading for the airport. I borrowed your car and caught up with the bus. I went crazy. I'd trusted this man and he'd taken advantage of me when I was vulnerable. I dragged him out the bus and into the road and demanded an explanation. He said he needed the money and it was all gone. Until then I hoped it might be a mistake, that the money was tied up in a savings fund. When I realised he'd conned everyone, but especially me, I started to hit him. Again and again. Luckily we were close to Bikenibeu Police Station. A couple of officers came out when they heard the commotion. They pulled me off and

298

took him away.' He shook his head wearily. 'I'd have killed him if they hadn't come. I was such an idiot.'

'Is he okay?'

'Oh yes. A few bruises. He's in jail now on remand. The church are determined to lock him up.'

'And what about you?'

His cheeks went red. 'I got off with a reprimand.'

'Hm? You were lucky,' said Louisa. 'And is he really a minister of the church?'

'Oh yes,' he smiled. 'A very bad one. The police think he spent the money paying back debts. No one knows what for.' He took her hand. She let him. 'I'm making no excuses, just trying to explain that I was an idiot. You talked about us living in Scotland and about me finding work there and I panicked. But instead of talking to you about how I felt I kept it all bottled inside. In Beru it all became too much. Maybe Mum being so ill was the last straw, but I lost it. I started drinking. Pastor Johan was visiting. In one of my drunken stupors I told him about flying back with you and the ridiculous cost of the tickets. He saw an opportunity and played me like the fool I was. Had I been more honest with myself and with you, well...'

Louisa blushed. 'I assumed you wanted what I wanted.'

'Johan conned me and I was ready to be conned.'

'You were very convincing.'

'He was very convincing.'

'Maybe I could have listened more,' said Louisa. She knew she wasn't perfect. 'But what a time to want to talk about our relationship. I'm leaving in a couple of hours. I have to go through security in ten minutes.'

Mataio cleared his throat. 'I don't know if you'll think this is good news or bad news but your flight has been delayed. Look.' He pointed to the departures board behind her.

He was right. The Brisbane flight had flagged up a twenty-four hour delay. Louisa groaned. 'I'm doomed to stay in this bloody country!'

'But it does give us time to talk some more, if you want?'

Louisa frowned. She'd hoped never to see him again but now the old Mataio was here beside her it was like they'd never been apart. 'But what else is there to say?'

'Can you forgive me, just a little bit?'

She chewed on her bottom lip. 'Maybe. But we're not getting back together. It's still over.'

He nodded. 'I betrayed your trust. I understand.' He let her hand go and leaned back in his chair. 'So, you're going back to live in Scotland when your contract finishes?'

'Yes. I am. And just to be clear, you don't want to live in Scotland, do you?'

'No. I don't know why I ever said I did.'

'I have to do what is right for me,' said Louisa.

'Yes,' said Mataio seriously. 'I think I kidded myself that I wanted to go with you because I couldn't face the idea of being without you.'

Louisa sighed. 'Maybe that's why I refused to listen to you when you voiced any concern. I didn't want to have to consider the consequence of what you were saying. But I don't want to stay on Tarawa any longer.'

Mataio leaned forward again and took both her hands. 'I'm really going to miss you, especially your obsessive cleaning and those ridiculous rituals –'

'I am not obsessive,' she half laughed. 'Just fastidious.' He had noticed her obsessive cleaning stuff. Why hadn't he mentioned it before?

'As for your moods–'

'I am not moody. In fact, I hate moody people!'

'But at least the moods don't last long.' His eyes glinted. 'And I'll miss your intelligence and mindfulness, and I'll especially miss your sexy body, and your soft lips and your smell–'

'I get it! I get it!' said Louisa blushing.

'You won't miss me just a little bit?'

'Of course I will.' Louisa cleared her throat. 'I'll miss everything about you.'

Mataio sighed and let Louisa's hands go. 'I wish you weren't leaving but you are. At least you know why I behaved like an idiot. It was nothing to do with you, it was just me cracking up.'

Louisa stood up. She'd made a decision. 'Do you need to be somewhere?'

'No,' said Mataio, looking at her curiously. 'I have no plans at all.'

She took his hand and pulled him to his feet. His rough fingers felt good in her smooth ones. 'There's this hotel I know. It's in a place called Denerau. It's very plush, not that you'll care about that, but I do. The thing is, they have the biggest, most comfortable double beds you've ever seen. They call them heavenly beds. Want to try one of them out, we've got twenty-four hours?'

Other books by Marianne Wheelaghan

The Food of Ghosts

DS Louisa Townsend has moved from Edinburgh to work for the Kiribati Police Service on Tarawa, a remote coral atoll in the middle of the Pacific. Locally she is known as the Scottish Lady Detective.

Louisa has been on Tarawa for six weeks when a man's mutilated, naked body is found in the middle of the island. No one knows who he is or how he got there. Louisa is put in charge of identifying him and finding his killer. She thinks it won't take her long to get to the truth and make an arrest – the island is very small, after all. But nothing is what it seems on Tarawa. With no forensics and no one telling the truth – and the bodies mounting up – Louisa couldn't be more mistaken.

Food of Ghosts is the first book in the Scottish Lady Detective mystery series featuring Detective Louisa Townsend.

"Food of Ghosts is a stunning new crime novel by an exciting Scottish writer"

"Set against an exotic backdrop, this thriller has a complex heroine who's as fragile as she is feisty – and who must tackle culture clashes and family ties as well as crime if she's to survive…"

The Blue Suitcase

"We think by now that there can be no more untold stories from the 1930s and the Second World War. Then a book like this comes along and we are once again astonished by the capacity of some humans to do unspeakably cruel things, and of others to survive them. The simple, almost mundane tone of Antonia's diary makes The Blue Suitcase all the more shocking. It's hard to read, but harder to stop."

James Robertson

"This is not an easy read but it is a compelling one. The simple narrative style of a diary is exactly right. The most appalling deprivations and gruesome events are related in a matter-of-fact way that makes them even more horrific.

This superb book is based on the life of Marianne Wheelaghan's mother, and she has seamlessly supplemented the facts with impeccable research. I found this story uncomfortable to read but couldn't put it down. It's a story that will stay with you for ever. This is a must-read book!"

Fenella Miller, The Historical Novels Review*

*For each quarterly issue of the Historical Novels Review, the editors will select a small number of titles they feel exemplify the best in historical fiction. The Blue Suitcase was an editor's choice in the May 2011 quarterly review.

The BESTSELLING The Blue Suitcase is the first in a series of three novels which tell the story of three generations of the one family and is inspired by real events. Book one (The Blue Suitcase) is based on Marianne Wheelaghan's mother's extraordinary early life and influenced by diary extracts and letters she found after her mother's death. The novel starts in 1932 and tells the harrowing story of a young Christian German girl, Antonia, growing up in Nazi Germany, surviving against all odds. Book two, The Brown Paper Parcel, due out in 2016, is the story of what happens to Antonia (and her family) when she arrives in Scotland and is set in the 1950s. Book Three (due out in 2017) is the final part to the trilogy and set in Scotland in the 1970s.